Escape From B-Movie Hell

Here are some things readers have said about M T McGuire's writing.

"*I loved it.*" – Joe, aged 14

"*I am now your number one fan.*" – Emily, aged 30 something.

"*My goodness this is good stuff; so brightly written and full of life. M T McGuire has the most remarkable depths of imagination and inventive flair.*" – Ken Shearwood, aged 90 something.

"*I have real difficulty getting my 12 year old son to read anything but he loved the K'Barthan Series. Please hurry up and write more books.*" – Sam, aged not telling.

Escape From B-Movie Hell

M T McGuire

HAMGEE
UNIVERSITY PRESS

First published in 2015 by
Hamgee University Press,
www.Hamgee.co.uk
Escape From B-Movie Hell 1st ed.

ISBN 978- 1-907809-25-5

Written by M T McGuire
Designed and set by M T McGuire
Published by Hamgee University Press
Edited by Kate Jackson and Mike Rose-Steel
Cover design by A Trouble Halved
This copy printed by Lightning Source UK Ltd, Milton Keynes

For Justine Raynsford: one gay heroine as promised!

M T McGuire is nearly 50 years old but still checks inside
unfamiliar wardrobes for a gateway to Narnia.
Boringly, she's not found any.

Thank you for buying this book.
If you enjoyed it you can keep up with
news of the author online by
visiting www.hamgee.co.uk

You can also sign up for the
M T McGuire mailing list by
visiting http://bit.ly/MTMailJNB
or buy MTM Book merchandise at
www.zazzle.co.uk/drawnbyhand*

Thank you to:-
The Editor – Kate Jackson
for help, advice and support over and above the call of duty.
Gerard, at ATH for understanding exactly what I wanted for the
cover... as usual.

And thanks to my husband and family, for their support and
understanding.

Chapter 1
Relaxing in the bath

The first time the voice found me was in the bath. As I lay back under the warm suds I tried to relax by thinking about the stars.

Prsssllllp, it said: right in my ear. Shocked doesn't do justice to my reaction. I just about went into orbit.

"What the?" I leapt to my feet abruptly, sloshing water over the edge with a splash, and stood still. I waited until the bath water stopped swirling backwards and forwards about my calves and listened.

Nope.

Nothing.

Then I noticed how much water had gone over the side and onto the floor. I shared the bathroom with three other girls and they were totally anal about mess … well … unless they made it, then suddenly I was the anal one. I didn't want to wipe the floor with my towel and hoped that, if I left the door open when I had finished, it would dry before anyone saw it.

You've no worries on that score. It's the middle of the night, I thought. Except that I didn't. It was definitely a thought, and it was definitely in my head, but it wasn't mine. It was somebody else's.

"How can I think another person's thoughts by mistake?" I asked. Was it even someone? 'Prssslllllp' didn't sound like any language I'd heard. What if the thoughts were some*thing's*?

No, it was OK, I told myself. I was not thinking anyone else's thoughts. There was only one me in my brain but it was acting a bit funny because it was five in the morning and it was knackered.

In case you're wondering what I was doing in the bath at five o'clock, let me explain. I was staying in the Paul Weller Student

1

Residency and I was at university, studying art restoration. But what I really wanted to do was stand-up comedy. That's why I picked a university in London.

That night was the first time my attempts to be funny had gone well. And when the set goes well ... trust me. There isn't a buzz that comes close. I was so hooked on the comedy drug that, afterwards, as I cycled back to the student residence, it was all I could do not to accost random strangers and attempt to be funny at them. But even in London, there aren't that many strangers on the street at four in the morning. And I doubted anyone who was would appreciate my biting wit. And I had to face reality. I had lectures in a few hours and I was far more likely to end up being an art restorer than a comedienne. So I needed to work at my course which meant I needed to sleep. Stopping to tell jokes to random strangers was right out. But so was sleep unless I relaxed. Which is how I came to be in the bath at five o'clock having a thought that was not my own.

Hello? said a voice. A voice that came from outside but was also inside my head with me.

"No, no, no."

I got out of the bath and began to towel myself dry. All the while the strange sensation persisted: that there was another mind looking through my eyes.

Two minds in my one brain.

"Am I mentally ill?" I asked myself, aloud, to make it feel real. No. This didn't feel like mental illness. But then surely it never does or people would know not to obey the voices that tell them to murder people and bury them under the patio.

"No. I've overdone it. That's all."

I shuddered as I left the warmth of the steamy bathroom and crossed the hall to my room. It wasn't because I was cold.

Oh come on: talk to me. I know you can hear me.

Goose pimples rose on the back of my neck.

No. Go away, I thought as I ran into my room and closed the door but the voice came with me. Well, it would wouldn't it? It was in my head.

It's alright. I'm not going to hurt you, I promise. What's your name?
I started to imagine myself building a wall across the inside of my skull with the voice on one side and me on the other.
Hang on, no, don't do that. Please don't do that, I need to find you.
No, you very much don't. I concentrated harder on the wall, picturing the bricks, and the mortar between, imagining it growing higher and stronger.
Wait, please. I have to know where you are. It's really important. We need to speak. Please don't shut me out.
I kept building the imaginary wall until the voice faded and was gone.

"What the hell happened there?" I asked my reflection in the wardrobe mirror.

Tiredness. That's all. I was knackered. And a bit buzzy from the stand-up. Yeh. I wasn't going mad. Not at all. I went to bed.

Two days later I met Eric or at least, looking back on it now I realise that what actually happened was, Eric found me. It's probably quite lucky that I didn't understand who he was: or at least, not until a lot later when we were already friends. Life went back to normal, sort of, although two things persisted; the feeling, from time to time that I was not alone in my head and occasionally, a *hello* from the voice. Each time it happened I would build my imaginary wall until it faded away.

It scared me, the thought that I might be getting ill in the head, but I didn't know what to do. It wasn't getting any worse so rather than acknowledge it, I justified my decision paralysis by telling myself I was evaluating the situation; after all, I reasoned, what could possibly happen? And then suddenly, one day, as I was minding my own business buying lunch in the student canteen, I found out.

Chapter 2
Scary visions

I dropped my tray. It crashed onto the canteen floor in a tsunami of overheated baked beans and orange juice; I retained a vivid mental picture of one of my Cumberland sausages skidding under the drinks machine and then, blackness. I woke up on the floor, blinking as a circle of blurred heads above me slid into focus. A group of concerned strangers were standing round, fanning me with empty crisp packets. There was a strong smell of cheese and onion fumes. I searched the faces, and behind them, I thought I saw something blurry and indistinct, just for an instant: something I really didn't want to see. Then I found the person I was looking for: Eric, my best friend, my only friend so far, at uni.

"Andi, are you OK?"

I couldn't speak. I nodded and the world faded again and sounds went a bit fizzy. Ugh. Keep your head still Andi.

"You're OK. You fainted," said someone.

Ah so that's what happened. I took my time. Partly because I was still seeing a lot of big green spots but mainly because I was still trying to process the thing that made me faint. The thing – or was that Thing? – I thought I'd seen.

Had I imagined it? What was I thinking? Yes. Of course I had. After all, I was imagining a lot of strange stuff these days. I told myself this was just the latest in a long line of events, which on the face of it, were best ignored.

Even so, this one was quite a biggie. Bigger than being afraid you're thinking someone else's thoughts; bigger than the voice that was in my head – but also not in my head – that kept saying, *hello*. It was even bigger than the feeling that someone else was sharing my brain. It was something so unbelievably scary it had made me pass out. For a moment I'd thought Eric metamorphosed into a giant lobster with seven eyes, three-foot pincers and antennae.

However, if he had, he'd gone back to looking like Eric now, and anyway, I seemed to be the only person who had noticed. It was probably some kind of optical illusion, I decided. Yes. That's what it was. Too many late nights, a glimpse of something out of the corner of my eye, my wacky imagination steps in and ... yeh. I was helped to my feet, given another portion of all-day breakfast by the kindly lady behind the counter and sat at a table in the corner. The concerned strangers – and Eric – surrounded me enquiring after my health. After a spell with my head between my knees I began to recover and I was soon able to sit up and mumble excuses about the time of the month. Eric was still looking like Eric and the concerned strangers, drama over, went back to whatever it was they had been doing. I wasn't feeling dizzy any more but I had a horrendous headache. It felt as if my skull was about to cave in.

Chapter 3
Lobsters from Norway

A short while later, when I had recovered a little more, I tried to tackle my meal. I noticed Eric was beginning to go a bit blurry round the edges. If I caught a glimpse of him out of the corner of my eye, I would see something ... else, but when I turned to look closely, he'd be Eric again. Whatever was going on, I decided it was best faced on a full stomach, so for now I'd cope with it the British way: ignore it and pretend nothing was happening. Eric kept drifting in and out of focus and the pain behind my eyes intensified each time his image sharpened. He was looking increasingly worried and uncomfortable, and judging by the expression on his face, he thought I was about to have a stroke. I was beginning to think the same thing.

"Andi," he began haltingly but I interrupted him.

"Eric, have you got an aspirin on you?"

"Yes."

"Can I have one?"

"What? Now?"

"Yes."

"Why?"

"Because I have a headache, you dolt." Blimey, what was the problem? I wished he'd hurry up, if he didn't give me one of those aspirins absolutely immediately the top of my head was going to blow off.

"OK, Andi, I can stop your headache but you have to promise me you won't go all limp and fall over again."

So Eric was Norwegian but surely he'd seen people faint before – I mean people faint all the time don't they? His expression was panicky but also slightly shifty.

"It's called fainting, imbecile and no, I won't."

He pressed me.

"You promise?"

"Yes I promise!" He eyed me sceptically. For heaven's sake! How much reassurance could a person need? "I will not faint again," I told him. As if I had some kind of control over it. "Satisfied?"

He nodded.

"Good! Now for God's sake give me an aspirin or I'm going to die."

"No. I'm not going to give you an aspirin. I'm going to stop your headache."

My reply died on my lips as Eric went into soft focus at the edges again. As he did so, my head began to hurt less. I didn't like this one bit, there was definitely a correlation between the amount of ache in my head and the amount of blur round Eric. I turned away from him and looked out onto the City of London through the plate glass windows which made up two-thirds of the Student Union canteen wall. I scanned the familiar skyline. The Post Office Tower and the Gherkin were where they should be. The Shard? Check. The Walkie Talkie? Check. All was right with the world and nothing, except Eric, was blurry. I faced him again and as I stared, something moved by his head. Was that a tentacle? No, no. My friend did not have tentacles.

"Andi?" Eric waved his hand in front of my face except …

Hang on. That definitely was a hint of a pincer there. Maybe it was a joke. Yeh that was it: a joke; a piss-poor one at that.

"Eric, what are you doing?"

"How's your head?"

"It hurts a bit less."

"OK," he said slowly. "Andi, this is going to freak you out a bit."

"Then don't do it."

"I don't have any choice."

"Yes you do."

"No, I don't. Your brain can't take it."

My breath caught.

"Can't take what Eric? Tell me right now or I swear to God I'm going to—"

I stopped. My headache had gone and this time, I knew I

7

wasn't imagining it. Slowly Eric became a translucent wavy outline and behind him something else appeared. It looked a bit like a lobster, but without a tail and with fewer legs: two pairs to walk on and a pair of 'arms' with huge pincers on them. It was about seven feet tall with two long antennae. It had mouth parts like a praying mantis and on top of its head were seven stalks, each with a human-like eye on the end: the eyes were blue, like Eric's. The creature's exoskeleton was reddish-brown and glistening with translucent slime. I sat there for a few moments with my mouth open.

"It's difficult to explain," he said.

Yeh. I reckoned that was the officially certified understatement of all time. When I spoke my voice was croaky and hard to control.

"Eric, does this freaky thing involve lobster hands?"

"What's a lobster?"

"You don't know?"

"No."

How? He was supposed to be Norwegian: from the land of fjords and smorgasbords. I looked at the wavy image of Eric and the thing behind it. Hmm. I was beginning to suspect that Eric might not be from Norway. Could I be bothered to explain a lobster to him? No. In one respect I was scared, really scared. In another, this was Eric, who had been my friend, my true and good friend, all term, when no-one else had. I tried a different tack.

"Do you have antennae?" I asked him. "Really, really long ones, like ... I dunno ... about from here to the window?"

"They're not that long. They're only eleven of your Earth feet. Here to the window is more like fifteen."

Eleven 'Earth feet'? My alarm bells began to ring. "Their length is academic Eric." I glared at him. "My point is that *I* don't have antennae, or lobster hands and I-I'm beginning ... I'm beginning to think, heaven help me, that you do."

"I honestly don't know if I have lobster hands. I don't know what a lobster is."

"They look a bit like ..." I paused to consider the crustacean

8

moving through the water of my mind's eye.

"Oh ..." he said in a relieved, penny-dropping sort of way. "Yes, I see. I—"

"Whoa, whoa, whoa there Eric. What do you mean, 'I see'?" The Thing gave off an aura of intense contrition and the wavy, out-of-focus human Eric looked sheepish. I leaned forward to stare into human Eric's face, nose to nose, but found myself leaning straight through him and coming up rather too close for comfort to the Thing's glistening, razor-sharp mandibles.

"Are you reading my mind?" I hissed, keenly aware that there were people around us who might hear what I was saying. "Because if you are, you're trespassing. Nobody gets to see my warped inner psyche without my permission."

"Andi, I have no choice. That's the problem. You're transmitting."

I put my head in my hands.

"I can't believe this is happening. Wait! I know! It isn't is it? It's a dream and I'm going to wake up any minute; or I'm hallucinating. We both know I've been overdoing it lately."

Another understatement there. That day I was feeling extra jaded. The previous evening's gig: a humiliation of epic proportions, was still fresh in my mind. Eric came along to watch me, which was kind of good and kind of bad. Dying on stage in front of my friend was embarrassing, squared, but in another way, the fact that he was there made my abysmal failure to amuse a single member of the audience, barring him, that little bit easier to take. Swings and roundabouts then. We went back to his flat afterwards and spent most of the night drinking whisky and making up put-down lines for the trolls who'd heckled. They were blinding, of course, unlike the ones I came up with on stage. Bus wit, as my dad calls it, because you think of your best lines on the bus on the way home. Never mind, at least next time I'll be armed with some pointy ripostes. I wondered if Eric's new, earthly challenged appearance was some kind of hangover symptom or worse, something to do with my recent attacks of thinking there was someone else in my head with me. What if I was ill? Really, properly, mentally ill. It was time to do something.

"Eric, I think that, maybe, I should go and see a doctor."

"No doctor on Earth can fix this Andi."

The wavy vision of Eric sat watching me and behind it the huge lobster thing cocked its head on one side. Despite it having a rigid exoskeleton, I got the impression it was looking quizzical, and sort of patient, as if it was waiting for me to catch up.

"What?"

You're not ill, he said. Only he wasn't speaking, he was putting the words into my mind. It was the most extraordinary sensation, as if they were arriving as little balls, taking root and growing there like mushrooms. No, no, no. I didn't want this. I was already Nobby no-mates but being a freak as well? Even worse.

"What are you doing?"

Talking to you, he was still using telepathy rather than speech.

"Do you have to do that? Can you not just ... you know ... use your mouth?" I asked, and before I could stop myself, I started to cry.

"Andi, oh Andi I'm so sorry ..."

He was totally perplexed, that much was clear. Mind you, so was I. I guess everything just overflowed. The fact is, I was utterly miserable. I'd had this weird head thing going on all term, and there was no-one I could talk to. Eric was my only friend. I had so little in common with my fellow students it was laughable. They were just kids and totally helpless.

Few had left home before, hardly anyone could cook and some of them couldn't even work the residency washing machines. Yet, at the same time, they were all faux grown-up and somewhere along the line had confused maturity with not having a sense of humour. Naturally, they hated me. I'd never thought of myself as mature until I met them but I suppose I must have been. I spent a lot of my childhood abroad, mainly in the Far East. Dad's work paid for boarding school in England until I'd done my GCSEs because his postings were mostly in the Gulf. Not the best place to bring up a bolshy daughter especially when he and Mum had probably worked out that I was gay a long time before I did.

When Dad's work moved him to Singapore I was able to stay 'home' with my parents and go to the international school. It was different there. Maybe the fact we were all from such a wide mix of national backgrounds made us look harder for common ground. Who can tell? Whatever it was, for those two years, I felt as if everything in my life had aligned. If I have a real home it's there, in those years, with my family and those friends. Nobody cared that I was gay, nobody cared where I was from or what my parents did. I was just taken on merit for who I was. Here at uni it was like going back to boarding school; all about wearing the same things the trendy people wore, liking the same bands, doing the same stuff. It was all about being an amorphous representation of the student next to you rather than being yourself. With one notable exception: Eric. I was in touch with my friends from Singapore, but they weren't physically here. So, apart from Eric's company, most of the time, I was alone.

"Sorry, what with the gig last night, I guess I've just had a bad week."

"I'm sorry too, Andi, I know this is hard for you."

The image of Eric looked worried but what surprised me was the sense of complete devastation coming from his lobster alter ego. He – or it, or was it they? I didn't know any more – was genuinely upset.

I sighed. I so wanted to believe I was sane but it looked as if I was going mad.

"Yeh. If you can really see inside my head, I guess you probably do know."

I searched my pockets for a tissue and in the absence of anything useable, wiped my eyes on my paper napkin. It wasn't really up to the job.

"Andi, you're really not insane, I promise. In fact you're one of the sanest, most grounded people I've ever met. You're just a bit more," he stopped for a moment, thinking of the right word, "evolved than other humans."

'Evolved': I'd been expecting 'sensitive'. And, 'humans' not 'people'. I blew my nose with a loud parp causing the napkin finally to dissolve. I screwed it into a ball and put it in my pocket.

"Seriously, you're fine. It's just telepathy. It's no biggie where I'm from."

"What about the huge lobster? Is that telepathy?"

"No silly, that's me. I know it's a bit of a new look but I'm still Eric. Here." He pressed one pincer against ... yes, well, I suppose that was his thorax and the wavy projection of human Eric put one hand on his heart.

I nodded.

He reached the end of one long, flexible antenna down to the table. The end of it was a bit like an elephant's trunk, in that it had an opposable grip of sorts, which he used to pick up his paper napkin. He passed it to me. Wavy projected human Eric used his hand.

"Thanks," I squeaked as I blew my nose a second time. I looked about at my fellow diners. Nobody else was reacting to Eric's earthly challenged appearance. I leant across the table.

"So we've established that you look like something out of Dr Who only with better special effects and less bubble wrap. What the hell are you doing here? What's going on?"

"What would you say ..." he broke off and glanced around the room. It's something he always does when he's trying to give himself time to think – or gather the courage to broach a difficult subject. In a bizarre way it was almost reassuring to see scary lobster Eric doing the exact same thing his human version always did. "What would you say if I told you I was an alien?" he muttered quickly. "There! I've said it! I've told you!" He sighed with relief, flopped back in his chair and waited for me to react.

"Well ..." There was an awkward pause. "Looking at you the way you are now, I'd probably say, 'that figures' at the least. I'm thinking, what with you not knowing what a lobster is, that you might not be from Norway."

"You're thinking along the right lines."

I sighed and scratched my head. If he came from another planet, it might explain his dress sense. Until then I'd put the leather drainpipes, Beatle boots, Regency-revival frilly shirts and crushed velvet frock coat down to some quirk of Nordic fashion.

Now a second, more sinister explanation offered itself for Eric's ignorance of mainstream trends.

"You really are an alien, aren't you?" I said.

"'Fraid so."

"Bugger."

I wasn't really in the mood to discover my best friend was from outer space.

"I should have been straight with you from the beginning."

"If being straight had meant looking like you do now there might not have been a beginning," I said.

"There nearly wasn't. Even though you were sending me all these thoughts, that wall thing you do ... It took me ages to find you."

"Couldn't you have found a more tactful way to tell me this?"

"I'm sorry. Events have overtaken me and forced my hand."

"Yeh." I glanced furtively round the room but our fellow diners still appeared to be blissfully unaware that there was a huge slimy lobster-shaped thing in their midst. "But on the up side, I'm not going mad?"

"No," he laughed, "you're just a telepath."

"There's no such thing."

"Trust me. There is. You can pick up thoughts, or share them, you can even disguise yourself."

I made an all-encompassing gesture with my fork.

"Is that how come they can't see you?" I asked.

"Yep," he tapped the side of his head with one antenna. "It's easy. Simple mind trick."

"Er ... right." I nodded vacantly. "And my being telepathic, is that why your mind trick doesn't work on me?"

"Yes. You've outgrown it."

"Is that a good thing?"

"Yes."

My eyes were drawn to the utility belt he was wearing. There were pouches and a metal box and, most notably, a thing that looked very like a weapon.

"Is that a gun?"

"What?"

"That. It's a gun isn't it? Either that or you're an intergalactic traffic cop and you use that to catch speeding—"

The wavy transmission of Eric smiled and the lobster-shaped one seemed to emanate the sense of a smile despite having rigid, immoveable features.

"Yes, it's a blaster, which is a gun: a laser. No, I've never used it."

"What never ever?"

"Never ever; I hope I never will."

"Not even to open a door, you know, like in films?"

He laughed.

"No."

"What about cutting metal?"

"By all that's holy, Andi, when do you find the time to watch so much crap telly—"

"At four in the morning after a gig when I'm coming down. It's all that's on and it relaxes me. And it's not crap it's classic sixties sci-fi." I reverted back to the subject of the gun. "What about cooking? If you were stuck out in the wilderness, could you use it to heat up a can of beans?"

"It does two things, Andi. If you are a highly trained weapons operative and you really know what you're doing, you can liquify some solid state stuff; ice, certain types of wax – even some plastics but for most of us it does two things, it kills or it stuns. You could use it to hunt in the wilderness but you'd have to heat your beans on the fire. Although, we don't eat food like you lot, it's one of the things I really like about this planet, the whole companionable eating thing," he waved one pincer expansively and a large lump of brownish translucent slime detached itself from the tip and plopped onto the table by my hand. It smelt faintly of Marmite.

"Eric, that's a bridge too far," I said.

"What?"

"The gloop."

"It's just life matter."

"Just. And what's life matter?"

"It's how I breathe."

"You mean you don't …" I inhaled and exhaled.

"No, I absorb oxygen through my exoskeleton. Life matter accelerates the process. Without it I'd suffocate."

"Seriously? You don't have lungs?"

"Gross. No."

He actually shuddered.

"Are you telling me you think breathing is vile?"

"Very."

"Well, I guess I can sympathise, I'm not too big a fan of slime," I said, before I could stop myself. "Sorry, that's—slime is not—well, you know how I feel about slugs not that you're a slug …" Flippin' Ada, mentally I was rolling my eyes at this point. I mean how big a hole could I dig? "No, that's not quite how I meant it but—"

"Are you saying you believe I'm real?"

I looked across the table at him, or was that it?

"A real alien? Yes. Unfortunately, I think I do."

"And you're OK about this!"

"Not exactly OK," especially not about the gun or the slime, "but I probably won't run away screaming just yet. It's weird but I guess I can tell it's still you, that you're Eric, who I know and trust, even if you look—" I was distracted by the slime which turned into a pool of spaghetti hoops. "Whoa. Is that a mind trick too?"

"No, I morphed that one," he unhooked the small metal box from his belt and held it up, "it has to stay like that after we've gone," he explained.

"Yeh," I cleared my throat, "right."

He put the box on the table in front of him using the ends of his flexible antennae and straightened it until it was just so.

"What is that?"

"My data pod." He anticipated my next question and continued, "It's a cross between a tablet, a mobile phone and a passport. It has all my electronic ID on it, I can even vote with it if I have to, it can be used to find me and transport me to my ship if I—"

"Your ship? You have colleagues nearby?"

"Only two."

"Right," I knew I was staring at him but I couldn't help it. He was so different and he was—yeh, come to think of it how did he—

"Eric, I have to ask, there are some technicalities I can't get straight. You're seven feet tall and your limbs outnumber mine by two to one if I count your ... antennae. How come you fit on the chair?"

He waved a pincer at the box on the table: the data pod. It had a purple LED on it so there were only two things it could be, an expensive piece of stereo equipment (too small) or something from outer space.

"Science: ours is a bit ahead of yours," he said. "With this, if I want to fit on this chair I will. That's how I ride a bicycle," he added, pre-empting my next question. "It's the Omega Three, it's a little long in the tooth now but it was state of the art when I got it. And it's still a fantastic piece of engineering. It's the think and type model and it's just so intuitive, the capabilities it has are mind blowing. They thought of everything and the battery life is brilliant and it just works really, really well."

"Yeh, I can see it knocks my crappy laptop into a cocked hat. It's very cool. But actually, Eric, I'm sure you didn't come to my planet so you could show me your personal digital assistant."

"Data pod, it's a data pod."

"Whatever. So, yes, I'm buying the alien thing, and I'm glad that makes you happy, but, as I may have mentioned, you have some serious explaining to do as to the reason for your visit. Why are you here?"

Chapter 4
The ultimate mission

While Eric and I were chatting, something important was happening. Far out in the silent reaches of space, several years away for human space flight, but just a short click from Earth for a more technologically advanced civilisation, something appeared. It was a sleek, dark, metal object and it was going very fast: it was a ship dropping out of hyperspace. In the silence of the vast emptiness around it, it made no sound, but aboard things were different. It was bustling with activity. Klaxons sounded, metal clanged and crew members made their way officiously about their business through the maze of corridors, or worked studiously at their stations. Each one of them was enjoying the posting of a lifetime. The big day was coming; the day that they would make history; the start of a new era.

In his quarters, the supreme mission commander tried to quell the anger that burned within him. It was no good being angry. He knew that, but someone was going to pay for this and it would not be him. He looked up from the report he was reading. He should be on the bridge, ready to give a rousing patriotic speech to the crew. He'd even compiled a few suitable sound bites.

"Today we stand at the dawn of a new forever: across the galaxy, for millennia henceforward, they will whisper our names with awe ..." he said.

He was not in the mood for the bridge or rousing speeches. Commodore Pimlip could deal with that. He turned his attention back to the report again. He must channel his rage, use it. He activated the keyboard and began to type. Something had to be done about this, and fast. It threw the whole mission into jeopardy. Naturally, it was not part of the plan but no matter, eighth hour it may be, there was still time to neutralise the situation.

He gave his précis a final read through before attaching it to a mail document, along with his own series of notes and the original report. He addressed it to his superior, copied in his co-commander – not that the idiot deserved the courtesy – and jabbed the send button.

There. That should do it. It had better.

Chapter 5
Three's company

Back in the canteen, Eric turned his pincers outwards and executed what I guessed was a Gallic shrug, although what with him having a rigid exoskeleton and all, it was a feeling, the telepathically projected essence of a Gallic shrug, that made me able to tell.

"Come on, out with it. What's a nice space lobster like you doing on a planet like this?"

"It's difficult to explain." A thought struck him. "The other girls on your corridor have their diet meeting this evening don't they? Shall I come round, while they're out? I can bring a bottle of wine and tell you everything."

"Aren't you seeing your—" I stopped. I was going to say 'parents' because a couple of days previously, when Eric was still human-shaped and everything was normal, he'd told me his mother and father were visiting from Stavanger. He was supposed to be going to collect Helga and Sven from Heathrow Airport this afternoon. It did occur to me now, that if he went to Heathrow at all, Eric would not be going to collect anyone, nobody human at any rate. Presumably it was the two colleagues he'd mentioned. Certainly, the odds against it being Helga and Sven were pretty high. "Tell you what, why don't I bunk off this afternoon?"

"Can't I'm—"

"I know you're not collecting your parents, Eric, and I know you're not going to Heathrow."

"Well, actually, I *am* going to Heathrow, but you're right, I'm not meeting my parents."

"Right, so I can come to Heathrow with you." I wanted to get to the bottom of this.

"You can't bunk off Andi, not after Desmond had a go at you. You told me he'd given you a warning."

"You're clutching at straws, Eric. It wasn't quite a warning, more an informal chat. He was worried about what he called my 'burning the candle at both ends' which I call 'doing too many things at once'. It's simple, I'll do fewer things, or at least, the same number of things but less often."

"And he had a chat with you because?"

I blushed.

"I fell asleep in his seminar."

"Andi!"

"It's the art module on my course. You try sitting on a comfortable sofa, in a darkened room, with a hangover, looking at slides! I defy you not to go to sleep. Anyway, he wasn't annoyed. He said he was concerned for my well-being. He actually *told* me it wasn't pique at my lack of self-discipline."

"It sounds like a warning to me."

"It's not official. Anyway, Desmond isn't teaching me today. We both have watertight excuses: you're collecting your mum and dad, I fainted."

"I'm not collecting my mum and dad though, am I?"

"No. But you have the afternoon off, right?"

"Wrong."

"Yeh right, don't tell me you're going to lectures after all."

"No, and don't get all sarcastic. I have to report to—"

"Report," I interrupted him. "I assume there are a lot more space lobsters up there than the two you've owned up to then."

"Don't be silly, I'll make the report via a telecommunications link. Nobody's here yet, it's just me – and my two partners."

"What, your business partners?"

"No, my spouses."

Spouses. Plural. Blimey.

"You're spouse-*S*."

"Yeh."

"You're polygamous."

"In a manner of speaking."

"In a manner of speaking, you are or you aren't, surely. Are you a space Mormon?"

"No, I'm Gamalian and I'm a threep. OK so look, it takes three of us to pod and incubate an egg so we marry in threes."

"There are three genders of your species?" I asked, in amazement. Wow! That was cool.

"No, Andi. There is one gender of threep, but, as I explained, it takes three to ..." he waved one pincer and the wavy insubstantial human projection of Eric in front of him waved one hand and took a deep breath. "It takes three to."

"Kinky."

"Yeh? Or are you the kinky ones with your weird extra gender?"

"I'm a lesbian. I don't use the extra gender."

"Yeh but there are plenty of Neanderthals who think that makes you kinky."

Good point. I suddenly felt a bit awkward. I said nothing.

"Andi, are you going to be OK? D'you need me to take you home?"

"I thought you had to go and report."

"I do, but I also have to look after you and there are ways I can transport you home a bit more quickly."

"Beam me up Scottie?"

He patted the box.

"Kind of. I want to take care of you because I may be Gamalian and you may be a human but I consider you to be my friend. And I *need* to look after you because if all goes well with my report, you're evidence."

"I *what?* And *NOW* we get to the nub of it. And I have to tell you, Eric, since it's been three-quarters of a term, I'd say it's about blummin' time."

He sighed or at least, the projection of human Eric sighed. The threep version just gave off an aura of weary resignation. And then he did the thought thing again; the speaking without sound.

Andi, I know this is a big ask for you but you're going to have to be

21

patient and trust me. I know I am a bit different from your original perception, but I told you, inside here, once again he pressed one pincer to his thorax, and the fuzzy projection of human Eric pressed his fingertips to his chest to emphasise his words, *I'm still Eric. If you've ever thought of me as a friend, if you've ever believed I have your best interests at heart then please trust me.*

I shrugged.

"I really don't know how or why, Eric but I do trust you. I'm keeping my eyes open, metaphorically, if you see what I mean." Even if, in the reality of this particular situation, things would be quite a lot easier if I kept them shut.

"OK, come on then, I'll take you home."

He picked up his tray and got to his feet. I followed suit.

So how come he was still bothering with the human Eric?

Because I don't want them to see me, he waved a pincer at the people around us.

"And you just answered my thoughts! Wow! Am I doing telepathy?"

Not as such, Andi, you just think really loudly.

He was trying to hide it but I got the impression that wasn't a good thing. As I slid my tray into a free slot on the high trolley he put his in the one on top, above my head. We walked into the hall outside and as I glanced back, to check that the slime—no wait, what had he called it? ah yes, life matter—on the table was still looking like spaghetti hoops.

It was.

Chapter 6
Personal chemistry

A voice broke into my thoughts: a human, female voice. "Hi, Andi isn't it?"

I was a bit thrown. Someone was speaking to me. A normal actual person, that was, who wasn't Eric except that he wasn't human anymore and ... yeh ... stop there. I must have looked mega stern as I wheeled round because she stepped backwards with a nervous expression. Something about her struck me at once. She had blonde hair, greeny-brown eyes, a seriously mischievous smile and I was prepared to bet that she was even gayer than me.

"Sorry, I didn't mean to look scary. Yes. I'm Andi. Do I know you?"

"You're on floor three with the undead, right?"

I snorted with laughter before I could stop myself.

"Is that what they're called?"

"Yeh, on account of the fact everyone is a fashion zombie and they all wear black, like vampires."

I thought of the people I shared a floor with, not to mention a bathroom and kitchen. They took their 'look', their course and everything else, very, very seriously. They wore black because they thought it was sophisticated. They were the most boring and opinionated bunch of people I'd ever met, and believe me, I've met some complete knobs in my time.

"Right." I glanced down at my home-decorated baseball boots; originally white, I'd given them red, orange and yellow flames. I was also wearing red drainpipe trousers, a long-sleeved Danger Mouse T-shirt and a thick checked shirt over the top of it. "So, you think I'm a fashion zombie?" I asked her incredulously.

"Nah, not really, or at least, not from this decade." She

grinned to make sure I realised she was joshing.

"Yeh, the girls on my corridor keep telling me this look's a crime. Eric here, has more fashion sense than me."

She seemed to notice Eric for the first time. Please let her be seeing a handsome Scandinavian man with leather trousers, boots and a velvet jacket and not the giant space lobster I was confronted with.

"That's true and it's why I thought it was time the normals on the fourth floor made contact," she said. The fourth floor. That meant she must be in her second year. Freshers were only allocated the rooms on the first three floors, four and five were for second and third years and post-grads.

"The normals?"

"Mmm hmm. You never talk to anyone but you don't look like you fit in with that bunch," she shrugged.

"I—to be honest, no-one ever talks to me."

"Ah, so you're a shy one."

I glanced helplessly at Eric but he just chuckled and said, "Yes."

"What course are you on?"

"Art Restoration and Museum Studies."

"Ooo," she sucked the air in through her teeth in mock surprise, "esoteric. No wonder you don't talk to anyone."

"What's that supposed to mean?"

"Your course is famous for being full of eccentrics."

"I don't see why."

"Oh c'mon, it's totally obscure and everyone on it is weird, except for you: the exception to prove the rule. I've seen your course mates, they're all about fifty."

Couldn't deny that.

"There are a lot of mature students. I suppose it's the chemistry module. Being an arty scientist is …" I shrugged, "quite rare. Most of them are chemists who've come to art later in life. I'm doing a curation module and the statutory art history modules, but the bulk is restoration of artefacts and that takes a fair bit of chemistry."

"I suppose it explains why I see you round the labs all the

time then, I'm doing chemical engineering."

I struggled to hide my surprise, failing dismally, I suspect.

"Chemical engineering? Geek central?"

"You know the nickname then."

"Um, yes." The chemical engineers were famed for the herdlike and cuboidal nature of their dress sense. This girl's T-shirt had a Blue Meanie on the front of it, her jeans were purple, and she was wearing a neat tailored jacket in dark blue, a scarf and black leather ankle boots. Her hair was cut short in a bob. We appeared to be dressing from a similar style book, sort of, although my hair is spiky rather than bobbed and she was definitely a lot cooler than I am. She managed to look both dishevelled and stylish at the same time, while I merely appear dishevelled. "That sounds like high-powered stuff though."

"Not really. I'm good at chemistry and useless at pretty much everything else. It's the obvious choice."

"Lucky you. I could do with having, well, even the vaguest notion about chemistry. I spend fifty per cent of my time trying to understand the chemistry modules on my course. I have to work like a Trojan to scrape a pass on every single one. The rest is a breeze."

"If-if you're having trouble, I can try and give you a hand if you like. I might not be the best teacher but I'm happy to have a go. You know, if you think I could help."

Was she—?

Eric's thoughts cut into mine.

Yes, she's gay, ah so he'd noticed as well, *and she likes you.*

I stopped to think for a few moments and Eric did the putting words in my head thing again.

I can read her mind. Ask her out for a drink. You're made for one another.

"Will you shut up!" I told Eric, out loud. Arse. "Sorry, not you," I told her quickly as she shot me a questioning look. "I'd really appreciate your help if you had time. I warn you though, I'm really thick."

She arched her eyebrows.

"Now that I cannot believe. I'm Jen, from room 424," she added.

"I'm Andi from room 317," I stuck out my hand, mock formal and she shook it, also mock formal. "It's a bit of a bad time now but later ... tomorrow maybe? Would you like to meet up?"

"Yep. Can't do tomorrow though in fact the first day I'm free is Friday. Would you like to come up to mine for tea, say four o'clock? – and bring your chemistry notes."

Whoa, she was so unfazed and so completely in control. So far at uni, I'd always felt like the calm mature one. I was a tiny bit in awe.

"That would be really nice," I said. I felt my cheeks colouring and cleared my throat. "Thanks."

"See you later then," she said.

Eric and I stood and watched as, with a wave, she went into the canteen.

"Aaaand Andi has a date," he nudged me.

"Gerroff!" It made my arm tingle. "It's not a date."

"Yeh right, you're going to her room to study chemistry."

"Yes, I am."

"Mmm personal chemistry and if you have time, I expect you might even look at your course work."

"You are so cheeky. It's not like that at all."

"Well, at the least you've made a friend." He nudged me again. More pins and needles. Come to think of it, I felt a bit pins and needly all over. "Stop that," I told him but Eric grabbed my hand.

"Quick, Andi."

"Wha—"

"This way." He dragged me across the wide hall to the glass outer wall of the building. I could feel his anxiety.

"What's up?" I asked. My hair felt funny and I had a worrying impression it might be standing on end, or at least standing rather more on end than its gel-assisted norm. I'd read somewhere that was a sign you're about to get struck by lightning. Hmm. Best get away from the window then. But before I could move, he took my hands with his antennae.

"Andi, I think events have just caught up with me," he said.

"Yeh, you told me."

"No, I mean *really* caught up, like NOW."

"Eh? What d'you mean? What's going on?"

"There's no time to explain," he glanced down, checking the machine on his belt; the Omega Three data pod. A red light was flashing urgently. Uh-oh. That looked like bad news. "The lads are transporting me up. Go back to your room and wait for me. This won't take long and I *will* return. I promise." He flickered for a moment as he looked down again and checked the box, "Plort! You're too close, you'll come with me if you aren't careful. Run away," he seemed to flicker again, "get out of here."

"But—"

"Quick."

"OK."

As I backed up, he started to turn translucent.

"Go!" His voice began to fade, "GO!" He waved me away, "Ru—" He disappeared.

"What the f—Eric?" I said.

No answer.

"Where are you?"

Still no answer. The tingling feeling under my skin increased. I was certain my hair was standing on end now, I could feel the roots pulling and a pinching sensation on my upper arms. On the face of the evidence, running away seemed like a good move.

I turned tail and fled down the corridor.

Chapter 7
Having a blast

In the absence of a better plan, I attended the slowest afternoon of lectures known to humankind. I swear I was sucked into some kind of time vortex that made every minute last about nine hours. It being a Tuesday, my last lecture was at five o'clock and for some reason the student residencies all chose to serve supper at half five – something to do with staff overtime, no doubt – but it meant that by the time I returned it would be closed. Skanky though the kitchen was on my floor, at least I could cook myself something. I'd made myself a curry the night before, to a chorus of complaints from everyone on the corridor about the 'disgusting smell'.

It was seven o'clock when I got home and I was looking forward to that curry. Needless to say, some total smeghead had eaten it. It's hard to live peacefully with people who are on diets. They are all po-faced and holier than thou about any food they are offered at mealtimes and then they eat everything in the fridge while you're out.

"What's the point of all this stupid dieting if you eat everyone else's stuff on the sly?" I shouted angrily at the empty corridor. I knew I was safe. They'd be at Weight Loss Support Group tonight.

Gits. They hadn't even washed the pots. Well, if they'd eaten my supper I was stuffed if I was going to wash up for them. I left the saucepans in the sink and with a disgruntled sigh I turned to the fridge freezer. I kept an emergency packet of fish fingers in the freezer compartment. They never looked there.

However, when I approached the fridge, I discovered someone had looked, probably several days ago, and then they'd left the door of the freezer half ajar and the whole compartment was now a solid block of ice. I could see the box of fish fingers in the middle but after a few minutes hacking at it with a knife it became clear that I couldn't reach it without an ice pick, or at the least, a chisel.

"Hello, do you want a hand with that?"

It was a strangely robotic electric voice, unnervingly reminiscent of a Dalek.

I spun round.

Standing facing me, were two space lobsters like Eric. One was grey, the other was dark brown, and was holding—

"Can we go easy with the gun?" Blimey O'Riley, I needed to sit down. "I said, can you not point it at me?"

The brown one made an incredibly loud screech that made me jump and my ears smart. Talk about an aural onslaught, it sounded like the noise you hear if someone is trying to send a fax to your landline; a high-pitched burbling combined with a fingernails-across-blackboard-style grating. It was finished off with a dash of breaking glass and shouting dolphins – yes, yes, I know dolphins can't shout but these threeps were doing a very credible imitation of sonic dolphin communication. It was only when the grey one did the same thing back that I realised they were actually talking to one another.

Blummin' Ada.

"Mrslsssp," said the brown one and, despite the fact his exoskeleton didn't move, I could tell that was definitely a shrug.

I felt surprisingly calm. Then again, 'do you want a hand with that?' is not a usual opening gambit for someone who's come to harm you, even if they are waving a gun. Eric had told me his partners were nearby so I reckoned these must be they, so to speak.

"What do you want?" I asked.

The brown threep turned to his grey friend. "Grlsp?"

I wasn't sure why they had suddenly relapsed into talking their own language but I hoped they were going to stop before my head exploded or my ears started bleeding.

As I watched them, the grey one curled the end of one huge, prawn-like antenna down to the top of its head and scratched the bottom of one of its seven eye stalks, thoughtfully.

"Grlsp." It stopped scratching and reached the end of his flexible antenna to a hole at the side of its head and removed something that looked remarkably like a bluetooth earpiece. It shook the earpiece and put it back.

"Pthfsk grlsp. Psrlcrgggggggggb?" it said.

The other one shrugged. "Sqularrrrrb?"

"Grlaaarb?" The grey one took a box from its belt and shook that. "Splorabundum?" It shook the box up and down, "Hrlllft." It banged the box against one pincer, "Mmrlssss," it said and banged the box harder. "Squlleeerrb? Norllsp," it smacked the box even harder, "—ucking piece of useless—hey, it's working Smeesch."

"Please, move over," said the brown threep. To my relief the electronic gizmo – some kind of translation device, I assumed – seemed to overlay their speech. In theory they should have been making far too much of a din for me to hear anything else. I supposed the box was fitted with noise cancellation. The brown threep waved the gun again. I stepped smartly sideways.

Before I could say anything else, like 'don't', or stop him, he fired. The blaster emitted a beam of green light which hit the fridge squarely in the frozen freezer compartment and made an absolutely text book B-movie pinging noise. However, I was more concerned by the, now melted, wall of ice, which fell out in a sudden, gargantuan splash. It spread rapidly out over the floor, leaving the packet of fish fingers on the strandline, as it were, at my feet.

"Oh my days," I said, as the grey threep reached a long antenna down, picked them up and handed them to me. I gave him a look and squinted into the box. There was a strong and unpleasant smell of burning but the fish fingers were fine. There were five left and the laser had thawed them so I'd have to cook them all. Perhaps it would be polite to offer some to the threeps. I turned to the oven, which was next to the fridge freezer, intending to put the grill on but I was distracted by the discovery of where the burning smell was coming from.

The top of the fridge – its freezer section – had disappeared and where the metal had survived it had melted in with its white plastic casing. The resulting mixture had run down the sides and then hardened. It looked like some saggy toxic candle.

"Sorry mate," said the brown threep, "I think I gave it a bit too much power."

Yeh. Just a tad. Oh dear.

"We've come to find Pers—" the grey one began but the brown one nudged him.

"It's n—qlurssceppp," said the brown threep.

"Blucscruwarrrp!" The grey one raised all seven of its eyes to heaven and smacked the box, which it was still holding, against its pincer.

While he fiddled with the box I went to the corner and turned the fridge off at the mains. I was going to have to report it as broken. What in the name of heaven would I say? Perhaps I could avoid saying anything and pretend I just found it like that.

"Sorry," the grey threep had got the box working again. "I was going to give you his Gamalian name. You will know him as Eric," it said. "He is our partner."

"You're his husbands?" I asked.

There was a moment while the translator, if that's what the box was, fed my answer to their ear pieces.

"Yes. We have lost contact."

My stomach lurched.

"But you beamed him up. Today. I nearly went with him but he—"

"What the hell is going on?" demanded a voice.

All three of us turned round. There, in the doorway, was the principal of the student residency and the caretaker, who was armed with a spade. Behind them, I could just make out two of the girls from my corridor. That's when I remembered. Jane and Laura were going to a new weight loss group because the woman who ran their old one had told them they were already thin enough. They must have seen me with the threeps and thought … who knew what they thought. I shuddered. Had they seen the brown threep shoot the fridge? Please no.

"Hello Mr Slimbridge, Bob, Jane, Laura," there was a kerfuffle in the hall and three more people arrived. Policemen? What on earth? Why were the police here? "Oh and ... hello ... sirs," I said.

They were all staring at me as if they weren't sure whether or not I was actually there.

"What are you doing, Miss Turbot?" the principal asked me. There was a forced woodenness to his tone.

"Er ..." I held up the packet of fish fingers, "just having supper."

"Hmm and who are these ... people?"

"My friends; they're in costumes for a play. We're just testing them out."

Lord above, what rubbish was I talking?

A large piece of Marmite-scented ectoplasm detached itself from the brown threep and landed on the floor with a splat.

Not good timing. At all.

Mr Slimbridge, the principal, looked down at the slime and then back up at me.

"What happened to the fridge?" His mouth outlined the 'w' of the 'what' several times before any actual sound came out.

"Ah yes, we had a bit of an accident—" began the computerised voice. There were two threeps and only one box. As a result, it wasn't always easy to work out which threep was doing the talking. Even so, I was pretty sure it was the grey one.

"That's more than an accident!" Bob the caretaker butted in, "that's pure vandalism, that is. It's—"

"I advise you to stand back, sir," one of the policemen muscled his way to the front. "We'll handle this! The one on the left is armed."

"Oh bum."

"There's no need for that madam," said the policeman.

"I'm really sorry, I know this looks bad," I said lamely, "nobody means any harm and I'll replace the fridge." I could feel goose pimples coming up on my arms and my head was tingling.

"I should hope you will madam," said the policeman, "but we'll have to ask you and your," he thought for a long time before he eventually plumped for the word, "friends, to come with us to the station."

"Is there any need?"

The tingling sensation increased.

"I'm afraid so madam. One of them is carrying an unlicensed firearm."

"What? This toy?" said the computerised voice of the threeps and the brown one waved it around. Jane and Laura screamed and everyone got down, except the brave policeman, who remained implacably where he was.

"Yes sir," he told the brown threep.

The tingling was getting really strong now, and the grey threep's pincer went to one of the boxes, on his belt. I guessed it was a data pod because it looked a bit like Eric's. At about the same time I realised what was happening. He looked up and I felt the same prickling sensation on my scalp as I had before, outside the canteen when Eric vanished. The threep's eyes met mine in alarm.

"Yes, of course," I gabbled at the policeman. "We'll all come with you right now. We'll all walk quickly down the hall away from ... here." I felt light, weightless. "And I think we should hurry up," I added. Except that nobody seemed to be listening, they were all staring at me. There was a fizzing sound, I felt an odd sensation, like being pinched all over, then there was a burst of light and ... nothing.

Chapter 8
B-Movie hell

When I woke up, it took me a moment to remember what had happened. I was lying on a bed, but while it was not a hard surface, it was gym mat soft rather than mattress soft. I was on my back so when I opened my eyes, I expected the cream ceiling of the kitchen in my student residence, or possibly that of a police cell, but not what I actually saw. This ceiling was not cream or police cell beige. It was metal: matt black with a yellow-gold sheen beneath it, like brass is sometimes when it's a bit tarnished or made to look old. But this was so much better than that, the gold underlay made it almost seem to glow. It was decorated, too. Except the word 'decorated' doesn't really do justice to what I could see. It was like Art Nouveau on speed. It was as if those green Parisian metro signs with the lamps on, the ones that I've always thought look like triffids, had gone on a drugs binge, begun to have an orgy and got tangled in the kind of hugantic Gordian knot that it would take the rest of time to undo. Well, no, it was more tasteful than that would be. It was barking mad, ornate and yet appealing – possibly even beautiful – in a steampunk sort of way. Panels giving off a soft ambient light were set into the, well, yes I suppose I could call those fronds. It would have been pleasing and quite restful if it weren't for the fact that I so very much wasn't looking at the ceiling I expected to see, in the place I anticipated.

I sat up and there was a click. It was the sound of a bunch of threeps. There were six – four with guns like the weapon Eric carried, the same type the visitor to my student residency had used to blow up the fridge. I was unimpressed to see the threeps were pointing these guns at me. In the middle of the group, flanked by a brace of gun toters either side, stood two more threeps who weren't brandishing any weapons – although they had similar blasters hanging from their belts. I didn't really notice one of them because the other had my full attention. He was jet black and the others, even the ones pointing the guns, were clearly petrified of him. Then again, I could see why. His eyes were dark, grey green and he had the kind of stare that would fry eggs at fifty feet. Currently he was directing it at me. If there was such a thing as a degree in caustic staring, this was a being who had studied to PhD level. He regarded me with distaste, yes, that was definitely a sense of distaste I was getting, and despite his rigid exoskeleton, I could tell that it was accompanied by a whopping dollop of snarling hauteur. If he'd had an upper lip, it would have been curled in a permanent sneer.

He turned and said something to the one beside him and even though I braced myself for the aural onslaught of threep speech, I feared for my hearing. Luckily whatever he was saying was brief. An order I guessed.

"What the—?" I whimpered. I cast a panic-stricken glance around for any signs of the two threeps who'd visited my student residence, or even Eric, but there were no friendly faces to be seen. Just before he disappeared Eric had told me to trust him, but it was difficult faced with such a menacing collection of his fellow species. I made to swing my legs off the bed and stand up but noticed that the floor was knee-deep in the same type of slime that had covered my friend, and which also covered them. The thought that it had fallen off them, and was second hand, made me queasy. Walking in it would be like wading through a carpet of other people's snot. Hmm. Standing up could wait then.

"Where am I?" I asked them.

"You are on the Eegby," said the black one, leaving me none the wiser. No translator box here, either. This was actually him speaking, in fluent English. He had a clipped BBC accent, but at the same time, his voice was gravelly and deep. It reminded me of Darth Vader without the heavy breathing. I wonder if he also found breathing repulsive the way Eric did. "You will be returned to your planet shortly, when you have answered some simple questions," he added.

My extensive knowledge of TV and film sci-fi had taught me that questions are never simple in a situation like this, so I hoped the returning to my planet bit wasn't conditional. I tried to quell my rising panic.

"Look, whatever you think it is I know I'm sure I don't. I can't help you." I spoke fast, my fear doing the talking.

The second of the unarmed threeps stepped forward. He was a light brown with the same human eyes except they were a shade of orange I'd never seen on earth. I felt an uncomfortable tightening round my head and a strange prickly sensation in the back of my neck. The black threep turned sharply to him and stood still for a moment, as if listening. Were they talking to each other? As I watched, he nodded and turned back to me.

"You can and you will."

"No, seriously, I'm just a bog-standard student. You've mixed me up with someone else."

Another pause while the two unarmed threeps exchanged looks. Yes, they *were* talking to each other. Bearing in mind what Eric had said about telepathy, I supposed it was possible. The two of them faced each other for a few moments while the guards stood implacably by. I wondered if they could read my mind: possibly, but I guessed it more likely that just the brown one could and that the pauses were him relaying what he saw. I tried to hide my thoughts. Not that I had the first clue how. The dark threep turned slowly back to face me.

"You have a friend, Eric. But he's not an earthling is he?"

'Earthling'? This was getting worse and worse. I didn't think this threep would be good news for Eric so I stayed silent.

"I asked you a question, human," it said and this time I noticed the flinty hardness in its tone.

I swallowed.

"Eric—" no, too wobbly, I took a deep breath and started

again. "Eric is one of you." Should I tell the ebony-coloured threep anything else about my friend? No, absolutely not.

"Where is he?"

Something in my interrogator's voice made me even more nervous, or perhaps it was the way the guns held by the flanking threeps suddenly seemed to get bigger. No, that would be a mind trick; I realised my head was aching the way it had when Eric had been doing his 'human' projection at full strength. Yes, it was definitely a mind trick. I concentrated and although I wasn't sure how, I found I could resist it. The headache abated and the guns somehow shrank and appeared less frightening. The brown threep became agitated, nervous and he burbled at length in his own language while the black one listened.

"Doubtless you are right, Advisor Mingold, and the human is a little more gifted than she appears," replied the black threep, still in English, when his colleague was finished.

'The human' I noticed again, and he'd clearly spoken in my language for my benefit, a warning shot to let me know he had the measure of me, which he undoubtedly did. This didn't bode well. I felt like an animal being examined by zoologists: old-school Victorian-style zoologists who would happily kill and dissect the last living specimen of a species to see how it worked. I hoped they weren't going to pickle me in formaldehyde and put me on a shelf in their equivalent of the Natural History Museum.

The black one turned his attention back to me.

"This Eric: where can I find him?"

He moved a step closer and I realised how much bigger than me he was. I cast another rapid glance round the room but there was no escape. The threeps with the guns moved in and the other unarmed one followed his colleague a couple of paces behind. Oh well, at least I could answer the question totally truthfully without compromising my friend.

"He disappeared."

"How convenient for you," said the black threep.

"Actually it's not. Not at all, but he did," I tried to keep my voice even because the black threep was clearly angry, as well as contemptuous, and I so didn't want to worsen his mood. "He vanished right in front of me a few hours before—" I stopped, before what? I didn't know. "Before whatever happened between me losing consciousness in my student residency and waking up here. And by the way, the authorities in my country don't approve of kidnapping our citizens. Not at all."

Lame: really, really lame. The black threep was right next to the bed now and the four guards close either side. Worryingly, I couldn't see the light brown one any more.

"Your authorities will not be troubling us, here. The Eegby is the flagship of the entire Gamalian fleet: and we are at a safe enough distance. Any rescue mission from your planet would take years to reach us. Your human compatriots, and their pathetic attempts at technology, can disapprove all they like. They pose no threat."

Please, please, God, let this not be happening. And don't let him kill me, I thought.

Despite his immovable features, I knew the black threep was smiling. It was not the kind of smile that had anything to do with friendship, either. He had detected my fear and he was seriously invading my personal space. As he towered over me I wondered if I was about to die. I began to shake and while I'm not one hundred per cent certain how you go about cowering, I reckon I gave it my best shot; shrinking away from him, pedalling backwards up the bed, the plastic squeaking as I went. He moved alongside me, until I was brought up short against the body of the other threep with an unpleasantly moist squelch. Ah. So that's where he'd gone.

"Eric disappeared?"

I stifled a scream of shock as my interrogator suddenly clicked one pincer in front of my face with a vicious snap.

"Just like that."

"Yes."

He cocked his head on one side. In the dim light, with the pupils dilated, his grey-green irises had all but disappeared and his eyes looked the same sinister black as the rest of his exoskeleton.

All seven of them glared into mine.

"I don't believe you."

The sense of cold determination emanating from him intensified as he burbled something to his unarmed companion in their own language. I felt nauseous as I watched them, close to blind panic, desperately trying to hold onto my self-control. Something told me that if I ever wanted to see my home again, I must stay calm and rational. Unfortunately, the rest of my body wasn't listening to that sort of logic.

"What's going on, what are you doing?" I asked, failing, abysmally, to hide the petrified wobble in my voice. No, no, no! Don't show your terror. This situation calls for a brave and fearless heroine and that's not how it's done.

The black one leaned forward.

"I need information. Information which I think you have but which I sense you are reluctant to share. So, I'm afraid Advisor Mingold here, will be forced to extract it from you using mental fusion. I'm sure he'll spare you as much pain as possible."

He might have been, but I wasn't. What in the name of the almighty was 'mental fusion'? This was like the worst science fiction scenario ever; like being stuck in a vintage space movie.

"I'm sure he doesn't need to do that to recognise the truth. But he's going to anyway, isn't he?" I said. *Because you want him to hurt me, just to see what I do,* I thought.

There was a slight pause.

"Correct. You are very cynical, human, but in this case, surprisingly astute," he said. Was he answering my thoughts as well as my words? It felt like it.

He turned, silently, to Advisor Mingold and I knew, now, that they were exchanging thoughts. Then he wheeled back round at lightning speed, catching me by the neck with one pincer. He slammed me back onto the plastic and squeezed so hard I began to see spots. Even so, I looked into his eyes and tried to pretend I was calm. Then the unhelpful realisation hit me that his giant pincers could probably nip my head off without trouble. It would be so easy he might even do it by mistake. I lay still or at least as still as a woman can while trembling the way I was.

He gave me a brief, appraising look and burbled something short and sharp in Threep. I guessed it was 'proceed' or some such, because Advisor Mingold stepped forward.

Mingold put one of his antennae on each of my temples. I didn't know much about telepathy but I had thought that touch was unnecessary. Perhaps 'fusion' was something different, perhaps it helped him to focus, or maybe they'd done some research on my planet and seen enough pulp science fiction films to know it would scare me.

Immediately, I felt a vile sensation, as if there were slimy worms trying to burrow and wriggle their way into my mind. There was a cold wetness – even though, like all threeps, Mingold had no slime on his antennae. I concentrated on building a mental wall. The worms would burrow through bricks so I made it solid metal: armour-plated, thick and strong to keep them out. I began to feel small pinpricks of pain, as if I could detect their gnawing at my metal fortress. I imagined them with sharp teeth, tearing and scraping at it.

No, no, that was him trying to undermine me. I must imagine harder.

I made the metal shiny, burnished to a bright sheen, I made it titanium. Still the worms attacked. I fought them with all my might, the pain increasing with every second and while I did so, I tried to put a part of my mind outside the metal barricade, with Advisor Mingold, and explain that I'd been telling the truth. I tried to say it with my mind rather than speaking so his jet-coloured, scary friend couldn't hear. Either it didn't work or he was under orders not to listen. Eric had told me that I thought loudly, but he'd also explained that I couldn't do telepathy with any proper control – or at all – even if I *was* telepathic. My fear took over. Except that what I actually thought was,

Please don't let me wee my pants!

Oh great, Andi. Act dignified in front of the mind reader why don't you?

Mingold made a noise, a half laugh, half snarl, and behind him, in the background, the other threep watched with ice-cool scientific detachment. I tried to think images and pictures, junk words, songs, anything that would keep Mingold from seeing into my head but the metal wall buckled and tumbled and I could feel his presence in my mind. I was outgunned and I couldn't protect myself. This wasn't anything close to an even fight. He was trained: fully trained and I wasn't. It was nuclear warhead versus toothpick. I didn't stand a chance. Somehow, I realised that if I didn't do something, my brain could end up toasted. But at the same time, I also realised that if I fought against him, a toasting was certain. So I did the honourable thing. I gave up all resistance: capitulated. Completely.

Alright. You win. Hello and welcome to Andi Turbot's brain. Please tread carefully and try not to break anything.

I felt the antennae clamped against my temples tense. Clearly, he hadn't expected cooperation.

Here's my cerebral cortex, my conscious thoughts are over here, and this rather ugly bunch over here, these are the thoughts I try to pretend I don't have. You know the thoughts everyone thinks only they have, the ones that are so embarrassing they make us squirm, or so gross that we can't look them in the face ... I saw pictures, I wasn't sure what of but I had the distinct suspicion they were from Mingold's brain. There were two threeps and they were ... I didn't want to know what they were doing. *Ew where did ...? Ah I get it, yeh, although I'm thinking more, socially unacceptable rather than forbidden thoughts like those.*

How had I known they were forbidden? Mingold's whole body twitched. I carried on with my tour.

My subconscious thoughts are somewhere around but because they're sub – under – conscious that means I don't actually know what, or where, they are. I'm afraid you'll have to find them on your own. In the meantime, you're welcome to have a browse through my paranoia and neuroses ...

Mingold was writhing and squirming as if in pain. I felt bad that he might be but at the same time, slightly bullish since he and his friend clearly didn't have many worries about hurting me.

Look mate, you're the one stomping around in my head. It's not much fun for me either. All you have to do is disconnect.

Something came back to me but it was in his language of fax/dolphin burbling.

I really, really need to learn the language.

The urgency of his beeping increased.

Sorry ... on with the tour. Where was I? Oh yeh, my neuroses. Look! There's an interesting one here about being kidnapped by aliens. Funny right?

"That's enough. You have made your point. Let go of him," said a voice, a voice with a lot of authority in it.

"It's her, actually," I corrected him, "but yes, seconded, if you're ready Mr Mingold I'm with your scary boss on this one. I'd quite like to stop."

"Don't toy with me human. I am talking to you, not him and I won't ask you politely again."

The black threep was speaking aloud and in English.

"What?" I gasped through gritted teeth, this whole fusion experience was ... well, let's just say it smarted a tad.

What's he on about? How can I? I tried sending thoughts to my assailant again. *Mingold, I want to stop but I can't. You have to help me here, you have to show me.*

Mingold started making a disturbing gargling sound.

"Let. Him. Go." The black one's voice was loaded with quiet, authoritative venom.

"Can't," I panted through the pain, "don't ... know ... how."

Mingold started clacking his pincers together and making a weird rattling noise.

Mingold, I'm sorry ... I don't want to hurt you ... blimey, even thinking was like pushing a rock uphill. Through the fog of pain I tried to send more thoughts to him but I couldn't do it, I forced myself to speak and the words came out as a strangled whisper, "Want to let go ... Mingold ... show me ... please."

"You are destroying his mind along with your own. He is beyond showing you anything."

The black threep released his hold on my neck and wrapped his antennae around Mingold's. There was a massive reduction in the pain levels and, at the same time, a sense of being overwhelmed as, suddenly, Mingold's telepathic ability dwarfed mine once more. I felt as if I was on the brink of understanding something important. Then the black threep pulled hard. The advisor disengaged from my temples with an audible snap and a bolt of pain so intense that I screamed like a … yeh well I am a big girl and I can tell you, that was a bellow of agony which more than measured up. Mingold screamed too. I rolled around, writhing in pain, and fell off the bed. There was a splat as I landed on my face, on the floor. Oh yes. I'd forgotten it was covered in an eighteen-inch layer of Marmite-scented slime, and now it seemed, so was I. The fact I'd inhaled a good lungful of the stuff did me no good whatsoever. I was going to drown in ectoplasm. This was not the way I wanted my life to end. It was all over my face and in my eyes. I couldn't see. I scrabbled and jabbed at my face, trying to get it off me. But my hands were covered in it too and I was merely smearing more on. No, no, don't panic what are you doing? Wipe … I ran my arm over my face and tried to think calm thoughts or, on an upside, ah yes, at least it didn't sting my eyes.

Coughing and retching I tried to stay on all fours. The last thing I needed to do was face-plant into it a second time and inhale another great chunk. It would probably be curtains. Oblivious of the threeps around me, I wheezed and gagged, and strove to stay conscious rather than fall back into the slime and drown. I doubt it was my most dignified moment. I didn't notice much of what was going on around me over those thirty seconds or so. They left me to my own devices. I was dimly aware of others entering the room and clustering around Mingold. When I had blinked away enough slime to see, the black threep was beside him cradling him in its arms – the first remotely sympathetic thing I'd seen it do – and barking out orders. Everything was still blurry and the two threeps stayed there, like some twisted, out-of-focus pieta. More threeps rushed in. Then, still holding Mingold in his arms, the black threep got to his feet. I tried to get to mine but my legs flew out from under me and I fell on my bottom with a squelch. Slowly I climbed onto my knees and knelt back on my heels while I got my breath. By the time I'd wiped my eyes enough to see properly, the black threep was no longer cradling Mingold. Instead he was towering over me, glaring down, his whole being vibrating with hatred and disgust. I felt as if I was shrivelling to nothing under the searing heat of his gaze. I tried to return his poisonous scowl with a look of fearless bravado but you have no idea how hard it is to stare someone down when their eyes outnumber yours by seven to two.

A couple of the guards took Mingold to the door. When I'd first seen him, I'd had an impression of his emotional responses to me, even if it was simply that he was hiding them. Now there was nothing; as if he was unconscious, or dead. Had I done that? And if so, how? Please don't let him be dead. I didn't know where I was, but I wanted to persuade the threeps to let me go home, not get myself put to death for murdering one of them by mistake. I didn't want to die. Life was looking up. After three-quarters of a term of just me and Eric it looked as if I'd made a friend. She might even be gay, too. I wanted to see Jen again and if I wanted to do that, I had to establish good interspecies relations but it was difficult when I had no idea what the threeps wanted. All I knew was that I'd been able to see through Eric's mind trick when other people couldn't and that he had called me 'evidence'. Evidence of what? Was I the kind of evidence anyone—this black threep, for example—wanted to get rid of? Were they going to kill me? No: not straight away, anyway. I was in trouble though, and I didn't have the first clue why. Worse, it was abundantly clear that, as an ambassador for the human race, I'd made a piss-poor start.

The black threep watched me intently. The irises of his eyes were still dilated, the colour hardly showing. The impression of calculated intelligence he gave made me incredibly nervous. I was glad he wasn't one of the telepathic ones, although at the same time, I suspected he was smart enough to know what I was thinking without that. I ran my hands through my hair, forgetting they, and it, were covered in life matter. Yuk.

"I'm sorry," I mumbled. "I never—I didn't—" I hugged my arms about me and my voice sounded very small when I said, "I just want to go home to Earth."

"Don't expect to see your planet again. Not after this."

"Please, I never meant to hurt him. I was trying to defend myself but I don't know how ..."

The aura of rage and contempt emanating from the jet-black threep intensified for a moment and then faded abruptly into resignation. I think if it had had lungs it would have sighed as it turned to the two remaining guards.

"I have all the information I need for the present. Take her back to the others," he said waving one antenna imperiously towards the door.

The nearest grabbed me around my waist and unceremoniously tucked me under one pincered arm, as if I was a ladder or something.

"Carefully you fool!"

"Sorry sir."

It was only halfway down the corridor, bouncing along with the guard's uneven strides, that I realised the black threep had been speaking his own language. I could see him looking after us for a moment, standing still, calm and thoughtful. Then he turned and walked away in the opposite direction.

Chapter 9
Imprisoned in space

At the end of the corridor was another door which the guard opened. He literally lobbed me inside, burbled something I didn't catch and slammed it behind me. I landed with a splash, globs of life matter flying everywhere. Oh well, at least it cushioned the impact.

"Great," and I stood up and looked around. The decor was similar to the previous room; matt black with a gold underlay. It was lit by panels in the walls and ceiling, which glowed with the same pleasant ambient light, and as I'd just discovered, the floor was covered in the same layer of threep life matter. Three threeps were at my side almost before I stood up.

There was the dark brown one with the matching brown eyes who'd destroyed the fridge at my student residency, his grey companion, who had violet eyes, and there was the familiar reddy-brown form of,

"Eric!" I flung my arms around him in a hug, not caring about close contact with his goo-covered exterior. We connected with a loud farting noise.

"Andi, are you OK? You look terrible."

"You think I look bad? You should see the other guy," I quipped and regretted it immediately. "Actually, sorry, that's not very funny. I'm really scared. I think I killed someone. Oh Eric what am I going to do? I just want to go home but I'll never see Earth again."

I was close to tears and annoyed with myself for being so pathetic.

"OK Andi, slow down. It's alright, we have time. Come on, let's get you sorted. But first, I should have said … Welcome, to our palatial quarters," and he waved a pincer at our accommodation.

Despite everything, I couldn't help but smile. "Yeh, total luxury."

I looked around. All along one wall were occasional panels and small trap doors, most with buttons next to them. The number of buttons varied: anything from one, to whole banks of the things like a keyboard. A table and some stools stood in the middle of the room. They were threep sized so they were a bit high for me but there was no life matter on them. Bonus.

"D'you want some water?" asked Eric.

I nodded.

The grey threep pressed a button on the wall beside us and a long hose popped out. He handed the nozzle to Eric.

"Here," Eric handed it to me.

I peered into it and looked up at him quizzically.

"You press the button on the side and suck it."

He showed me but when I tried, a jet of water squirted into my face at high velocity. Never mind.

The grey threep bent his long antennae down and tapped away with the ends of them at a panel in the wall, a few feet from the water hose. A hatch opened and a box of paper handkerchiefs, just like the ones produced on my own planet, slid out. The threep removed it by wrapping the end of one long antenna round the box to hold it. He squished over and proffered them to me. I used several drying my face, wiping my eyes and blowing my nose. When I was done, I was amazed at how much better that one small act made me feel.

"Thanks," I smiled wanly and I tried to think 'smile' too, projecting my emotional response telepathically, the way threeps do. The fridge destroyer pressed another button lower down the wall and a small drawer popped out. I shot Eric a questioning glance.

"Rubbish chute," he said.

"Right," I lobbed the ball of used handkerchief into the drawer and it closed with a snap. There was a whump from inside, like flames igniting. Oh yes, I remembered, all the rubbish chutes on the Eegby self-incinerated the litter using a thermonuclear disposal system which converted it to—hang on. No I didn't remember that. Not at all. "Eric—"

"Andi, you know, I should probably tell you, my name's not Eric. It's Persaaaaluuuub."

"It's what?" I put my hands up to run them through my slime-laden

47

hair and then thought better of it. "It's alright, you don't need to repeat it. I'm not sure I am actually physically equipped to make that noise."

"You can carry on calling me Eric, if you like, or call me the shortened version; Persalub. I think you've met my spouses, Neewong," the grey threep made a bow, "and this is Smeesch," the brown threep did likewise.

"Well, hello. It's good to see you again," I told them and said to Eric, "yes, we have met although it didn't get as far as introductions."

"They tell me it went well."

"Yes and no," I said.

I glanced over at the pair of them. Neewong winked the two of his eyes that Eric couldn't see. Smeesch held his pincers out sideways either side of him. I thought about our meeting and notably, the fridge. I was desperate to go home but at the same time, aware that, were I to do so, I might be arrested and at the least would have to help the police with their enquiries and stump up a lot of cash I didn't have for white goods. Chances were I might be better off temporarily where I was. I took a deep breath and felt my tension levels reduce a couple of microns.

"It's nice to meet you two properly. How do you do? I'm Andi," I said.

"Hi," said Neewong, or at least, he said the threep equivalent just at about the same moment as Smeesch leaned in and said something approximating to 'wotcher', also in his own language.

Eric translated and I smiled and had another go at transmitting my facial expression telepathically.

"Ah," said Neewong, "I wondered why she was showing her teeth like that."

"Yeh, sorry, I didn't mean to scare you."

"Whoa! You understood!" said Smeesch.

"Yes. It's taking me a while to get this telepathy thing down but I seem to have absorbed your language."

"Wow, that's amazing, Andi," said Eric proudly.

"Very interesting," said Neewong.

"Do you guys understand much English?" I asked him.

"A little, it's hard for us to speak it," he screeched.

It hurt my ears a bit, listening to him talk, but being able to communicate with all three of them more than made up for it. I tried to say, 'Hello, my name is Andi Turbot,' in their language. They squirmed in horror like Parisiennes being subjected to tourist French.

"Sorry," I switched back to English. "Is my Threep that bad?"

There was a moment of silence.

"Um, let's say your pronunciation needs work," said Neewong.

"Yes, maybe it's best you stick to English," said Eric.

"And we actually call our language Gamalian, not Threep," said Smeesch.

"I thought you said you were threeps, though."

"We are," Eric explained. "But we come from the Gamalian Federation of Planets, the way you come from England, so we're Gamalian and we speak Gamalian the way you are English and speak English rather than human."

Yes. I suppose that figured.

"I see. Well, talking should be easier now," I told Neewong and Smeesch. "You won't need the translator box."

"Useless piece of rubbish that it was," said Smeesch.

"Yeh," I smiled, "so you three are married?"

"Yes, we call it a marital unit," said Eric proudly.

"Well no," Smeesch interrupted him, "we'd say—" he made some kind of screeching noise that could probably rupture eardrums and blow the doors and windows off houses up to three miles away.

"Marital unit it is then," I said swiftly. "Congratulations."

Eric gave me the impression he was smiling.

"Shall we go and sit at the table, out of the plastic matter?"

"Plastic matter?"

"Plastic, ersatz. You didn't think it fell off us did you?"

"Er ..." I shrugged.

"You are a wally!" he laughed. "Come on." He stood up and squished over to the table.

I waded after him. I noticed the other two exchange glances before they followed us.

We sat down.

"Thanks, I feel so much better here, talking to you guys."

"Good, so what happened?"

"I was questioned," I shuddered at the recollection and my carefully acquired sangfroid cracked a bit. Cold sweat began to prickle around my temples and I felt Eric's transmission of concern. I put my hands flat on the table, leaned back in my seat, took a deep breath and tried to sound cool and collected when I spoke.

"There was this threep," despite my efforts to be calm about this I could feel the tears of fright and frustration welling up. Eric put the end of one of his long antennae gently on my arm.

"OK Andi, take your time."

"Eric, they wanted to know where you were, although I can't begin to understand why, since clearly, if you're here, they already do."

"Not exactly, they knew I was here but they didn't know I'm Eric."

"They do now. I suppose it depends if—" I stopped. I couldn't actually say it out loud. *If the threep who read my mind is still alive,* I thought miserably. Eric clearly picked it up. I could feel his concern. I blundered on, speaking aloud, "There were two of them and some guards. One of them put his antennae on my temples and went into my mind. They called it 'fusion'. It hurt a lot. His name was Advisor Mingold. As far as I can tell, he knows everything about me, and a lot of things I wish he didn't know. But I think something went wrong, because there seem to be a lot of things I know about him and I think I may have hurt him. He's unconscious."

I stopped while Eric translated a couple of difficult bits for the other two.

"Serves him right!" said Smeesch.

"I don't think he wanted to do me any harm but I was scared. I was trying to cooperate because I was afraid he'd fry me. But I didn't know what to do. I thought I was surrendering but then it all went wrong and now it looks like I fried him."

The four of us sat in silence for a moment.

"I was alone and afraid and I had all these questions. And it's as if I plundered Mingold's mind for answers but I've come up with the wrong information. My head's full of weird random stuff that I don't need to know, apart from being able to understand your language," I shrugged. "That's handy. I also know we're in the brig – which seems like really bad news. I can put that with the things the one asking the questions told me, ergo that we're on a ship called the Eegby, that it's the flagship of the Gamalian space fleet. I also know that we're far enough out from Earth to be invisible to human technology and that I'm beyond rescue. He made very sure he told me that."

"I'd say he's trying to scare you," said Smeesch.

"Yeh well I can tell you, he's succeeded. If I look at this head-on, it's all I can do to keep a lid on it, even here, with you guys. And apart from the language, why haven't I absorbed anything that could help us?"

"All the random stuff might be helpful," said Eric. "You might just not know what it's for yet."

"How can knowing that this ship has a thermonuclear rubbish disposal system be more useful than knowing the name of the guy who questioned me?"

"His name might have been better protected than the information about the rubbish chutes."

"Perhaps, but it would be good to know something pertinent, like what the hell is going on."

"I think we can tell you that," said Eric, "but it's complicated."

I looked around me.

"Yep, I get it, so come on then."

"I'm so sorry Andi, I really, really didn't mean it to happen like this."

"Yeh, I understand that. Now get a move on."

"Well, let's start at the beginning. You know we're Gamalian and that we're threeps."

"Yes."

"And that we come from the Gamalian Federation of Planets."

"Which is?"

"It's five worlds, orbiting a sun called Blindock, in the Huurg Quadrant of the Bubblejox system."

"Yeh fine, but why am I here, Eric?"

"We're from Gamma Five, the most recently settled planet. As such, we are in the Fifth Gamalian Space Corps—"

"Eric, is there a point to this?"

"YES. I'm getting to it. As I said we're in the space corps and from the fifth planet: Gamma Five. We are currently halfway through a three-year secondment to the Second Gamalian Science Corps – the science corps of Gamma Two – for our mission here. Gamma Two has a fantastic climate for Gamalians – it rains all the time – but Gamma Five is more like Earth. You might like it."

I wasn't sure about that. Not if there was life matter everywhere, even if it was 'plastic'.

"So what brings you all the way out from the Huurg Quadrant to this neck of the woods?" I asked.

"I'm getting to that."

"Can you get to it faster?"

"OK, the first thing you need to know is that we threeps breed fast, so we're always on the lookout for new places to live."

"Uh huh."

"Just tell her, Persalub," said Smeesch.

"In a minute! I'm building up to it, Smeesch."

I eyed Eric warily and wondered, idly if I could uncover the truth of this in the minds of either of his partners, although it didn't feel like the sort of thing I ought to do unasked, not to a friend. I concentrated for a moment, subtly testing. No, he was protecting them, and I couldn't break through his guard without it being obvious what I was doing or worse, turning into a full-on confrontation. He continued.

"We've settled on all the planets orbiting our sun. Future lack of space is a big worry so we are surveying all the habitable – or potentially habitable – planets in nearby galaxies that fall within a certain radius of ours. But if it was just that, we wouldn't bother looking this far out. There's another reason, and I guess it's the one that changes everything for you: The Baldock Project."

"The what?"

"Thousands of years ago we discovered that there's other intelligent life, like us: the Garboldians. We found each other telepathically."

"The way you found me?"

"Pretty much, they're crustaceans, too. They communicate

expression the way we do, with weak telepathic transmissions. Every Garboldian is a telepath to some extent, the same way we are, but back then, they'd learned to take their skills to a whole other level and we hadn't. They taught us that skill; gave us the gift of sage advice and showed us how to pick out and train the really talented telepaths. At first contact they promised to send a ship. Five hundred years later, it arrived. I guess it was more like a probe than a ship—"

"And there was a robot, don't forget the robot," said Neewong.

"Yep! The robot sounds like the coolest thing ever," Smeesch cut in.

"Yeh that was pretty amazing. I'd have loved to have seen the robot as much as the guys here," said Eric. "But it went home. There was no living crew. The robot brought us samples from the Garboldians' home world, seeds, minerals, science, including a super-light-speed engine; stuff which brought us out of the dark ages and changed everything. We gave the robot thank-you gifts. We have this yellow metal which is abundant in our system, 'gold' you guys call it. They valued that, so we loaded some into the ship along with the same kind of stuff they sent us; things the robot identified as appropriate – and then it took off for home. Meanwhile, our leaders were in contact with the Garboldians the usual way, telepathically, and suggested our two species should try to meet, in the flesh, as soon as scientifically possible. They agreed, although both sides knew it would be many centuries before it could happen.

"For hundreds of years since, we have exchanged ideas, cultural views, art … everything, using our minds. Then a few years ago, Baldock—"

"One of the greatest scientists who ever lived in the Gamalian Federation of Planets," Neewong interrupted.

"Yeh, Neewong's quite a fan." Eric transmitted a fond smile at his partner. "He was an incredible guy though, Baldock. Anyway, he invented the universal transporter. Naturally, we shared the technology with the Garboldians, and then, one of our politicians, a guy called Sneeb, came up with this brilliant idea that we could make it possible to visit their planet if we could set up a string of base stations between there and here and use a universal transporter to go from one to the next."

"I have to give him, it was really smart," Neewong jumped in,

"UT-travel is short range, and will always be so, but it's instant. Sneeb posited that if we set up enough relay stations between there and here the journey time to the Garboldian system would drop to a couple of weeks. He did pretty well out of it, too. I said he was a politician right?"

I nodded.

"Yeh, his career trajectory looks like a rocket at escape velocity."

"I guess he's bound to do well out of it. So, you've started building these stations, but won't it take you another five hundred years, at least, to build the infrastructure?"

"About three hundred, we will meet in the middle. That's why we need to get started."

"The trouble is, we can't rely solely on relay stations based in space: not for the whole trip. The physical and mental effects of using the UT for so long do not allow it. Even though the actual transit only lasts a few seconds, doing it repeatedly in too short a time frame causes the molecules in your body to lose adhesion."

"What does that mean?"

"Well, it's like this," Neewong explained. "Travel by UT maps the molecules of your body, disassembles them, beams them at super-light speed to another location and reassembles them there. That's all fine but it throws up two problems: one, if you transport too many times in one day it affects your mind. We call it brain lag. Basically, if you transport over fifty times in a row you start to get confused and it takes a while for you to catch up. Two, if you transport day after day without a rest as well as totally losing your mind you lose molecular adhesion, which means that, on a microscopic level, the parts of your body just float away from each other. This second factor may be why we get brain lag anyway. Whatever the reason, if you transported again and again for too long, about seven hours we reckon, you'd cease to exist. So, allowing for safety margins and the like, the passengers on the route can only be in transit for a maximum of one hour at a time for three days straight. After that, they will need two days off travelling for molecular grounding somewhere where there's gravity; proper planetary gravity. We don't know why it has to be a planet, both ourselves and the Garboldians are researching that, but there is something about being on an actual world which is different to the gravity we create in places like this ship. It is also essential, for the re-adhesion of our molecules. Until we get to the bottom of that, it means we have to have planets along the way to provide us with a space for travellers to recuperate; somewhere with recreational facilities, real earth, water, air, gravity and such."

"Exactly," Eric agreed. "Also, there's still our population growth to deal with. It's always worth searching for new places to live, and with the transporter system in place, even planets this far out have suddenly become viable. So the idea is to rent space on some and colonise others along the way."

"Colonise." I began to have a horrible feeling I knew where this conversation was going.

"Yes. The number of planets capable of sustaining life is finite, and only a few of those are capable of supporting it now; any useable ones that we can, you know, use, will save us several years. You guys have a pretty plum gig. Earth is just … Ah you have no idea Andi. Earth is stunning."

"Even after the human race has stuffed it up?"

"Even."

"So about this colonising thing you mentioned, you know, of the suddenly viable planets out at the arse end of the galaxy—"

"It's not the arse end, Andi, it's just … rural."

"Whatever. Are any particular planets involved yet?" I was beginning to feel numb, as if I was standing outside my body, watching myself ask the questions.

There was a long silence.

I leant my elbows on the table and felt the weight of their silence upon my shoulders. It was worse than an out-and-out admission. With a sigh, I put my head in my hands.

"Great news: sodding marvellous," I raised my head and faced them. "So this ship we're on is here to take over the Earth is it? Is that why they told me I'd never go back?"

"Yes and no."

"What do you mean 'yes and no'? It either is or it isn't."

"To tell the truth, I don't have enough information to say."

"Oh get real. You must do."

"Keep your hair on. It's complicated. Look, as far as we're concerned, me and the guys here, the Gamalian code of ethics is very clear. We aren't allowed to let another sentient species die. We have to help them to survive. However, if a species is not sentient – by Gamalian standards – and if their planet is about to undergo some kind of natural disaster, then, as long as we preserve some specimens, we are at liberty to colonise the devastated planet after—after the disaster."

"Disaster? What disaster is this, Eric?"

He made a noise like clearing his throat.

"For heaven's sake! Smeesch? Neewong? Will one of you blummin' tell me?"

"There's this meteor," said Smeesch.

Something cold gripped the pit of my stomach.

"It was discovered a few years ago," said Eric, "we are the advance reconnaissance team."

"And …?"

I was pretty sure I knew what was coming but Eric, tactless plank that he was, had to spell it out anyway: a large rock hurtling through space, Earth, directly in its path. The hideous impact and the imaginary camera panning over the City of London: the bent and twisted remains of razed buildings, debris littering the streets, charred upturned cars and dead humans in suits everywhere. Everyone and everything on the planet would be destroyed. I'd read once that for a meteor to destroy Earth it only had to be 500 metres across. If it hit in the right place it would wipe out all civilisation and plant life in seconds. There'd be tidal waves – whole oceans emptying themselves across continents, the earthquakes would be off the Richter scale, volcanoes would erupt and the sky would be black with dust for years. No light meant nothing would grow and any survivors would starve. Yikes! I began to protest vehemently but Eric cut me off.

"You must have known it was going to happen sometime. Nothing significant has hit your planet since the dinosaurs. You're well overdue for a big strike. Few of the rest of us have been that lucky."

Maybe but now was a very inconvenient time for me. I didn't want to die. I had things to do with my life: important things, like helping the police with their enquiries and buying a fridge—no, not those, things like being a stand-up comedienne and other things; deep and meaningful things. Things that were so important I didn't know what they were.

"ERIC!" I held my hands out either side of me. "Why the hell didn't you tell me when we first met? I could have done something."

"What?"

"Oh I don't know do I? I could have called our leaders, or NASA or someone."

"I had to gather evidence. I had to be sure humans were sentient. And I was under orders not to tell you. In fact I was under orders not to fraternise with the human race at all: I still am. And if you had warned your leaders would it have made any difference? It's too small for your science to spot yet and it's too far away."

"We can spot quite a lot of them," I shot back. "We have lists of the ones that cross our path."

"Yes, you understand they're there but what can you do about it?"

"It may not hit us, they wobble around, meteors, it's really difficult to predict whether they're going to hit or not until it's almost too late."

"That's why they're so dangerous," said Smeesch. "Anyway, we have an algorithm for that."

I put my hands up to my temples, blinking back tears of anger and frustration as I tried to clear my mind: to think. My planet was going to die and I was stuck here, unable to save it. But there must be something I could do.

"Come on Andi," Eric's blue eyes looked into mine. "We both know the score," he put one of his antennae gently on my shoulder. "The only place telling people would have got you was a mental home. Instead, you're here, now, with us. Surely you'd rather live?"

"NO!" I wrenched myself away from him and stood up. "Not if I'm the only human left," I ached with loneliness at the mere thought. "Anyway there's you and this ship. That would convince anyone." I couldn't be still, I had to move. I began to pace backwards and forwards across the floor, "I must get back there Eric and you have to come with me and bring … I don't know … something that proves you're an extraterrestrial with—with—technology. You have to use it to help us."

"That was an option but not anymore. We're in the brig of the Eegby. We can't go anywhere."

It's difficult to pace through knee-deep slime so I stopped and returned to the table.

"Then what can we do? We can't just sit here," I said, flinging myself back onto my stool and doing just that.

"No. Somehow we have to convince mission command that you're sentient, by Gamalian standards. If we can get an audience with Commodore Pimlip – he's the commander of the Eegby – it should be a start, all we have to do is show there is enough doubt."

"How, though?"

Eric and his marital partners exchanged glances.

"The evidence they have should be enough. I sent an updated report back this morning, just before you and I met at the canteen. I recommended that the colonisation be aborted. But the thing is, there's a complication."

"Surprise, surprise, there always is."

"Yes, and I think it might explain why we're here in the brig."

Chapter 10
Honourable doubts

A few floors above my friends and I, in his private office, next to the Eegby's bridge, the officer in command of the Eegby, Commodore Pimlip, was having an uncomfortable time. It was bad enough that his sage advisor was out of action, even if only for a few days. Mingold's telepathic powers were at the lower end of the spectrum but his excellence as a tactician more than compensated. If ever the Commodore needed Mingold's advice it was now, with the mission commander aboard ship. But worse, from the Commodore's point of view, Mingold's predicament might be regarded as a failure by their superior and he would not be pleased. When his commander was angry, it took a sizeable chunk of Commodore Pimlip's courage to face him, although, the commander seemed displeased by pretty much everything and in a near permanent state of irritation. He was fair, Commodore Pimlip couldn't deny that, but he did not suffer fools, and the ice-cold calm, the unruffled logic of his demeanour merely served to enhance the impression of bottled-up volcano about to explode. It caused a certain tension in those who served under him.

After the events of the morning, Commodore Pimlip had some niggling misgivings about the mission, and as the threep in charge of the ship, it was his duty to raise them, tactfully, with his boss. It was not a thought he relished. He had sent a message suggesting he visit the commander's pod at a mutually convenient time, and in lieu of any reply, said commander had arrived in his office, suddenly, unannounced.

"Sir," said Commodore Pimlip, leaping up from his desk and snapping to attention.

"You wish to speak with me."

"Yes, sir."

"I assume, after Mingold's injury, you have doubts about this colonisation."

Straight to the point: Commodore Pimlip's boss was not a telepath but for someone without such abilities, he seemed uncannily adept at guessing what others were thinking.

"I wouldn't call them doubts, sir, but this morning does raise … questions. Mingold is—"

"Not quite as powerful as you anticipated?" asked the commander. The sharp edge of his displeasure was clear in his tone.

"Perhaps, but I fear the alternative. That the human we have captured is more sentient than we thought," said Commodore Pimlip evenly, "I wonder if some more research would be appropriate. We have time." He was stepping close to the line, his words dangerously near to insubordination.

The commander did not like that and eyed him coolly, projecting an aura of even more extreme control than usual. It betrayed the rage burning beneath it more eloquently than any display of actual temper, and there was a life, an energy in that pent-up anger, a power that seemed to fill the room.

"Are you questioning my orders, Commodore?" he asked, softly.

"No, sir, I merely seek clarification," said Pimlip swiftly. Plort! Too swiftly.

"Do you?" All seven of his grey-green eyes locked with Commodore Pimlip's in a sinister stare. His black exoskeleton glistened in the light of the desk lamp and Commodore Pimlip couldn't stop himself from putting a nervous antenna to his forehead. The commander wielded the power to make or break those who served him at a whim, and he often did.

"You read the report we intercepted?" the commander asked.

Pimlip swallowed.

"Sir."

"And ...?" The green eyes never left his.

"I noticed that the reconnaissance team posit a theory about the creatures on Gamma Six; that they are sentient."

"Yes they do," said the commander slowly. "And what do you think, Commodore?"

Pimlip swallowed, it felt as if the commander could see into his soul, "I could not say."

"Really," the wattage of the green-eyed glare intensified but the Commodore stood firm. "Cannot or dare not?"

Commodore Pimlip bridled at that, straightening his back and raising himself up to his full height, and said,

"Cannot, sir: not without further examination of the evidence. We have three weeks. There is time."

"Yes," a pause, "I thank you for being so frank." The commander subjected him to a few more seconds of staring, turned abruptly and stalked over to the window. "The ship's physician tells me Mingold is still unwell," he said as he gazed out into space. "Since I have inconvenienced you, I will assign my own sage advisor to assist you."

That's all I need, someone watching me and reporting every move, thought Commodore Pimlip but what he actually said was, "There is no need sir. The ship's doctor says Mingold will be well in three days."

"Even so, you will accept my offer," said the other.

He doesn't trust me, thought Commodore Pimlip. "If you are sure you can spare him, I thank you, sir," he said.

"Excellent, he will join you directly. If you have no further questions, I will be in my pod."

The door closed. Commodore Pimlip stood watching it for a moment, lost in thought. He had done the honourable thing, voiced his doubts, but had the interview gone badly or well? He had no idea. He sat slowly down at his desk.

Chapter 11
Pending Armageddon

S till stuck in the brig of the Eegby I sat glumly at the table with my friends.

"So come on then, why are we here?" I asked.

Silence.

"How much worse than Armageddon does it get? You may as well tell me."

"Several times, now, since it's been discovered, the meteor heading for Earth has drifted off course but every time it reaches the point where it's going to safely bypass the planet it seems to collide with some other bit of space debris and swing back onto an impact course. Smeesch, Neewong and I—" I sensed his unwillingness to actually say what he was thinking so it came as no surprise when I felt his words arriving in the back of my head, as thoughts. *We suspect foul play.*

"What?" I said before I realised one of the more useful things I'd plundered from Mingold's brain was how to think a reply back. *Do you mean someone's actually trying to wipe out life on my planet?*

Yes. I think so, he thought back. *It's difficult to prove.* He switched back to speech. "As you rightly pointed out, with the gravitational fields of all the other objects around, working out the course of any meteor, even with our algorithm, is very difficult. But the speculative programme we have keeps throwing up the same anomalies. They're only small and the powers that be have discounted them because they're so slight. But coupled with the way it's happened, the timing and everything, the meteor's movements seem more than coincidental to us."

"Oh this just gets worse and worse." I stood up again and waded through the slime to the water hose. "Doesn't anyone see it the way you do? Presumably millions of other Gamalians are tracking this thing. Not to mention your news stations. Surely they all saw what you did."

"Not millions and definitely not the news stations. Our state runs differently to yours. We're more risk averse and our leaders dislike losing face. It's not public yet. It's still top secret and will be until it's a done deal. Our scientists, the military, the government; they know what we think but they interpret the data differently. Looking at it their way, it's debatable whether the first one's even a nudge at all. There's no unusual or damning evidence on the meteor. The guys and I, we've been over it inch by inch. Everything looks natural. There are a couple of burn marks which might possibly be suspect. We documented them and flagged up the data weeks ago, but command discounted them because they're so small. The biggest evidence is just the way it's conveniently happened now: perfect planet, perfect place, perfect moment. It seems too much of a fluke."

"But out of the Gamalians who know already, you guys are the scientists right? Shouldn't your interpretation of the data carry more weight?"

"We're *some* of the scientists yes. In that, we're science-trained members of the space corps. We were seconded to the science corps for this mission because they wanted a team who could liaise with both, and our original qualifications make us a good fit for either. We've been surveying Earth; working out where the worst volcanic eruptions might be, how to get the dust cloud down as quickly as possible after impact, that kind of stuff. But it's so beautiful, Andi; all your weird plants; like trees. We don't have trees anywhere in the Gamalian Federation. And your oceans and your strange creatures, and you humans; you may be wrecking the place but there is so much that is honourable and good in you. I guess the three of us are a little in love with your planet the way it is. When I heard your thoughts I had to find you. We couldn't stand by and let the meteor hit if there was any doubt. It's totally unethical. And then from the moment you and I met, I'd seen enough to convince me you are sentient.

"The trouble is, I also have to convince my superiors." He switched to thoughts again. *They've a lot riding on this to the point where I don't believe they want to be convinced. I've tried the Science Corps on Gamma Two and Mission Command on Gamma Five and anyone else I can tell without committing treason,* he held his pincers out either side of him and let them drop. *We've had nothing from anyone but standard official acknowledgements – you know 'we received your excellent idea and we will be back in touch' kind of stuff. Bearing in mind that our information is pretty hot, the least I was expecting was a call from one of them. So clearly, nothing's getting through. In the end, I even contacted the Arch Doge, who, well, he's kind of like a President but of the whole Gamalian Federation. Finally, someone from his office contacted me back.*

I pressed the nozzle and actually managed to get a drink of water, only squirting about half of it in my face, as Eric carried on with his train of thought.

They arranged that I should make a personal report by comlink.

"So ...?" I asked.

They gave me a date, a time and a secure comlink number and code. I was to talk to one of the Arch Doge's aides; that trip to 'Heathrow' to meet my 'parents' that I told you about. But when you saw through my projection of human Eric this afternoon, I had the conclusive proof I needed. My actual intention was to blow the meteor up first and present my findings as a done deal.

"Which is ..." Smeesch began and projected a subtle signal. From the information I'd gleaned from Mingold, I understood this was, basically, an invitation for me to read his mind ... *Insubordination,* he was thinking. Reading his thoughts was a different sensation to receiving Eric's projected ones. *And that's a capital crime in the Gamalian Federation.* I realised that Eric was somehow amplifying Smeesch's thoughts so that Neewong could 'hear' them too.

When Eric answered he reverted to speech.

"I wouldn't go that far, our orders were pretty general," he said.

"The one about fraternising with the natives sounded pretty

specific. Have you been arrested for talking to me?" I asked him.

"None of us has been arrested," said Eric. "Or formally charged; no-one's been near us."

It's academic what they arrest us for. They just want to shut us up, thought Smeesch.

Eric projected something that was very like a sigh, bent the end of one of his long antennae round and rubbed the back of his head.

"What about the comlink report? Did you get to make it?" I asked Neewong.

"No. That's why we came to find you. That was the plan if the three of us lost contact with one another. Smeesch and I were waiting up in orbit with the comlink transmitter ready to go and the slot approaching fast—"

"And no Persalub," Smeesch chipped in.

"Yes, we were beginning to worry that one of us would have to stand in so I got a fix on Persalub's data pod," Neewong explained.

"Then the Eegby turned up," said Smeesch.

"Almost immediately I lost Persalub's signal and our sensors picked up universal transporter use," Neewong continued. "The perfect text book signature of a single Gamalian: planet to ship. We were surprised that he hadn't warned us but he didn't answer when we hailed him, so then we wondered if the Arch Doge had sent his aide for a report face to face."

With the dynamite we'd found it made sense, thought Smeesch.

"So we hailed the Eegby and they confirmed that he was on-board but that they were not at liberty to say more."

"We totally assumed it was a face to face then – especially when the Arch Doge's office contacted us and cancelled the comlink call," said Smeesch.

"Yes!" Neewong agreed. "So we set about looking busy with what we were doing; some survey work on your moon and when the time came to meet you, and Persalub still hadn't returned—"

"We came to get you," said Smeesch. "We had the coordinates of your pod."

"He means your corridor at the residency," Eric chipped in.

"Yeh whatever," said Smeesch. "We had to wait until the time when Persalub had told us you'd be alone."

"Yes, because we can't disguise ourselves without him," Neewong added.

"Yeh, so we came to get you and you know the rest: they got us," said Smeesch.

"So did you get to meet anyone?" I asked Eric.

"Not yet."

"Then what are we doing here?"

"I reckon Smeesch's answer to that question was spot on," said Eric. We're being gagged. Someone really did move that meteor but they want the colonisation to go ahead anyway.

There was a fraction of a second's pause as I received the same signal from Neewong giving permission to read his mind as I'd had from Smeesch and Eric performed the same amplification technique to allow Smeesch to hear.

In view of your sentience, it is ... an abhorrent action, Neewong thought and his grey colouring lightened a shade.

"Who questioned you, Andi? Can you describe him?" asked Eric.

"I've already told you I don't know his name but ..." I realised I could do better than a description. I pictured the black threep in my head and tried to transmit it to Eric, Neewong and Smeesch. When Smeesch made a noise that my new-found knowledge of Gamalian identified as the equivalent of 'ouch' I feared I'd been heavy handed, but before I could apologise, Eric said,

"Is that him?"

"Yeh."

"Plort!" said Smeesch.

"He's called Plort?"

"No, Andi, that was swearing." Eric explained. "Just thinking ... you're not making him look blacker or anything are you?"

"No."

There was a long silence.

"What?"

"If that's the guy who's in charge of this ship, we are in big, big trouble."

Having met him, I was kind of inclined to agree.

"Although even he can't deny your status," said Neewong. "Not if you can do that."

"Unfortunately, I think he can. I can only do the transmission because of Mingold's training. He's passed it on to me somehow."

"No, you've absorbed it. He tried to fuse his mind with yours, and with no training and no idea what you were doing, you took the information you needed from your opponent to defend yourself. You won."

"It doesn't feel that way."

"Well you did and it's an amazing thing to have done. Your telepathic abilities are easily up with ours – possibly beyond. The problem is, that if anyone has altered that meteor, the prime suspect is the one with the most at stake—"

"And that would be our supreme mission commander, Sneeb, whose whole idea this is, whose scientists discovered the meteor, and who let his sage advisor run rampant through your head," said Smeesch.

"Which he should not have done," Neewong added.

"It's a violation," said Smeesch.

"Well, it probably doesn't matter. I think in the end, *I* ran rampant through *his* head."

"It does matter. What he did was unethical and just proves we're right about the meteor."

"We don't know that Smeesch," said Neewong.

"We sure as hell do."

"No, Neewong's right," said Eric, "we don't – and we must keep an open mind. Yes, it looks like somebody moved the meteor but it wasn't necessarily Sneeb."

"That's true, but we do suspect him rather a lot," whispered Neewong, very, very quietly.

"Yeh just a tad," said Smeesch.

Chapter 12
Space politics

"So this, Sneeb – is Sneeb his name made easy for me to pronounce or does he have a Gamalian squeaky name?"

"That's his name; in English and Gamalian."

"So are you telling me my nemesis is your mission commander, the one who started it all?" I asked.

"Yeh."

"That doesn't sound good."

"It isn't. Like I told you, it was Sneeb who began this and it was his scientists on Gamma Five who wrote the software that alerted us to the path of the meteor," Eric added.

"It's very interesting it's based on weather prediction software and—" Neewong began but Eric transmitted a gentle smile and shook his head. Neewong stopped.

"So we have to bust our way out of here, find a comlink and go over Sneeb's head, right?"

"Well … it's a bit more complicated than that. He's *Doge* Sneeb."

"Which means?"

"It means he's—well we don't run our political system quite the same way as you but I guess a Doge is the equivalent of your Prime Minister."

Arse. My mouth made a round o but no words came out. I tried again.

"He runs a country," I whispered.

"Er no, Andi, we don't have countries any more. He runs a planet."

"Right," I croaked, "and he's mission command. Brilliant. Do we have a second in command?"

"There's Vippit but he's not strictly second in command, he's the Doge of Gamma Two so he's co-commander, Sneeb's equal."

"Except he's not because Sneeb has the Arch Doge in his pocket," grumbled Smeesch.

"But someone'll listen to us, right?"

"Possibly," Eric sounded doubtful. "But they might not act."

"All the Doges are involved in some way or another," said Neewong.

"Yeh," said Smeesch. "There's money to be made and a chance to go down in history. They're all eager for a slice of the action."

"The problem is that, as mission commander, it's Doge Sneeb who decides whether the colonisation goes ahead," said Eric. "But this is the first colonisation outside our own solar system, and it's the making of him. His ethical stance might be a bit ..."

"Fluid?" I suggested.

"Exactly, and then there's the Garboldians. This is a big deal. It's a lot of pressure. It may be nearly three hundred years away but it's first contact."

"What about me? Aren't I first contact?"

"Not yet Andi: not officially. Your planet is in the perfect place. There's another route but it would involve establishing a base on a dead planet. We'd have to spend an extra seven years building three more relay stations to get there and another ten years seeding life on it—"

"You can seed planets?"

"Yeh, it's no biggie but that's not the point. This project is the gateway to Gamalian intergalactic expansion and it's all under Doge Sneeb's command. When this goes through, his name will live forever. He'll be up there with our equivalents of your Columbus and Cook. And the first planet on the route ... to find a place so perfect it's ... well, he'll never turn his back on that. Never."

"I'm so sorry, Andi," said Neewong.

"Not as sorry as I am," I muttered. "There must be something we can do. Isn't Doge Sneeb accountable to anyone?"

"Only the Arch Doge."

"Who's in his pocket."

"Right."

Oh dear.

"How 'in Sneeb's pocket' is the Arch Doge?"

"Sneeb is his adopted son."

"Bummer."

"Yeh, that's why if anyone did intercept our messages to the Arch Doge, it has to be Sneeb. He's very protective of his adopted 'dad'."

"Also, Zebulon, the Arch Doge, is very old and he has a lot to contend with," said Neewong.

"But surely, from what you say, the colonisation will be the most important thing he's done in his life," I said.

"He might think the elections are more important," said Smeesch.

"What elections?"

"The elections for his next term are right after the colonisation," Eric explained. "Arch Doge Zebulon is an uber-dude, everyone loves him and he's been Arch Doge half his life. He's clever, kind, wise, far-sighted; he's like everybody's dad. He's been elected unopposed for three out of five terms. He hasn't fought a campaign in years and a lot has changed. Now, out of the blue, Doge Sneeb is talking about standing against him. Arch Doge Zebulon should walk it. But Doge Sneeb is popular and Neewong's right, Zebulon is old—"

"Old? He's practically a fossil," said Smeesch.

"Another three years and he'll be the oldest Gamalian ever to have lived," said Neewong.

"Sure, but his age has never held him back before," said Eric. He stopped. "Although, yeh, this time, the commentators are worried, I guess. Like a lot of us, they are thinking that even if Zebulon gets in he will die midterm anyway. I reckon most Gamalians think that since he clearly wants to die in office, the decent thing for Sneeb to do would be to let him stand unopposed this one last time. I guess a lot of us are thinking, privately, that the rigours of conducting an election campaign may kill him, anyway. Then again, Doge Sneeb hasn't confirmed his intention to stand."

"Yeh but he will, won't he? He wears his ambition like a rash," said Smeesch.

"Easy Smeesch," said Eric.

"It's true! He's basically going to campaign one of his own fathers to death because he can't wait a few years."

"Well, Vippit's no better," said Neewong.

"Sadly true, I'm afraid," Eric told me. "He is also positioning himself to contest the Arch Dogeship but his line is that political stability under Arch Doge Zebulon is paramount, and he will not be standing against an elderly being for what will almost certainly be his last tenure."

"So Sneeb is happy to stand on dad's hands to get to the prize and Vippit is making a big thing that he can wait for the Arch Doge to die?" I wasn't sure which approach was worst. If Sneeb's was ruthless, then at least he was honest, but it painted both of them in a bad light: like vultures, circling a dying animal. "That's unbelievably creepy."

"Yep, it is a bit," said Eric. "But Sneeb's not the kind of guy who lets anyone get in his way. The only good news, for us, is that he and Vippit can hardly stand to be in the same room as one another. We might be able to use their enmity for leverage, if we can get a message to Vippit, of course."

"Except he's ignored all our reports to him so far," said Smeesch.

"And anyway, we're in prison," I reminded them.

"Yep."

"Flippin' Nora, we are stuffed aren't we, unless we get out of here?"

"Yep."

"Can we get out of here?"

Nobody said anything.

I put my head in my hands.

My throat felt so tight I could hardly speak.

"I think I'm going to hurl."

Neewong got up, squished over to the wall and pressed the button to open the rubbish chute.

"Be our guest," he said.

71

Chapter 13
Stir crazy

Time dragged slowly. I didn't hurl, despite feeling physically sick with dread, but my fear and frustration at being trapped were almost overwhelming unless I walked about. Something about moving seemed to deaden it. I therefore paced the room, despite the vileness of wading through an eighteen-inch layer of plastic life matter, not to mention the fact I felt mentally and physically exhausted after my encounter with Mingold. I suppose it was less pacing and more wading that I did. Every now and again I would stop and immediately I would start to sweat, my stomach would churn and my guts would feel as if they were tying themselves in a ball. So, round and round I went: exhausted, catatonic almost, but too wired to stop. I was grateful for the small comfort brought by the presence of Eric, Neewong and Smeesch but no matter how hard I concentrated on their goodwill towards me, their kindness, I couldn't quell my horror at what was to come: my planet, my species and my life were all doomed, and there was nothing I could do. My friends sat at the table deep in whispered conversation. I didn't need telepathy to know they were talking about me, the aura of concern they were projecting and the odd eyestalk flicking round to glance in my direction was enough to go on. I stopped walking.

"Is this it?" My insides started knotting themselves at once so I had to start moving again. "Is he just going to leave us here, stewing, until the meteor hits?" I demanded as I paced to and fro.

A couple of Eric's eyes flicked towards Neewong and Smeesch. Neewong seemed resigned and Smeesch projected something like a shrug.

"Who can tell? I'm surprised he hasn't done something," said Eric.

"Yeh, at the least I'd expect him to come here and gloat," said Smeesch.

"What about your ship? If we could get to it, do you think we could escape and blow up the meteor?"

"Unlikely. It'll be disabled and it'll be heavily guarded. They'll be searching the flight recorder, the computer records."

"They'll be *trying* to search the computer records," said Neewong.

"Yeh, there's nothing we can do about the flight recorder but they won't get into the mainframe, Andi. Not with the security protocol Neewong's put on it," Smeesch explained. "If we want to leave, and we can get to the docking bay, we would have to take one of the shuttles. They're armed well enough to blow a meteor I'd say."

"Won't the Eegby give chase? Presumably when we leave there'll be alarms going off all over."

"Not necessarily if we can swing it, and not straight away," said Neewong. "If we get the codes right and get out before anyone has raised the alarm, the computer will release us automatically. That's the thing. If nothing is remarkable enough to be flagged, no conscious beings will be involved so we won't be noticed at once, not until they check our course."

"But even if we can escape this cell without being noticed and get to a ship they'll work it out and come after us eventually, right?"

"Yes. This is a battle cruiser, it will have a whole squadron of short-range fighters," said Smeesch. "But if we get the codes right they won't reach us in time to stop us blowing the meteor."

"Then we have to get out of here first. What about pretending I'm ill? I roll around, when the doctor rushes in we thump him and do a runner." I couldn't believe I was even suggesting that old chestnut.

"We cannot harm fellow Gamalians and certainly not space corps members," said Eric.

"We can but only in self-defence," countered Smeesch, "they have to attack first."

"Never mind," I said and I started to pace again.

I knew my constant movement was driving them crazy. It wasn't going to help if they ended up as jumpy as I was. It was time to get a grip. I stood still and turned my attention to the ranks of buttons and the various openings and trapdoors in the wall.

One of the sets of buttons was a lot more complicated than the others. I wondered what it was for. Each button carried a character from the Gamalian alphabet and the part of my brain which was newly informed by Mingold understood, instinctively, that it was the Gamalian equivalent of a qwerty keyboard. It also seemed that Mingold knew the equivalent of touch typing so I began to type 'I want my mummy' – or at least daddy. With only one gender threeps don't have mummies or daddies, per se, they just have a single word meaning 'father' and then they number them: first father, second father, third father, or fathers, alone, for all three.

Having rethought, and typed, 'I want my daddies,' I pressed the red button to send. A belching noise came from a hole in the wall next to it and an electronic Gamalian voice repeated back the phrase I'd typed and announced that it did not compute.

"Why won't you compute?" I asked it, aloud.

"Because it's a food replicator, Andi," said Eric.

"You mean I could make edible stuff?" Food was the last thing I wanted right now but I quite liked the idea of something to settle my churning stomach. I wondered if it could make an antacid tablet. I explained what I wanted.

"The replicator might run to that. It depends what model it is," said Neewong. "Do you know the constituent parts of an antacid pill?"

"Bicarbonate of soda? Peppermint essence? Chalk?"

"Can you describe those chemically using the Gamalian periodic table?"

I examined the knowledge I'd newly purloined from Mingold. He wasn't much of a scientist, it seemed.

"No not really."

I pressed the keys randomly and the replicator burped again. Nothing came out of it though.

Neewong glanced up suddenly. I wondered what he was thinking. However, from Mingold's knowledge on sage advisor's etiquette I knew it would be rude to read his mind without asking unless he invited me as he had before, or was a fellow telepath, or had a sage advisor of his own.

"Andi, is that a Spectrum EFPP?"

Eric and Smeesch were both watching him with questioning expressions.

"I dunno. How would I find out?"

"I'll come and look," he said, getting up and coming over to join me.

"Let's see ..." He tapped away at the keys for a few moments and the machine burped again. "Ah. Wonderful. Yes it is."

"Why, 'wonderful'?"

"It's difficult to explain."

Again, I felt the subtle invitation from Neewong to read his mind and the same, shortly afterwards, from Smeesch. In both their minds I saw a single word, *Surveillance*.

Is that why nobody's come? They're listening?

And watching, thought Smeesch.

Are they reading our thoughts? I asked Eric.

I don't know. If they are, I can't feel anything, but I've a few light defences in place.

It doesn't mean they aren't though, does it?

No. It depends how many sage advisors there are on the ship and what other duties they are assigned. Doge Sneeb may have more than one and the ship's commander, Commodore Pimlip, will probably have one too.

I tried to reach out with my mind, subtly, stealthily. There was nothing obvious but there was a feeling, an undercurrent, a distant presence.

There's someone there but ... I stopped to concentrate. *We don't seem to be a priority. Perhaps they have all they need. What with the three of you sitting here talking to me they have you bang to rights for insubordination, for starters.*

I doubt that will satisfy them.

"I wish we could escape. I'm not very good at being cooped

up in here while my planet faces Armageddon."

"Give it a few moments," said Neewong.

"What do you mean?"

There was a melodic bing-bong sound and a smooth Gamalian voice informed us that the first rites of Twonkot would begin in three minutes.

"Excellent," said Neewong, transmitting a huge beaming smile at the rest of us.

"Come on Smeesch," said Eric, getting up from the table. "We need to show Andi how the food replicator works."

"What are the first rites of Twonkot?" I asked as Eric and Smeesch joined Neewong and I in front of the food replicator.

"It's our religious service. We make our devotions on the middle day in our week, Twonkot. At the end of that day, we stop work to pray and sing the holy antiphon. On a ship like this they run it twice so only half of the crew is praying each time while the other runs the ship."

"What, you all pray?"

"Of course."

"What kneeling down in the ...?" I glanced down at the plastic matter around our feet.

"No we pray like this," Eric stood with his pincers and one pair of his legs stretched out either side of him. He flicked his antennae straight up in the air, they were too long to fit in the room extended so the ends of them bent at right angles when they reached the ceiling. "But the point is that it's prayers so," he winked and thought the rest of his answer, *only half the crew will be concentrating.*

How do we know which half?

We don't but we know this is the first service.

We do?

Yes, because it's the first Antiphon of Twonkot as opposed to the second. And what that means is that, for the next hour, only half the crew will be on duty instead of about two thirds, with a third on break. And what THAT means is that this is the best time to escape without detection.

"What's your god's name?" I asked.

"Plort."

I remembered Smeesch's swearing.

"Our religion is more than a belief to us. We know there is an afterlife. Scientists have been there and brought back evidence. He's difficult to contact—"

"Very difficult," said Neewong.

"But he is ... listening."

"Kind of," Neewong added.

Smeesch burbled something which I didn't catch.

"He says mostly to music."

Chapter 14
Holy death metal

If you'd asked me what to expect from the first Antiphon of Twonkot, I certainly wouldn't have guessed screaming voices, thumping bass, crashing drums and thrashing guitars, all playing at breakneck speed and full volume. I think there was a melody of sorts but it was barely discernible over a wall of aural chaos that made death metal seem quite light and middle of the road.

"BLIMEY! THAT'S LOUD! I CAN'T HEAR MYSELF THINK!" I shouted as loudly as I could.

"NEITHER CAN ANYONE ELSE!" bellowed Eric.

Good point. Perhaps our captors thought of it too because the volume reduced a bit, not much but enough for it to hurt my ears less and for us to have to merely shout normally.

"How long do we have?"

"A Gamalian hour: half for each antiphon," replied Eric, he turned to Neewong. "Will it take that long?"

"No."

"Neewong can make the food replicator malfunction so badly that they'll have to move us to another cell. When they do, we can appeal to the Arch Doge. Then they have to give us an audience with the most senior Gamalian on the ship, by law."

Why would we want that if it was Doge Sneeb? Stuff appealing.

"No, too complicated. Let's give them the slip and do a runner. You know that transmission thing you did on Earth to disguise yourself? Can't you disguise us as some other guards, then when they come to move us, tell them we jumped us, locked us in and legged it … if you see what I mean?"

"It's a great idea Andi but I can only do three, max, after that I won't be able to walk and talk in a straight line, it's hard enough doing me and the guys here."

Yeh. I could imagine.

"OK, let me think about that for a minute."

Eric and his husbands pretended to pray, or perhaps they really did, and the aural assault of the antiphon continued. I was glad it only lasted half an hour, even so, I worried it would cause me permanent hearing loss if I had to listen to it again.

Right, so I had to do my own disguise. That was OK, Eric had called it a simple mind trick. He wasn't even trained in sage advice, or at least, not formally. If it was that simple, surely a fully trained sage advisor like Mingold knew how it was done. It was just a question of whether I could access the knowledge and produce a realistic enough threep. The antiphon screamed on. I closed my eyes, trying to blank out the decibels and concentrate. I felt myself receding into my mind, felt the noise lessen as if it was coming from further away, my temples tingled and flickers of an insubstantial image appeared in my mind's eye. I concentrated more. They coalesced into something tangible and cautiously, I opened my eyes. Yes, I was surrounded with black shiny insubstantial exoskeleton, like a woman buried in jelly. If only I could make it look denser, more real. I gazed through it at Eric, Neewong and Smeesch. As suddenly as it started, the antiphon ended. In the abrupt silence I could hear my ears buzzing. The three of them stopped praying and turned to look at me. Neewong took an involuntary step back.

"Wow," said Eric.

"Is it … working?" I asked.

"And some," said Smeesch, projecting an expression of what I guessed was slack-jawed amazement, if he'd had jaws rather than mandibles, that is.

"Can you do anyone else?" asked Eric.

I shook my head.

"I don't think so." I projected what I hoped was a suitably sinister smile. "Can you do guards, Eric?"

He nodded.

"Yep, I reckon."

I turned to Neewong, concentrating on making my pretend self turn with me. He flinched, as if to take another step back.

Told you it was good, Eric thought.

I smiled.

"You ready?" I asked.

Neewong nodded. "Andi, your tiny hands will make short work of this," and, after the usual invitation, I read his mind.

I dropped my threep disguise. Even for a few minutes the effort had really tired me. I found it harder to access the mental pictures Neewong was trying to show me, but I understood that he wanted me to look up into the opening at the bottom of the replicator. I knelt down with a squelch and sure enough, there was a space between the chute the food was delivered down and the casing, through which I could see the machine's interior. I aligned my mind and read Neewong's thoughts.

The component parts to these machines are manufactured on different planets. Everything is colour coded so they can be constructed on site. There's a red circuit board and a yellow one in there, side by side, yes?

I craned my head in while my friends tried to mask me from any surveillance cameras.

"Yes."

Undo the clips and switch them.

"That's it?"

"That's it."

I did as he instructed. I'd worried that, what with the gap in strength between threeps and humans, the fastenings would be too stiff for me to undo. In the event, it was surprisingly easy. I switched the circuit boards, withdrew my hands and stood up.

"Done," I said.

Neewong started on the control panel. The tips of his antennae flew over the buttons. The replicator barked staccato half words as he tapped away until finally, with a strange burping sound, it began to belch out an orange foamy substance in great quantity. The nearest thing I had seen on Earth is that expanding stuff builders use; or those indoor fireworks. We all backed up swiftly as it poured over the tray and down the wall. As it started to writhe and tumble across the floor, like giant squishy orange worms, I experienced a few misgivings as to the wisdom of our decision. Then we heard noises outside. We backed up and Eric motioned us to stand along the wall, the way he and his husbands had done when I originally entered the room. I could hear running feet squishing through the life matter outside in the corridor. There were alarmed burbles and shouts from beyond the locked door, then it burst open and three guards rushed in.

In the end, we didn't need my disguise to escape. Eric projected an image of himself and his husbands over by the food replicator, it just held the guards' attention long enough for us to duck out into the hall and slam the door. The two threeps in the corridor turned to us in surprise but before any of them could react something flew past me at speed and charged headlong into the first of them. It was Smeesch. He and his victim fell to the floor in a tangle of writhing pincers, antennae and legs. The other drew his gun and aimed at Smeesch. There was a ping as he fired but the round hit his colleague instead. Before he could fire a second shot, a line of green light from Smeesch's antenna hit him. He fell backwards and I turned to Smeesch, who was disentangling himself from his opponent.

"They're not dead are they?"

"No. Stunned," he said as he threw a gun into the slime by the first guard's prone form. "And I hope I squared it with Plort just now or I'll be baking in Nardy Pimlock with Doge Sneeb when my time comes. You're right, though, Andi. There's no other way. Appealing won't get us anywhere. We have to do this ourselves."

"Yeh, I guess so." I turned to Eric, "Nardy Pimlock?"

"It's what we call hell."

"Should we take their guns?" I asked.

"No, if we're captured, it will go better for us if we're unarmed," said Eric, "but let's hurry, these guys will have called for backup."

"Right," said Smeesch shakily, "and shooting in cold blood like that. I can't do it again, not even with a whole species at stake."

Wading through the life matter was harder than my threep friends made it look. Eric and his spouses were at the end of the corridor before I'd gone a couple of yards. He came back and tucked me under one arm, the same way Doge Sneeb's guard had done.

"Sorry, don't mean to be condescending," he said. "But while no-one's around …" He ran to catch up with the others.

The three of them set off at a jog.

"Ugh, where do … you get all this … stuff?" I asked him as we bounced along. "Your flat in London was never like this."

"Well, to be honest, Andi, I didn't live there, I lived on our ship and even if I had lived in my flat, it isn't a battleship. If we go into shock our life matter will fall off. Likewise, in the heat of battle it could be blown off. Lose too much and it's fatal. If I get injured and fall to the floor then, even if I lose my own matter I won't suffocate. The plastic matter will keep me absorbing oxygen, so long as there is any in the air: even if I'm injured or unconscious."

"You mean it's a … health and safety initiative."

"More like a lifebelt, if that makes sense."

Kind of, but I wondered why they couldn't pressurise it in cans on the belts around their waists or something. Threeps wore no clothes and seemed to use their belts the way we use pockets; to carry tools, guns, ration packs, electrical gizmos and all sorts of other stuff – although Eric and his spouses were wearing belts with a lot of empty clips. It looked as if our gaolers had taken most of their stuff away.

"It doesn't keep in cans," Eric said.

"OK, look. Can you not answer my thoughts unless I want you to?"

"Sorry: only trying to help."

It's alright. Where are we headed? I thought as Eric and I bumped along behind his partners, with me clinging to his pincer for dear life.

"We have to get to the docking bay, and fast," Eric said out loud.

Do you know where it is? I asked, knowing that if need be, with the knowledge I'd acquired from Mingold, I did. It was making me feel queasy, bouncing around like this. Hanging on with all my might, trying to get a purchase on Eric's slippery pincer covered in life matter, I could feel my grip beginning to loosen.

Yeh.

The slipperiness won out, I lost my hold on Eric and my upper body flopped towards the floor, my head bouncing off the surface of the plastic matter round his feet like a stone skimming over a pond.

Urgh! Can you find it soon?

"Yes, I'm sorry Andi," he said as he scooped me up, "it's just up here."

We squelched speedily along one final corridor and then Eric and the other two stopped. My friend plonked me on the ground and I leaned against the wall, jelly-kneed.

This is where we need your help, Andi.

I closed my eyes and concentrated.

"Wow," said Neewong and I heaved a sigh of relief.

"Hmm," said Eric. "Can you really not do anyone else?"

I opened my eyes and considered my telepathic projection in the shiny surface of a nearby door. If I say it myself it was a pretty impressive replica. After a few minutes of concerted effort it soon became apparent that, no, I still couldn't do a projection of anyone other than Doge Sneeb.

"No." I tried again. "Definitely not: sorry."

I suppose I couldn't get my fear of him far enough out of my head, or maybe I hadn't dared look at anyone else in enough detail. As Eric kindly explained, a generic threep would be difficult when I'd only seen a few.

"Alright, let's go."

We rounded a corner and stopped. In front of us was a huge chamber, I'm talking massive here. You could probably fit about five football stadiums into it: maybe more. The walls were the same black with gold highlights as the rest of the ship. Or is that gold with black lowlights? It was hard to tell. Here the architecture was less ornate and more linear. Long slender columns drew my eye upwards to the vaulted ceiling. Despite this, there was an even more pronounced feeling that the ship was organic, living: that it had grown rather than been built. Everywhere the walls and ceiling were set with the same lighting panels as there had been in our cell, giving off a restful ambient light, like daylight. The floor was black and shiny. Unfortunately, it was still covered in the ubiquitous layer of slimy plastic matter but even I could ignore that when I took in the drop-dead beauty of the rest of it. Doing museum studies might make me more of a sucker for these things than the average person but I couldn't help being impressed. At the far end was the exit, through which I could see the dark serenity of space. Thousands upon thousands of stars glowed against the inky blackness like holes in a piece of velvet.

"It's so beautiful."

"Yeh, it's not bad is it?" said Eric.

"That is a glass door right?"

"No, the door's only closed during battle."

"How come we're not being sucked out into space?"

"There's a force field across it. It's specially calibrated to allow ships in and out without loss of pressure. We need to get an access code though, or it won't allow our ship out and we'll be smashed to smithereens against it."

I watched a threep driving a hovertanker stop by one of the lights set into the wall a few yards away. He got out, popped open a small panel beneath it and inserted a hose.

"What's he doing?" I pointed.

"Feeding the lighting system. The lights on the Eegby are provided by phosphorescent plankton."

"No way, that's fantastic."

"It's pretty standard."

"What if it bursts? Won't they die and you all drown in the dark?"

"No, there isn't that much water in them and the life matter will keep the organisms alive," said Eric.

"The feed is pumped in by technicians like that one, there," Neewong added, "it circulates round through a series of one-way inlet valves to each tank. That way, were one tank to rupture it could be isolated or, if the organisms inside become ill, it could be shut off for repair or replaced with healthy plankton from another tank."

"That's so cool."

"It's also important that the tanks can be isolated, as much of the water in them serves as the mainframe for the ship's computer."

"Water?"

"Yes, water molecules can be positively or negatively charged: zero or one, that's all you need."

"Whoa," I said as I tried to process this idea.

Parked around the sides of the chamber – or is that docked? – there were several things which might have been ships. Hoses and cables ran from them to walls or service vehicles. Threeps squished backwards and forwards, going about their business, some on foot, others in teams on hovercars.

"Do you have any idea how amazing this is?" I said.

"Yeh. Trust me, all cadets are given a tour of this ship or at least, some of it – you know, learn well my friend and you may serve here one day. I'll remember mine until the day I die. They didn't show it all of course, the technology is seriously advanced. It's not just the flagship of the Gamalian space fleet. It's state of the art. You know those planes back on Earth, the black triangles."

"Stealth bombers," I corrected him.

"Right, well, compared to this ship, even our version of the black triangle is a skateboard. And you should see the recreational area at the centre of the ship. It's mind blowing."

It was then that we encountered the sentries, who moved in from my right. I wheeled round and they all stopped.

"Sir," said the leader. He was certainly surprised. The conversation dried up.

Eric, I need your help, 'Doge Sneeb' has to say something.

What?

I don't know do I? Say that I'm going to look at the meteor and you're my security detail. You are disguising the three of you as guards aren't you?

Yes.

Great, well tell him I'm taking you and a shuttle.

They'll never buy that.

"Sir?" said the leader of the guards again.

Of course they will, I'm Doge Sneeb for heaven's sake. For a second I wondered if something had gone wrong with my telepathic disguise; if others were seeing what I was seeing, *I am still Doge Sneeb, aren't I?* I asked, to check.

Yes.

Right well, say something. And throw your voice.

"Sir?" the guard asked again.

"Uh …" said Eric.

Oh for heaven's sake. If a thing's worth doing … I cleared my throat, took a deep breath and tried to speak Gamalian. I knew I couldn't do it properly so I had to use my telepathic skills in other

85

ways. Mingold was able to get into the heads of other threeps and alter their perception. That meant that because he was … I barged into the heads of the guards and tried to convince them that the caterwauling they were hearing was the calm, smooth voice – well Gamalian smooth, which would still be caterwauling to you and me – of their leader.

"I am taking a shuttle to the meteor. I want to know what is driving the human and the mutineers to such heights of intransigence," I said while Eric and his husbands stared on in bug-eyed horror, "I believe the key is on the meteor and I intend to find it. That is why I want a shuttle. Now—"

Aargh! What rank was he?

"—captain, if you please," Eric cut in.

The captain was perplexed at best, at worst suspicious. Maybe my replica Sneeb wasn't so perfect. I concentrated for a moment. No, I was as sure as I could be that he had the right number of limbs and other appendages. Although I didn't sound a bit like him and while I got the impression that Eric did, he clearly hadn't quite got the Doge's tones off pat. The voice sounded right to me but then I'm not aurally equipped to tell. To my ears, all threeps sounded similar; perhaps, as a human being, I am unable to hear at the right frequencies to spot the difference. I tried to compensate by moving closer to him and hoped it was enough.

"Well? Why are you still here?" demanded Eric, in what I suspected was still a poor imitation of Doge Sneeb's voice. I tried to project an impression of sneering condescension.

"We had an all stations message that the prisoners had escaped," said the guard. "We're on emergency lockdown."

"Tell me, captain. Do you think denying me access to a shuttle on my own ship is a constructive part of that process?" I waved my arm at the scene in the background: the giant chamber, the force-field-protected doors with the stars beyond and the many threeps coming and going about their business, although there was a bit less coming and going now that a couple of them had noticed us.

"No sir," said the guard hastily.

"Excellent, then go and get us the k—" I began and Eric swiftly spoke over me.

"—departure codes."

"Er yes ... the um ... those."

"Sir."

All three guards snapped to attention.

"Permission to speak, sir."

"What?"

"Please accept my apologies, sir," said the captain with a bow.

"Accepted, minion, and your zeal is also noted. Now get me the codes and get out of my way," I barked, while Eric, Neewong and Smeesch tried to look unfazed. Despite having a rigid exoskeleton and no way of making facial expressions, it's amazing how much non-verbal information threeps can get across with their eyes. All seven of them.

The guards were clearly perplexed but none of them actually summoned up the courage to challenge Doge Sneeb. Their leader ran swiftly to a safe, set in the wall, which he opened. He came back with a grey cube with sides of about an inch in length.

"The Thesarus, sir. It's in bay nine," he said.

"I'll take that," said Eric, in his own voice and he stepped forward and took the cube. "Thank you."

"Sir." The captain and his team saluted me and then turned and marched smartly away like the soldiers they were, but their emotional response was more like that of chastised children. Our Doge Sneeb's actions were slightly wrong, that much was obvious, but I couldn't tell how.

"Let's go." I strode past them and waded, as quickly as I could towards a silver saucer-shaped thing with the equivalent, in Gamalian numerals, of the number nine on the side. I tried to ensure I made enough squelchy noises for a seven-foot-something space lobster, as opposed to a five-foot-something human. After about five strides, Eric caught up with me.

"That's storage pod nine Andi. The ship's this way."

Bum.

I turned back to the corridor entrance where the guards we'd just encountered were watching us. Even from there I could pick up their incredulity. They were probably going to go report to someone that Doge Sneeb had flipped. Time to hurry this up. Eric, Neewong and Smeesch led me to the most bizarre-looking vehicle I'd ever seen.

The ship, if that's what we were approaching, was gourd-shaped and covered in spikes. It reminded me of a puffer fish in full puff: where a fish would have eyes it had two headlights, there were fin-like outriggers either side, there was a mouth-shaped hole recessed into the bodywork at the front and the hull above that came to a point like a nose. The hole housed the radar and detection systems. The 'headlights' were really torpedo tubes, the outriggers had laser cannon mounted on them and there were more laser guns at the back. Between the rear lasers was an aileron like a fishtail, which swivelled up and down, serving the same purpose as a tail plane when the ship was flying in atmosphere. It stood on sledge-like runners.

We got up close. Oh. No door. Eric handed Neewong the grey cube which turned orange and then green. Orange lights on the outriggers flashed on and off and the ship beeped twice. As I watched, a hole morphed out of the metal at the tail end.

"On you get," said Eric transmitting the threep equivalent of a cheeky grin.

I did as I was told, dropping my projection of Doge Sneeb with relief, the minute I got in.

Inside the cabin was a single room. To my disappointment, there was even more life matter in here than there was in the main ship. Neewong soon seated himself in what I guessed was the pilot's chair. There was a joystick in front of him and a ludicrous number of displays and flashing lights. He was tapping away at the computerised controls and talking to the Eegby's equivalent of a control tower through a headset. Smeesch sat at a station to the side, also wearing a headset. Eric told me he was priming the weapons systems and then gestured to two seats side by side next to a bank of computers.

"You sit here Andi and do up your seat belt. When the meteor explodes there may be a shockwave. Things could get bumpy."

"Dangerous bumpy?"

"No, just uncomfortable bumpy," Smeesch chipped in.

"So long as I don't chuck up, I don't care."

"Ah, the thing about that—" Smeesch began.

"We'll deal with that one when and if we come to it shall we?" said Eric. He transmitted a smile and ruffled my hair with one antennae. "Don't worry Andi, by that time the meteor will be history. You won't care." He turned to Neewong, "We clear?"

"Yes," Neewong tapped the headset he was wearing with one antenna.

"Hit it," said Eric. Neewong pulled the joystick towards him and we took off.

Eric pressed some buttons and a huge screen where the windscreen should be flickered into life and showed us the view ahead, as if it were … well … a windscreen. We flew through the gaping doorway and out into the stars.

The windscreen went milky white as it transferred our view from forwards to backwards. Despite the fact I was on tenterhooks, waiting for pursuing fighters, I had to take a few seconds out to admire the Eegby. It was made of the same dark metal outside as inside and had the same matt black finish with a hint of gold underneath. It was sleek and covered in sharp pointy bits in the most beautiful, aerodynamic and yet menacing manner. Everything about it said, 'Don't mess with me buster,' and I didn't want to. It made James Bond's Aston Martin with the missiles behind the headlights look like a Reliant Robin. That's the level we're talking here.

Neewong set a course and we headed out into space.

Chapter 15
Pursuit

As the sleek lines of the Eegby receded we watched for signs of fighters in pursuit but none came.

"OK, we have an hour and ten minutes before we reach the meteor. Guys, can I leave you to keep an eye out? I'm just going to see if there's any kit we could use on this thing," said Eric.

"Can I come?"

"Sure."

We undid our seat belts and I followed him to some hatches at the back of the shuttle. It was less ornate, inside, than the Eegby but made of the same matt black and yellow metal.

"This metal is really cool, what is it?" I asked Eric.

"It's an alloy. It comes out black but it made everything so dark that it caused depression among space crews. Now we include a soft yellow ore to add colour. It's the same stuff we sent to the Garboldians, you know—"

"Gold?"

"Yeh."

"Any spare lumps knocking about?"

"There probably are on the Eegby, why?"

"It's quite rare on Earth. I could probably live a life of leisure on a few lumps of that. Not that—" I sighed and cleared my throat, best not to dwell on my planet's potential doom. "Yeh, right, what are we looking for?"

"I'm hoping they might have a couple of UTs somewhere; universal transporters," he reminded me.

"Beam me up Scottie. Like yesterday?"

"Exactly, although, I'm talking about the actual UT units; yesterday the Eegby's system did the transporting, it used our data pods to find us and then locked onto our bio signs, and yours. These

UTs enable us to travel independently, ourselves, wherever we want to go. No need for help from the ship, just the right coordinates ... within a certain range." He opened the first locker in a row of three at the back of the ship and started rummaging through the contents. It seemed to be electrical spares: wires, connectors, bits of circuit board and the like.

While Eric searched that locker I opened the next one. I found a rack of five brushed aluminium metal boxes. They had round corners, like those really cool American briefcases. I took one out. It had a green and red button on it and hinges in the middle of one side, as if it opened, but I wasn't sure how.

"Are these any use?" I showed them to him.

"Yes. Nice going, Andi. Lads!" he said, holding up one of the boxes with a red and green button. "We have UTs," he waved the box I'd given him. "Five."

"Now we're on autopilot I'll sort those if you like," said Neewong squishing back to us from the pilot's seat.

"Thanks, Neewong," said Eric, as I handed them to his partner. "We're lucky he's here to programme these, I'm rubbish at it without the attachment for telepaths but Neewong's a UT whizz, right Smeesch?"

"Neewong's the computer whizz, full stop."

Neewong, who was already working on one of the UTs looked up from the keyboard and winked four of his seven eyes.

"Yeh, you know, I've been meaning to ask you about telepathy," I said as we moved onto the last locker. "You're clearly gifted. You found me. How come you're not a sage advisor? I can see you're more telepathic than Neewong and Smeesch. In fact, I'd say you're easily as telepathic as Mingold. Presumably more so, since you found me, and he didn't. So if he's a sage advisor, why not you?"

"I wanted to find you. I wanted an excuse to save the Earth. That probably helped, but I'm not that telepathic, I'm a kind of halfway house. Some of us are incredibly gifted; like you," I could feel myself blushing as he said this. "They are the ones who get to be sage advisors like Mingold."

"But he isn't gifted," I said as I helped him heft a box out of the last locker. "He's nowhere close to where you are."

The box was heavy and I was breathing hard when we finally got it onto a nearby surface.

"He must be. He probably kept it from you," said Eric as he tried to open it.

"Maybe," I wasn't certain. It had felt as if I'd blown his mind right open, until the very end, when he rallied and disconnected … or I did. "Why haven't you applied for training though?"

Eric straightened up and put one antenna on the box.

"I did. They turned me down. They said my skills weren't fully developed."

"That's not exactly turning you down flat, Eric. Didn't you try again?"

"I would have done if they'd meant it but they were just letting me down gently."

"How d'you know?"

He tapped his head.

"I'm telepathic, remember? I read their minds." He projected something like a shrug of the shoulders and turned his attention to the box again.

"Do you ever wonder what it would have been like?"

"No, not as much as I expected, I'm happy being a pilot now. At the time I was gutted. It's an incredibly interesting job if you're assigned to the right being. You get to go on diplomatic missions and take part in intergalactic negotiations with other races. I'd have been able to travel, see space, meet new species before anyone else did—"

"My dad says business travel is overrated," I said as Eric tested the locks on the box, jiggling them this way and that. "He said it might sound glamorous but that it was just the insides of offices, taxis, chain hotels, city ring roads and airports. Anyway, you've already done the first contact thing with me, haven't you?"

"Not officially," he said. "The species has to be acknowledged as sentient."

"Oh that old chestnut."

"Yeh," he jiggled the locks again and they popped open but when he tried it the lid remained firmly closed. "It's not locked, it's stuck. We need to get it open."

"This might loosen it," Smeesch came up behind us and thumped the box with one pincer. It didn't. "Or we might need to force it. I'll see what I can find in the toolkit."

"You're probably better off, I doubt sage advice is all roses," I said, reverting to our original topic. "You might have ended up working for someone like Doge Sneeb."

"He's not a monster. He's doing a good job. Gamma Five is profitable, the crime rate is low, the economy booming, the local laws are sensible ... If he's called upon to mediate, he is surprisingly balanced and fair." Eric sounded as if he was trying to convince himself as much as me.

"It's true. He explains things, gives reasons for his actions. It's as if he thinks we're all as intelligent as he is," said Neewong from where he was programming the UTs.

"Yeh, I'll give him that," said Smeesch as he returned with a wrench and a screwdriver, "it makes for a refreshing change."

"Yep, he's a good leader," began Eric, "even if ..." he trailed off.

"Even if what? He's a bad character?"

"Hold it still, can you?" said Smeesch.

Eric clamped one pincer each side of the box and carried on his conversation with me.

"I can't really comment on that. Sneeb and I, we have a bit of a history."

"What sort of history?"

Smeesch stuck the screwdriver under the lid of the box and hit it hard with the wrench.

"Well, when I failed to get onto the Space Academy's course for sage advice I signed up as a pilot."

"He's a damn good one!" Smeesch chipped in as he gave the screwdriver another whack.

Eric's colour deepened a little, as if he was blushing.

"I'm not bad," he said.

"He graduated in the top five of his year," called Neewong, from the front.

"That sounds a little better than 'not bad'." I flashed Eric a smile but he just shrugged.

"Maybe, but at my passing-out ceremony Doge Sneeb took me aside and told me I shouldn't be a pilot: that I was wasted," Eric took the wrench from Smeesch and gave the screwdriver an almighty whack with it. "He said I'd better wake up and use the skills Plort had given me because I wouldn't be getting anywhere in the space corps as a pilot any time soon," he whacked the screwdriver again. "Isn't there a hammer, Smeesch?"

"No, that's the best I could find."

"Oh well then," Eric hit the screwdriver again and carried on with his story. "I hold the rank of Acting Captain. To progress to being a fully accredited captain I need to rack up enough flying hours, which I've done, and pilot different ships, the more the better, which I haven't done," said Eric, as he jammed the screwdriver under a different part of the box lid. "I've been passed over for every single transfer and promotion I've applied for since then," he added, smacking it with the wrench extremely hard. "I didn't want to believe it. Of all the planets in the Gamalian Federation, Gamma Five is the least corrupt, the closest thing to a meritocracy we have. But last time, my commander actually told me my request had been refused," he belted the screwdriver with all his might, "on Doge Sneeb's orders. He is sabotaging my career."

"Why though?"

"You tell me. Because he can?" he gave the screwdriver another pounding and the corner of the lid moved a little. "Even Neewong and Smeesch are marred by association," said Eric as Smeesch turned the box for him and he positioned the screwdriver at the opposite corner. "A few months ago Neewong came up with a new formula for universal transporter use. We used to be limited in the size of stuff we could move with a UT. We still are, but not nearly as much if you apply Neewong's formula. With that you can move huge stuff – maybe even a small ship. Normally, at the least, he would get a commendation for that but there was nothing. We wanted to get some investment or sell a licence to the UT makers to add the formula to their software but nobody read his paper, nobody was interested," Eric hit the end of the screwdriver so hard the box lifted, despite Smeesch holding it. "It's as if it's been buried," he said.

"It has," said Smeesch.

"That's really unfair."

"Yeh," Eric hit the screwdriver even harder. "But that's life," he put the wrench down for a moment. "When this opportunity came up, flying the survey mission for the—" his voice faltered a little, "colonisation, I jumped at it. It's under the domain of the science corps on Gamma Two so it's not directly under Doge Sneeb's control, it's under Doge Vippit's."

"Persalub didn't apply though, they came looking," said Smeesch. "He's that good."

"You flatter me Smeesch," said Eric, "they did request me, and our qualifications, from school upwards, are pretty much the perfect fit for the job, but I suspect Doge Vippit found out about Sneeb's little vendetta and chose us: me, specifically, to wind him up. Rumour has it he agreed a deal with the Arch Doge without letting Sneeb in on it. How are we doing for time, Neewong?"

"Forty-five minutes."

"Not bad, but we'd better get this thing open. I'll bet it's the gun case and we may need blasters," said Eric. He picked up the wrench and this time, I joined Smeesch holding the box.

"As official mission commander, Sneeb would have taken that as a massive insult, but once the Arch Doge ratified it there was nothing anyone could do."

"So is that why Doge Sneeb is so angry?"

Eric stopped, wrench raised as he was about to hit the screwdriver again. He seemed surprised.

"Is that what he seemed to you?"

"Absolutely; most of the time he was burning with this boiling white-hot rage. The rest he was just vile."

"Hmm ..." Eric was thoughtful for a moment and then turned

his attention to jemmying the box open again.

"Can I ask you something?"

"Go ahead."

"Why do your politicians need sage advisors? I mean, if this was Earth, telepathy would give them such an advantage that before long all our politicians would be telepathic anyway, you know, all that mind control and stuff."

"Telepaths aren't allowed to enter politics in the Gamalian Federation because, as you rightly say, 'all that mind control and stuff'."

"But what's the difference when the sage advisors just do it for them?"

"They don't though. At the top level, every politician has one, some have more than one, so they cancel each other out."

"What about with the actual voters, do the politicians use their sage advisors on them?"

"No. They're not allowed to and they don't, other sage advisors would pick up on it. The Guild of Sage Advice has a strict code of ethics and that's forbidden. If one breaks it, the others will blow the whistle on him."

"So, could someone like you be a politician?"

"Not even if I wanted to. If you have any telepathic ability at all, beyond expressing your emotions, you're barred. And those of us with enhanced ability aren't usually the political type. Genetic happenstance I guess."

Eric hit the screwdriver again and at last the lid came off. The box contained a lot of packing material and some guns. He removed one. It looked like a Luger only with circular foils round the end of the barrel and a squeezy handle instead of a trigger. He attached one to his belt, handed a second to Smeesch and then moved to the front of the ship and gave one to Neewong. When he returned to my side he took another gun from the box and held it out to me.

"I don't want it."

"You might need it."

"I hope not," I said.

"You don't need to fire it necessarily but it makes a good

deterrent. Or you can stun them. Here," he showed me how to change the settings, set it to stun, locked the trigger so it wouldn't accidentally go off and handed it to me. It had a clip and a retracting string. "I'll put it on your belt."

He helped me attach it.

"Hey," said Neewong as Eric put the battered remains of the box back into the last locker. "Take a look at this."

We moved forward to the viewing screen, which was showing the stars ahead. In the distance, growing all the time, I could see the tiny outline of a rock.

"What the—" Eric was tense, "zoom in can you?"

Neewong put a cross-hatch over the rock and suddenly it filled the screen.

"You've double-checked it, right?"

"Right."

"Is that it?" I asked.

"Yes, but it shouldn't be here. It should be another forty minutes away at our present velocity."

"Which is another few hundred thousand of your miles and a couple more weeks of your time," said Smeesch.

"So that's why the Eegby is here," said Eric.

"Looks like it."

Neewong tapped rapidly at the control console. He glanced up at Eric beside me, "That's the ship out of autopilot," he said.

"Why has the meteor speeded up?" asked Eric.

"Good question," said Neewong.

"Yeh," mused Eric.

"I'll bet my mandibles it's foul play," said Smeesch. "We should investigate."

"Yeh."

"How long do we have?"

"Give me a second. Scanning and tracking," said Neewong, tapping at the keyboard in front of him again. "Oh," he seemed surprised. "Impact in … that can't be right," he turned slowly round to face us. "It's going to hit in thirty-six Earth hours."

"We're going to blow it up now, aren't we?" I said.

"Yep," said Eric.

97

"Yeh, I've calibrated the lasers to—" began Smeesch, then the screen next to him caught his attention. "Whoa! Where did they come from? Bogeys at ten o'clock!" he yelled.

"Persalub?" shouted Neewong. I could feel the aura of panic coming off him.

"Don't worry, I've got the stick," said Eric. "Strap yourself in Andi," he added as he leapt into Neewong's recently vacated seat.

"Can you take the rear guns?" shouted Smeesch as the ship started to accelerate.

"I'm on it!" called Neewong rushing past me as I belted myself in.

"Who is it?" asked Eric.

"Short-range fighters, they're from the Eegby," said Smeesch.

"They bear no markings," said Neewong. "They might be from another ship."

"Yeh right," said Smeesch, "if they are where is it? There's nothing on the scanners and nothing on visual."

"They're targeting us!" said Neewong.

"Shields to maximum," said Eric.

There was a massive crash and the Thesarus shook.

"Plort! They fired without even hailing us!" shouted Smeesch. "And the shields are already down to seventy-three per cent."

"How come?" asked Eric. "Is there a malfunction?"

"None that I can see, it looks like they have upgraded weapons."

"Then let's blow this thing and get out of here," said Eric.

"Targeting ..." said Smeesch.

"Enemy ships on screen," said Neewong from his position at the back of the ship. "I'm sending out a distress signal."

There were three of them. The viewing screen showed a pinpoint of red from one of the fighters. The Thesarus did a sudden barrel roll and the red beam of light sped past us.

They were closing. I felt useless as well as frightened.

"How can I help?"

"Sit tight and stay cool, we'll handle it," said Eric.

"I have a lock," said Smeesch. "Firing in three, two, one, steady ..." he sounded remarkably calm. The ship jinked sharply upwards, rolled again and then did a loop the loop. It stabilised for a few seconds, "Now," said Smeesch and I felt the kick as our lasers spoke.

Dots of red light flew towards the meteor but instead of hitting it, they exploded against the empty space around it in an eruption of boiling fire.

"Why isn't it working?" I wailed.

"There's a force field round it," said Eric through what would be gritted teeth, if he'd had teeth and been human of course. "Plort's bottom! Who in the name of Nardy Pimlock put that there?"

We were moving very fast now, in an erratic weaving course to evade the laser fire from the fighters, but still towards the meteor. Every now and again, Eric held the ship steady for a split second and Smeesch fired. Our repeated efforts to blow up the meteor met with the same result.

"Save the power, Smeesch, we need to get closer," said Eric.

Another round of laser fire hit us broadside and the ship juddered and bounced as the shields absorbed the energy.

All three fighters were shooting at us at once and the cabin was beginning to smell of hot metal.

A klaxon started to sound.

"We can't get closer. The shields are down to twenty per cent!" shouted Smeesch. "We have to return fire, or leave."

"We can't fire on our own species, not if it means we might kill them," said Eric as he flipped the ship sharply downwards.

"Why not? They started it," I shouted as the ship bucked and dipped. I knew he was keeping us alive but I wished he didn't have to shake us about so much. It was like being the ball bearing in the bottom of a spray paint can. Thank heavens I had done up my seat belt. The ship spun round and round, and for the second time that morning, I was thankful it was so long since I'd eaten.

"We can fire in self-defence to disable their ships!" shouted Smeesch. "And we should."

In the middle of the chaos, finally I realised how I could help. I closed my eyes, concentrated on the pilots of the other ships and reached out with my mind. I could stop them, if I could just disrupt their thoughts a little.

Chapter 16
Mental fusion

Reaching out to the pilots of the fighters pursuing us I felt my head aching which I took to be a good sign.

"We're losing cabin pressure," I heard Neewong say, as if from a very long way away.

"We have to abort, Persalub," Smeesch was shouting, "we can't do this now. We will have to come back." I could feel his frustration and distress. Were he human, I had the impression he would have been close to tears.

The lights went off, leaving nothing but the glow from the banks of instruments and a single red emergency bulb; no plankton in these lights, they were electrical. The stupid klaxon kept on sounding. Smoke started coming out of one of the vents and the air was filled with a strong smell of burning. The ship shook again as it took another hit. Smeesch was tapping away at a keyboard with his antennae. "I've rerouted as much power as I can to the shields but we're taking a lot of damage."

"We're venting oxygen," said Neewong.

"Yeh, we're leaving," said Eric bitterly.

There was an almighty crash as another round hit us.

"Where's the hyperdrive?" he yelled.

"Rebooting," shouted Neewong.

"Shields down to ten per cent!" Smeesch reported.

"Plort in the afterlife! Can you hurry it up?"

"No."

"Weapon systems at twelve per cent of power," said Smeesch.

"Neewong. How long?" said Eric.

"Thirty seconds."

"We don't have thirty seconds," shouted Smeesch. "Let me fire at them."

"No, it'll make it worse: hailing enemy ships. I'm sending a message that we're going."

Another round of laser fire struck us.

"There go the stabilisers!" said Neewong.

"And there's your reply," said Smeesch.

The Thesarus started shaking us about like the beans in a maraca during a particularly energetic salsa number.

"If we don't go soon the ship will break up!" shouted Neewong.

"What ... about ... escape ...to ... Earth ... with ... the ... UT?" I said, molto vibrato, because of the insane level of vibration.

"Need to be closer," said Eric. "Won't work this far out."

I made one last effort to connect with the threeps in the fighters but they were faint, distant, as if they were being shielded somehow. Had Mingold recovered enough to protect them? Or was there another sage advisor back on the Eegby? Then I felt it, something else; a tingling. Only a little, as if my skull was contracting and pressing on my brain. I was afraid the cabin air pressure had changed or suddenly become too high for me and that I was about to be crushed to death. Then there was a massive bang and the ship lurched.

There are no words to describe my fear. I thought it was the end. I tried to speak but time seemed to have ground to a halt and the words that came out of my mouth were like a slowed-down record. I could see my friends, see that they were busy about their stations. The pressing, slow feeling didn't abate but at least the ship had stopped rocking and shaking. It occurred to me that this might be hyperdrive, and further that my human brain might not be able to withstand its rigours. Then I began to see something else, another reality superimposed on the one I was in. It was like staring at one of those Magic Eye pictures and I had to use the same method of focussing and yet not focussing at once in order to get a result. First it was just blurry blobs – vague outlines and shapes of objects – then, as I began to concentrate, my eyes felt as if they were sliding together somehow and the image appeared. It started from the bottom of my field of vision and rose like floodwater, becoming more sharply defined as it progressed. As my visual world changed, my head changed too, I felt a drop in temperature, as if I was submerging myself slowly in a cold bath. I saw the Thesarus from a distance, crippled and limping. I saw it disappear, leaving behind a huge explosion and shards of twisted broken metal. I felt another being's pleasure at our distress, at what it believed to be my own death. One antenna reached out, pressed a button and the picture disappeared. The creature turned and moved to a glass window. Beyond was Earth, a beautiful blue-green jewel hanging in space.

Behind it, all I could still see was the inside of the Thesarus' cabin, the eerie red light and the bloody annoying klaxon that wouldn't switch off. I heard the whine of the engines failing and felt the ship judder to a stop.

"Andi. Andi?"

It was Eric. I couldn't answer.

"Don't be afraid Andi, it's cool ... don't be afraid," he said, his words, quite clearly, as much for his benefit as mine.

When I sent him a thought, I could sense that we were both extremely scared.

Am I dead?

No. It looks like you're fusing with someone's mind. Where are you? he asked, except his voice wasn't coming through my ears, he was telepathically planting the words in my brain. It was different to when he had done this before. They were louder, brighter and there wasn't the same feeling of a time lag between their arriving in my mind and resolving themselves into speech.

I don't know, I thought back fearfully.

Describe it to me.

Stuff that! How do I get back?

By listening to me, he answered. Take a deep breath, calm down and describe where you are.

I looked around me. I was me, except I wasn't me at all, I was someone else. Whoever this was, they were thinking, except the thoughts were disguised, only his emotions were readable. I glared out of a glass window at my own planet, except that whoever was doing the glaring wasn't me and it wasn't their planet either. I was hooked into someone else's brain. OK, that was fine, so I had inadvertently managed to meld with somebody else's mind. The burning question now was, how the hell did I reverse the process before whoever it was found out? It was most important they didn't find out, too, because this mind did not belong to the type of individual I wished to meet, ever. We are talking about an awesome level of malice here, a mind powered by pure hatred.

While I couldn't have told you any of his specific thoughts, I was aware of the background knowledge of his existence; his goals, his malicious bile, his frustration and impatience, and his anger. I knew, in an instant, why Eric had been worried about the course of the meteor. It had been diverted, twice, from its true innocuous path onto a collision course with a populated planet, and this was the creature responsible. All his emotions were expertly channelled, even the hatred was controlled and focussed. There was nothing positive in there, no compassion, and love was dead to him. His mind was dried up, broken, yet there was a shadow of something else; something different and noble, the way it had been before illness had killed everything in it that was good. He was disciplined, ruled by logic and yet somehow detached and out of kilter. He had a formidable, calculated intelligence, yet his thinking was warped by paranoia and driven by bitterness and envy. Where he had once rejoiced in the success of his peers he now wanted to crush and destroy them. He burned with ambition, to achieve more than he had, and wreak vengeance on those he had once helped, who he now believed held him back. He wanted the colonisation because he wanted to be a god and he wanted to see the galaxy at his feet, his puny plaything, making obeisance. He was an inhuman being, in every negative sense of the word, and he was lurking out there, waiting for the end, with more eager expectation than I thought tasteful or necessary.

Then his mind changed, as if illuminated by some dark mental sun. I'd given myself away. He knew I was still alive and where we were and he was going to come and blow us to pieces because he wanted me dead. If the parts of his mind I was reading showed true, he was excited at a second opportunity to watch me die, for real.

And I will make certain of it this time … he thought, in Gamalian.

God in heaven! Eric!

Oh yes, you are wise to fear me little human, I know where you are.

"Eric!" I screamed. "He's reading my thoughts. Get him out! He's in my head! He's talking to me."

No he's not, Andi. You're in his head and he's thinking things he knows you can hear.

"But he won't let go …"

He can't! You're the one fusing with him. You have to break the link.

"I don't know how—" I began. I was beginning to panic again.

Yes you do.

"No."

Alright, don't be afraid. Relax and trust me, I'm going to show you.

He might have been a Science Corps captain but Eric could have been a doctor, he had that special soothing way of talking that bought me back from the heights of fear, grounding and calming me. I have no idea what he did but I shut my eyes, and with his help, I finally realised how to let go. The connection between myself and the evil threep began to stretch like rubber until somehow I was able to turn my mind away and feel it snap. Reality appeared and with it the red-lit cabin, the stupid, stupid klaxon that wouldn't stop and Eric, who was sitting opposite me. His reddy-brown colouring had paled significantly and he seemed exhausted.

"What are you doing?" I asked.

"Talking to you!" he said. "I had to take drastic action to reach you in there. You're not going to like this," he added, "but I'm going to let go of you."

"You're not holding onto me."

"I mean unfuse."

I swallowed.

"OK."

Neewong and Smeesch were still at their stations but they weren't fully concentrating and I picked up a sense of expectancy.

"Hi guys!" I said and they waved cheerfully.

"Pay attention!" said Eric, and to his better thirds, "don't distract her!"

"Ready Andi?"

I nodded.

"Here we go. One, two, three."

He let go. Even though he was sitting three feet away from me, I felt a physical sensation; as if he was pulling a slimy, wriggling, invisible extension out through my ears.

"Yuk! What was that?" I asked.

"That was a low-grade mind fusion: stage one."

"Like Mingold tried to give me?"

"Exactly like that," said Eric. "Although I think Mingold tried to give you a stage two." He looked drained. He was still a lighter colour and when he returned to the pilot's seat he was clearly relieved to sit down. "I'm sorry I did it without your permission but it was the only way I could—"

"It's OK Eric."

"Your mind is much more powerful than mine and way too difficult to manipulate. If you hadn't trusted me you'd have fried me."

"It's not much good being so all-powerful if I can't control it either," I said sullenly.

He transmitted a smile.

"You will. Believe me. You can't expect to work like a pro right off," he said.

"I don't. The trouble is, I need to don't I?" I shivered as I contemplated the mind I had just read. If we got out of this alive,

Eric was going to have to teach me all the skills he knew, and I was going to have to work out how to access the information I'd learned from Mingold, fast.

"You might not, and it isn't as if you aren't learning. You won't get trapped like that again."

Too right. I wouldn't be trying anything like that in a hurry, at least, not if I saw it coming.

"Eric," I said. "Could you see any of it?"

He shrugged.

"Some."

"Then you know he was watching those fighters destroying our ship, and enjoying it." I was shaking with rage as well as fear. I couldn't help it.

"Yeh, I know, Andi."

"So you also know that, stupid moron that I am, I've stomped through his brain and he's realised I'm still alive."

"Yep, and he's coming to get us."

"Why don't you sound worried by that?"

"Military training," he said and winked three eyes.

"You're making jokes!"

"Gallows humour, isn't that what they call it? You're British, you should be good at it."

"Yeh, well this isn't so funny. Someone is coming to kill us Eric and I get the impression we're not moving very fast. Are we going to escape?" I wanted to sound as calm about all this as he and the others did but I could couldn't stop my hands from shaking or keep the panic from my voice.

"We're not going to die. We're going to survive this. We're going to survive if I have to put on a space suit, get out and push this benighted ship, because we have to. What he's doing is against everything Gamalian civilisation stands for and I will see he is called to account. Did you get a name?"

"No but he's a high-up politician so I'd kind of assumed it was Doge Sneeb."

"You think?"

"I don't know, I won't know for sure, unless I meet the two of them together, or do fusion on Sneeb's brain."

Neewong and Smeesch were still firing the lasers.

"What are you guys doing?" I asked them. "There are no baddies out there," I shuddered, "yet."

"Engine's dead. We're using the recoil," said Smeesch.

Clever but—

"How long is that going to take?"

The alarm was still sounding.

"Can we—oh for heaven's sake is there a way to turn that bloody thing off?"

Smeesch unhooked the blaster from his belt, fiddled with the settings for a moment and shot the alarm, which slowed down and stopped.

"Thank you."

There was silence in the ship except for the sound of Neewong firing the lasers at the back. Smeesch returned to firing the set he was controlling.

"Do they need our help?" I asked Eric.

"No, there are only two stations."

"I can't just sit here! Isn't there anything else we could use, are there jets for landing or anything?" I asked hopefully.

"No, all systems are dead except for the ship's computer, weapons and life support. The engine's totally burned out. I managed to drop it out of hyperspace and we should be close enough to Earth to use our UTs soon."

I could feel a knot of dread in my stomach. 'Soon' was not enough. It needed to be 'now'.

"How soon?"

"About ten minutes."

I looked up at Eric and all seven of his blue eyes turned to mine.

"If he knows our location those fighters will be coming after us by now, so do we have ten minutes, Eric?"

"No. There is one other way," he said haltingly. "We can vent the oxygen tanks."

"What are you waiting for?"

"Andi, it'll be three minutes without oxygen. We have life matter but you—"

"Just do it Eric, there's enough air in here for three minutes. Anyway, somebody has to save my planet. If it can't be me it has to be you."

Neewong and Smeesch glanced over at us transmitting questioning expressions. When I nodded, Smeesch turned to Eric and shrugged.

"OK," said Eric.

He turned to the bank of computers beside me and called up a holographic screen. The tanks were on the sides, and we had to turn. Neewong and Smeesch gave a couple of bursts of the lasers on one side and stopped firing. I could feel the movement as the ship drifted round.

On the viewing screen, which showed the stars behind us, there was a tiny dot of light which seemed to be changing. I watched it closely. Yes, it was getting bigger.

"Are you ready Andi?"

"Yeh."

"The pressure in the ship won't change, just the oxygen. Stay calm."

"Hurry it up Eric. They're coming."

"Firing oxygen thrusters, in three, two, one …"

There was a hiss and the ship jerked forward. Eric vented the oxygen from the tanks in short bursts, adjusting the course by varying the length of the burst from the tank on one side or the other as he went. There were only two tanks so there was no control for up or down, though Smeesch was able to help a little with the lasers.

Neewong came up to us with the UTs.

"I've programmed them all for Andi's pod at the university,' he said, as he handed them out, and showed me which button to press.

"Oxygen levels at five per cent," said Eric, "how are you doing Andi?"

"OK," I lied. I tried to breathe evenly, calmly, but I was sweating and shaking. I transmitted a smile to them, to show I was alright. In the viewing window, we watched the pinpoint of light growing bigger.

"We'll be in range of their weapons soon, how long?" asked Smeesch.

"Just a few clicks ..." Eric kept venting the tanks in turn, keeping the ship on a steady course towards Earth; towards safety. I realised I was panting. No. Breathe calmly. My stomach was churning and the sweat was running into my eyes but even so I could see the pinpoint resolving itself into a shape; a ship. I was beginning to feel light-headed. No, the oxygen was fine, it was just fear.

"Come on," Eric was saying, although whether to himself or the ship I couldn't say.

There was a long hiss from the oxygen tanks as Eric gave it full thrust. On the viewing screen a tiny spot of light flashed from one of the pursuing ships.

"It's a missile, this is it."

I watched as the dot grew bigger. I was dizzy now, big green spots were appearing in my vision, my head was hammering and I could feel my friends' fear as well as my own.

"Just a little bit more," said Eric pressing rapidly at the buttons venting the tanks. "OK, activate UTs in three, two, one, now!"

The last thing I remember was the missile looming in the viewer as I pressed the red button on the box Neewong had given me. Then I was lying on the carpet of my room in the university residence gasping for air. There was a splat as Neewong landed next to me, followed closely by Smeesch, with a squelch. After a second, which felt like an eternity, Eric arrived with a bit less of a splat. I hoped to God no-one else on my corridor was in.

Chapter 17
Back to Earth

I leapt up, rushed to my room door and listened. No sound from beyond. What day was it? Wednesday? Possibly. There was another diet club meeting tonight, please God let them all be at that. Or had they evacuated everyone on my floor after what Smeesch did to the fridge freezer? Possibly.

"Stay here," I told my friends and without waiting for an answer I slipped out into the hall. I'd forgotten I was covered in life matter until I noticed the trail of slime I was leaving behind me as I went.

"Oops."

I looked about me. Nothing amiss except for the yellow and black striped tape stuck in a cross over the closed kitchen door.

"Laura? Jane? Anyone?"

I listened.

Nothing. It looked as if the coast was clear. I ran back to my room.

I realised something was wrong at once. Eric hadn't got up. As I entered the room, Neewong and Smeesch were at his side bending over him. The concern they were transmitting was so strong that it felt as if it had a physical texture. Something terrible had happened to my friend. There was a black burn mark across his thorax and the flesh seemed to be bubbling, or was it the life matter? No, there was hardly any life matter on him. I started to cry.

"Eric," I sobbed as I joined his spouses beside him.

"Cut it ... a bit ... fine ..." he said and all seven eyes rolled and closed.

"Eric," I couldn't stop crying, "Eric." I tried to read his thoughts but he had lost consciousness. There was nothing.

"What's wrong? It's more than just the burn isn't it?" I asked Neewong, in English.

"Yes. He has matter loss." He answered me in Gamalian and I felt another wave of relief that the other girls on my corridor seemed to be out.

"How do we cure it?"

"He needs more life matter," said Smeesch, "he is suffocating."

"There's some on me."

"Not enough."

"Can't you add some of yours?" I asked.

"Yes," said Neewong, "but there won't be enough to do anything more than keep him alive a few extra minutes. He needs plastic matter, until he has generated more of his own, and he needs treatment for the burn," said Neewong.

"How long does he have?" I blubbed, my tears showing no sign of abating.

"A couple of minutes," said Smeesch.

"Then we have to go back."

"What about the meteor? You need to try and contact your leaders."

Stuff my leaders! I'd known from the outset that we had no chance there. However, I had entertained hopes that NASA or the UK space programme might listen. Had. But now things were different.

"There's no point is there? Even if our space organisations could get a mission together, and even if it's capable of reaching the meteor, it will be blown to pieces before it gets near," the tears ran faster, "this is over," I wiped my nose on my sleeve. "It never even began. We can't save Eric or my planet on our own," I hiccuped. "Our only hope is the Eegby. We have to take him back and find a way to use your technology to blow up the meteor without Doge Sneeb realising."

Neewong reached one antenna down and placed it gently on my wrist.

"Are you sure?" he asked. "If we take Eric back you don't have to come, you can still try to contact someone here."

I shook my head.

"I can't convince my leaders without you guys and I get the impression you can't convince your leaders without me. Between the human race and yours it's no contest. Now that the meteor has speeded up, I'll bet the only way we can stop it is with the weapons on the Eegby."

"If you will come with us, perhaps we can find a way," said Smeesch. "I swear I will do everything in my power to ensure we do."

"Amen to that," said Neewong, "but Andi, you do not have to come."

I transmitted a wan smile.

"I do. Eric's out cold, who's going to project a cover for you? You need to get him to a doctor, not arrested. Do you even know the way to the medical pod?"

Neewong shook his head.

"Well, I reckon Mingold does and because I fried his mind, that means I do too."

"I'll programme the UT," said Neewong. For a few seemingly endless seconds, he concentrated on the box, while I concentrated on Eric. Guided by Smeesch, I scraped off some of his and Neewong's life matter, along with as much of the stuff on me as we could remove, and we spread it over my friend.

"We're in luck," said Neewong, with surprise. "There is an automatic setting. It will transfer us to a special area of the Eegby's medical bay."

"Is it near enough?" I asked him.

"It should be – it's between us and the coordinates we've just come from – but if it isn't we'll get an error message."

"We won't die then?"

"No, Andi."

But if we were too far away to transport, Eric would. No he

wouldn't; not on my account.

"Let's go."

Smeesch called up the emergency setting on his own UT. While he was doing so Neewong took mine and Eric's and set them up.

Following Neewong's instructions for the transportation of unconscious beings, I put Eric's pincer against the green button on his UT and he disappeared.

"Looks promising," I said.

"Yes," Neewong agreed.

"Good," I said and the three of us pressed the green buttons on ours.

Chapter 18
Noble gesture

The medical area of the Eegby was a fully operational hospital. I guess on a battle cruiser it had to be. It comprised a round hallway with a series of doors and corridors leading off it. Here and there, along the corridors, I could see strange pieces of equipment lying about, which I assumed were the Gamalian equivalent of the oxygen canisters, empty wheelchairs, gurneys and other paraphernalia you get in a hospital on Earth.

Gamalian doctors wear stethoscopes, too. I suppose that means your average threep has a heart under all that exoskeleton even if there aren't any lungs or bronchial tubes to listen to. A doctor greeted us with an air of bemusement, which turned to glassy incomprehension when he saw me. I was disguising myself as Doge Sneeb and I had managed to disguise the colours of my friends so that Neewong and Smeesch weren't instantly recognisable.

I wished I could project a disguise for myself that was a bit less conspicuous. I wasn't imagining it quite right, either. That much was obvious, even if I couldn't work out why. Luckily, the doctor seemed to forget about my disguise and any irregularity I might be displaying when he saw Eric. He ushered us all quickly into a consulting room. Two assistants arrived, seemingly out of nowhere, pushing something that looked like a hovercoffin. However, it was full of plastic matter, so I was pretty sure it wasn't. They lifted Eric into it and all but his head and antennae sank beneath the surface accompanied by a noise like someone blowing an enormous raspberry. Then they began to wire the bits of him left sticking out to what I assumed was life support. The doctor was small for a threep – so that's still a good foot taller than me – and beady-eyed. His ocular pieces were such a dark shade of brown they were almost black. They were never still and mostly looking in several directions at once. He waited until his assistants had left before he spoke.

"This is no ordinary case of matter loss and the burn ..." he said, shaking his head in incomprehension and darting my projection of the Doge a sideways glance. "I might almost think it was deliberate. How did it happen?"

I nodded at Smeesch who started on a feeble excuse about an explosion in engineering. We could all see the doctor wasn't buying it, but it was Neewong who cracked first and cut Smeesch off.

"Yes, well now it doesn't do to talk about this type of work," he said fussily. "But he was on a TOP secret reconnaissance mission on the planet we are about to colonise when he was attacked. We were lucky to get to him in time. We patched him up as best we could and brought him straight here."

"Then why did you not bring him through the proper channels?" asked the doctor. "If you'd followed the correct protocol I would have had a team on standby."

There was an uncomfortable silence.

"Er," said Neewong, "I thought we had."

"No," said the doctor.

"There wasn't time," said Smeesch abruptly.

"I changed the protocol, you should have received the memo," I said in my shockingly bad Gamalian.

"No you didn't," said the doctor.

"Do you dare to contradict me?"

The doctor laughed and said, "Yes."

"Wretched communicator's bust," said Neewong.

To add credence to the story, I pointed half-heartedly to one of the metallic gizmos on my pretend Doge Sneeb's belt.

"That's not a communicator," said the doctor, sounding less than happy. "Tell me, Your Loftiness," he said and I realised he was talking to my projection of Doge Sneeb. "What is your reason for bypassing the procedures you, yourself, drew up?" All seven brown-black eyes concentrated on my fake Doge. Two large threeps with cattle prods came in and stood either side of the door.

Bum.

He was onto us. He must have pressed a panic button without our noticing. Lord in heaven please don't let me have to try and speak any more Gamalian. I could do it telepathically, I supposed. I made Doge Sneeb look angry and implanted my reply in his head as if no-one would notice.

I do not have to explain my actions to you, minion.

The doctor had one antenna behind his back.

"That may be so," he transmitted a hurt expression. "But putting that last uncharacteristic rebuke aside for a moment, I am your personal physician and I would have thought you might want to discuss the trauma of growing an extra ocular piece." That's when I realised what was wrong. I had inadvertently been thinking eight for my ersatz Sneeb's eyes. I'm logical, a straight A mathematician. How could I have got that wrong? No wonder the doctor had been giving me funny looks. I felt the colour draining from my face and the doctor flipped his antenna round from behind his back to reveal a glass tube, full of fluorescent green liquid. "Perhaps a sedative would make you feel more yourself."

"Don't come near me," I barked.

I heard thoughts in my head.

Andi, what are you doing?

Eric was awake.

"Who are you? What have you done with the real Sneeb?" asked the doctor angrily.

Yikes, Sneeb on its own, no 'Doge', I hoped they weren't friends and that if they were, the doctor didn't know how much his boss loathed Eric. As I began to back away Eric surfaced from the life matter that covered him and moaned feebly. There was little else he could do but it was enough to bring about a change of emphasis. I ducked as the doctor made a grab for my arm.

"OK, OK, you win. I'm human," I said and stopped disguising myself, although I carried on my efforts to mask Neewong and Smeesch's colour. "I haven't done anything to Doge Sneeb – wherever he is I'm sure he's fine – I just borrowed his identity for a while, that's all. I come from the planet down there, Earth, only you probably call it Gamma Six."

"Not yet."

"Look, I'm sorry, but my friend is dying and it's my fault. He tried to blow up the meteor because he believes I'm sentient; Gamalian sentient. Then these fighters came—"

"Where from?"

"I don't know do I? They weren't marked but they were Gamalian. They attacked us and we escaped to Earth to see if we could contact my leaders instead. But my friend was injured in the attack, and human medicine can't fix him, so we had to come back here. His name's Persalub and these are his spouses Neewong and Smeesch. He's Gamalian and so are you. You have to treat him," I gabbled. "You can arrest me afterwards – I promise I'll go quietly – but please, help him. I won't try anything. Here take my gun. I really, really don't want it anyway." I unclipped the blaster Eric had given me from my belt and held it out with the handle towards him, thankful for an opportunity to be rid of it. He seemed shocked but also impressed by my melodramatic surrender. He took the gun from my hand and put it on a trolley behind him.

"Persalub is lucky you know our law better than our anatomy," he transmitted a smile and turned to the cattle-prod-wielding heavies by the door. "If you will, wait outside please, I must examine the patient. I will send the alien out to you shortly." He was very sure of himself. He showed no sign of fear and hadn't even bothered to check whether or not Neewong and Smeesch were armed, in his position I wouldn't have been so magnanimous.

"Begging your pardon," said the more stolid of the two guards, "but we are under orders from Commodore Pimlip not to leave the room without …" clearly, he didn't know what to call me. "That," he eventually said, pointing.

"Very efficient of you, I'm sure, but as the ship's medical officer, I outrank Commodore Pimlip on medical matters concerning the crew and it is on those grounds that I'm countermanding your orders from him. Rest assured I will take full responsibility. Now, if you will please wait outside," said the doctor.

"Sorry sir, these orders are from the Doge himself, sir. Via Commodore Pimlip. No can do," said the larger one.

The doctor tried a different tack.

"You do realise I'm the Doge's personal physician?" he said. "He won't be very pleased when I tell him you've been forcing me to break the law by stopping me from doing my job."

"We aren't stopping you, sir," said the other guard politely.

"Yes you are! This room is supposed to be a sterile environment!" retorted the doctor, clearly resorting to the if-in-doubt-blind-them-with-science approach.

"They're not sterile," said one of the guards gesturing to Neewong, Smeesch and I.

"They're next of kin," said the doctor. "Now, out!" He opened the door and held it open.

They left like a pair of chastened schoolboys. When they had gone the doctor brushed aside my effusive thanks and with at least two eyes watching me the entire time he took another glass tube, full of pink liquid this time. He fished Eric's arm out of the life matter, held the flat end of the tube against it and the liquid disappeared with a hiss, Star Trek style. Eric surfaced almost immediately and tried to sit up but the doctor pushed him gently back into his bath of slime.

"Easy, my friend, you need to rest. It's incredible that you're awake."

"Must stop the colonisation," burbled Eric feebly.

"He's delirious," said the doctor.

No he wasn't.

"Don't be afraid, we'll have you right in no time," he told Eric. "I'll give you something to help you sleep and then—"

"No—" began Eric but the doctor put a second syringe against my friend's exoskeleton, and injected the green liquid into

118

him. Eric flopped back, unconscious, under the surface of the plastic matter.

The doctor put his antennae into the life matter and examined the burn on Eric's thorax for a few moments before turning gravely to us.

"This is very serious," he said.

We'd gathered that. The three of us watched mutely while he examined Eric from head to, well, I suppose those would be his toes.

"Your friend is lucky enough to have an iron constitution," he told us all. "His exoskeleton hasn't dried out as thoroughly as I had feared – already he is producing his own life matter. He will make a full recovery. However he will take longer to recover than he would from an ordinary instance of matter loss and the burn will need an injection of regenerative cells which will take time to fully knit. He will find it painful while the damaged section regrows. I will have to keep him sedated for the first three or four hours. I could not ethically allow him to face pain of such magnitude while conscious. Then he will have to take it easy for a day or two. I will watch him carefully and let you know when his condition improves."

"When will that be?" I asked.

"As I said, in a few hours," replied the doctor. "Maybe less. I'd say by this evening he'll be ready to receive visitors. It depends on his stamina."

There was an awkward silence.

"I'm afraid I must ask you to accompany my colleagues outside to the brig," said the doctor. This was the worst bit; where I had to keep my part of the bargain. "I can't make you," he said giving Neewong and Smeesch an appraising nod. They were both bigger than him.

"We don't want to hurt anyone," I said. "The whole reason we're in so much trouble is because we're trying to stop people getting hurt."

There was another awkward pause.

"If I don't go out there they'll come in and get me won't they?"

The doctor nodded.

I'd had enough violence for one day. The last thing I wanted now was to be poked with the Gamalian answer to an electronic cattle prod. If it was set to stun threeps it would probably kill me, anyway.

"Do Neewong and Smeesch have to come to prison too?" I asked.

"Not until your friend is recovered. They are family. Indeed they may be pardoned for their trouble. You escaped from containment here on the Eegby and it would have taken valuable time to track you down. It was a noble gesture, surrendering your freedom to bring him back here."

"What else would we do?"

The doctor transmitted a smile.

"Are you really Doge Sneeb's personal physician?" I asked.

"Yes," he said slowly. He sounded doubtful which worried me.

"Does that mean you're friends?" I asked.

"It's—" I didn't dare look too closely into his mind uninvited, but from what I could gather the word he wanted to use was 'complicated'. He didn't use it though, he said, "The Doge is not ill very often."

"But you know him a little, don't you?"

"Just a little, yes," he said.

"I realise it's a lot to ask but I don't suppose you'd put in a good word for us would you?" I asked hopefully.

He transmitted another smile but the strength of the transmission had increased. I was afraid there was a hidden agenda here, which I hadn't picked up on. He was plainly even less frightened of Doge Sneeb than he had been of us. And I realised why I couldn't read his thoughts. It was not because he was like Eric but because somewhere, out of sight, another far more powerful mind than mine was protecting him. Either Mingold had recovered or there was another sage advisor on the ship.

"I have a small amount of influence with my employer and I can but ask," the doctor was saying. He made to open the door for me.

"Shouldn't you warn them?" I asked.

He was surprised but he opened the door a crack and looked out, at me and back out again. "Prisoner coming through," he said and closed it momentarily. "They want you badly don't they?"

"Yes." I sighed and to my dismay he handed me my blaster.

"If you give them this the way you did me it might help."

"Thanks."

I tried to shove the wretched gun into my back pocket but it wouldn't go because the UT was already in there. I thanked the doctor, anyway, and went out into the hall to be greeted with a chorus of clicking sounds as a sea of threep guards primed various pieces of ordnance and pointed them at me.

"Hello," I said. Both my hands were still behind my back but now I had a plan. I felt for the reassuring shape of the remote transporter. I hadn't exactly lied to the doctor. I was going to go quietly, I just wasn't going to go with the guards. I pressed the button and materialised just behind them, where we had arrived with Eric. Then I turned and ran.

Chapter 19
Stunned

As soon as I landed I knew this had been a bad idea. Never mind, too late now. I leapt up and bolted down the corridor; a round of laser fire pinged off the wall as I turned the corner. Yikes! The passage forked and I took the right hand which seemed to go uphill. A few yards along I found a door. I dived in. It was a cupboard by the looks of things, with some kind of gas cylinder and a lot of complicated valves and pipes. I hid behind it and waited, listening as the pursuit squished past me at full speed. After their shouts died away I crept out from behind the cylinder and moved stealthily over to the door, or at least, as stealthily as anyone can who is squelching through eighteen inches of Marmite-scented ectoplasm.

I waited, listening.

Silence.

Just in case, I took the blaster out of my pocket and put my other hand on the door. It opened with a splat and I staggered out straight into the path of Doge Sneeb. He was with another threep, who I instinctively categorised as a sage advisor, mainly because I could read nothing from his mind, not even the kinds of signals normal threeps usually sent, the non-verbal stuff that we humans do with facial expressions.

That was the point when I also noticed their armed escort of three who stepped up and levelled their guns at me. But they left me with a clear shot at their leader. Without thinking my actions through I pointed my blaster at Doge Sneeb. The sage advisor didn't project his anxiety, indeed, he displayed a conspicuously impassive exterior but he couldn't hide the effort it was taking to maintain his emotionless facade or his physical reaction; he turned pale. What with me pointing a gun at his boss, I assumed he was worrying about future job prospects. I took a deep breath. Oh deary me. More speaking required. I just hoped I could make it intelligible, because if I wanted to get out of this alive, they had to understand me.

"OK, I don't want to hurt anyone," I screeched. It wasn't bad, I'd definitely got the fingers down the blackboard and fax burble aspect, but I suspected my efforts at the shouting dolphin side of it were falling short. Especially when I had the distinct impression that Doge Sneeb was appalled and almost physically squirming while, at the other end of the spectrum, one of the guards was trying not to laugh. Never mind, they were obviously getting the gist, plough on. "I'm warning you. I'm desperate," I continued. "Let me go and I promise nobody will come to any harm. Otherwise, the big guy gets it."

"May I humbly suggest you stop this preposterous charade and give yourself up," said Doge Sneeb, in perfect English. The irony sounded even heavier in his BBC 1960s newscaster accent.

Subtly, surreptitiously out of the corner of my eye so that no-one could see, I checked that the gun was set to stun.

"I can't," I said.

It's checking the gun, I picked up the sage advisor's thoughts to his boss.

"I mean what I say," I told the guards in what was, quite obviously, risible Gamalian. "Let me go or I'm going to shoot the Doge."

"This is the Eegby. There are seven hundred Gamalians on board who are loyal to me, and no way off. Where, precisely do you intend to go?"

The truth was, I hadn't thought ahead that far. Doge Sneeb took a step forwards. I ignored him and continued to address the guards.

"I mean it!" I screeched. My efforts at Gamalian were beginning to give me a sore throat. "For heaven's sake!" I shouted in exasperation, and in English this time, "which part of 'let me go' don't you understand?"

"All of it I should imagine, your pronunciation being what it is." Doge Sneeb took another step forwards. His voice was flat, his thoughts completely hidden and the surface of his mind was smooth, cold and impenetrable, like alabaster. There was nothing in his demeanour but icy calm and the hard edge of his anger. The Doge was not pleased, that much was clear but then, based on my experience so far, he never was.

He moved closer still.

Arse! Was he near enough to get the gun? I didn't know. I couldn't back up, it would be defeat.

How come this always worked in films, I wondered, with more than a little pique. I was going to have to shoot him now. I just hoped that stun meant stun. I took a deep breath and let it out slowly. My hands began to shake. He looked calmly down the barrel of the blaster.

"Your human peers would have to travel for over six months to reach you. You are all alone. Do not make this harder for yourself than it has to be."

"Let me go."

"No." The power of Doge Sneeb's glare intensified. I should have known not to try and outstare him when the ratio of eyes was so unequally biased in his favour. Seven dark green eyes, each displaying the same negligible amount of warmth as the rest of his personality, glowered at my two. I started shivering and sweating all at the same time. I couldn't hold the gun steady and my clammy palms were making the handle slippery.

"I'll give you one last chance, sir," I half whispered, half begged.

"I think not," he flicked one antenna towards me and I knew he wanted to make a grab for the gun. The world slowed down and the blaster kicked as I squeezed the trigger. A green beam of light flew from the barrel and hit the Doge full in the thorax. In his shock, he dropped his impassive facade and I saw his surprise. He plainly hadn't believed I'd have the gumption to shoot him but then, neither had I. The impact of my shot sent him flying backwards into the arms of one of the guards and took the rest of them down in a heap. Turning in horror, the sage advisor rushed to his aid.

Throwing the gun from me I backed away, revolted by what I had done, and fled back down the passage in the confusion. I had a good head start on Doge Sneeb's guards and at the place where the corridor forked I turned right.

Surely I could find the launch bay I'd been to with Eric and his husbands. If I could nick another ship and get it to NASA the human race might yet save itself. I could hear the burbles and chitterings of Doge Sneeb's guards close behind me as I ran. I was seeing stars. My breath was rasping and I was exhausted but the adrenaline kept my leaden legs moving. I reached another fork in the corridor. Which way? Mingold knew the ship like the town he grew up in. But now, when I tried to access his knowledge it was gone. Was mental fusion temporary? Had it worn off? I glanced at a sign to my right and easily read the words, *'Lighting access'* in Gamalian script. No.

I plumped for the left fork and struggled on. My legs were really burning now and the shouts behind were getting closer. It was as if they knew where I was going. Bum. The sage advisor must have got into my head during that last encounter.

I was hardly moving now, gasping for breath. As I rounded a bend in the corridor, I met a group of threeps coming the other way.

No time for thought. Doge Sneeb's guards had nearly caught up. I reached for the UT in my back pocket. When I arrived back outside the medical pod I landed awkwardly, rolling painfully to a halt against the door to the room where the ship's doctor had examined Eric.

Flippin' Ada, I must work out how to programme the UT, and fast, but first I'd better start running.

Again.

Except ...

When I tried to get to my feet I found that something had

happened to my knee. It felt weird, and when I put my weight on it, it collapsed under me.

No. Not now.

Gritting my teeth, I staggered to my feet again. My right knee was numb and once again, when I put my weight on it to walk, it crumpled beneath me, dumping me back in the slime. I got up and had another go with the same ignominious result. For heaven's sake! This was the pits. I might yet escape, though. If I could hide in the cupboard or if only I could get inside the medical pod, maybe I could convince the doctor to help me. I began to crawl through the slime. I suppose I had managed a couple of yards before my pursuers returned.

It occurred to me that standing up, albeit on one leg, would make me look more dignified but as I tried to get up, a sudden pressure against my back pushed me down, I lay gasping and coughing for air with my face in the slime. An antenna reached round under my chin and pulled my head up. My vision blurry with life matter, I looked up into the dark green eyes of Doge Sneeb. He was angry, no, more than angry he'd gone right through anger and out the other side into ice-cold rage. He leaned down and looked into my face.

"This may hurt a bit," slowly, deliberately, he put a blaster against my temple. "Tit for tat as I believe you humans say."

He transmitted a small, self-satisfied smile as he squeezed the handle. There was an overwhelming glare of green, a bolt of searing pain and then silence.

Chapter 20
The doctor calls

I lay on my back, gradually assimilating the fact that I was awake and not dead. On the other hand, the ceiling above me was black, and gold, and looked as if it had been designed by someone who had dropped an acid tab and looked at a runner bean plant for a long time.

Bollocks.

I was still trapped in B-movie hell.

Good points to the situation? I was alive; bad points? Everything else. Yes, a meteor was about to kill life on earth and no, the activities of the last forty-eight hours were not a dream. They were real. I rolled over and immediately felt a stab of the most unspeakable agony in my knee. It was so bad I actually whimpered. Slowly, wincing at the pain with every move, I sat up. I was on a bed in a room that had been cleared of life matter. I noticed my baseball boots and socks on the floor by my bed. That was the point when I also noticed my hands.

"What?"

The nails were long, world-record attempt long, and judging by the way I could feel my hair hanging about my face it had put in a similar amount of growth. My heart sank. Actually 'my heart sank' doesn't really do justice to what it did because it implies there was an actual bottom to the pit of my despair. I must have been unconscious for weeks. The meteor would have reached earth by this time and every other human being would be dead or dying. I was the last of my kind, a novelty for the Arch Doge of the Gamalian Federation of Planets' private zoo.

"No," I whispered. "No, no."

The door squished open and the doctor who had treated Eric strolled in all bright and breezy. He stood watching me for a moment, fidgeting.

"I'm glad to see you are awake," he said, in English.

"I wish I could say I was," I put my head in my hands and began to sob.

He seemed completely taken aback but in my misery and utter loneliness I didn't care. I cried for the people I loved, who were gone, I cried for the places I would never see, the life I would never have, the soulmate I would never meet and the days that would never dawn on a human population of Earth.

"It's not so bad, it's just a sprain," I felt the tentative touch of one antenna on my shoulder. "You'll be alright. I promise. Trust me, I'm a doctor."

I sobbed some more.

"My name is Apreetik."

I made a noise like a sea lion and cried with renewed vigour, wishing, all the while that I could stop.

"I am also a trained counsellor, if you'd like to talk about it."

"Th-th-th-there's n-n-n-n-nothing t-t-t-to talk a-a-a-about," I said doing that stuttering thing you do when you've cried so much you can't really breathe any more. Although it wasn't something I had ever expected to do again after the age of about five. Blimey, communication was hard work during a fit of hysterics. I realised that, in theory, I should be able to put the words in his brain, without the hiccuping, so long as his sage advisor would let me. *I've slept through the death of my planet.*

Had it worked? He stared at me for a moment projecting a puzzled frown.

"Death of your—what do you—" he began, out loud.

I sent him a thought, the way Neewong and Smeesch had to me but in reverse, asking if I could put words into his head. He nodded.

The meteor: the extinction of my species.

For a moment he seemed completely perplexed. Did he not know about the meteor? I got the impression it was more polite to talk out loud than blunder into someone's head and dump words in their brain so I reverted to speaking aloud. Apart from the odd hiccup I managed to be a bit more intelligible.

"If I've been – hic – out long enough to g-g – hic – grow all this hair and talons l-l-l-like th-th-th-th-this," I held up my hands to show him my giant fingernails, "I must have s-s-s-s – hic – slept for weeks."

"Oh forgive me, I'm so sorry," he countered, "I should have said something sooner – I didn't understand ..." I think he wanted to add that he hadn't realised medicine on my planet was so many centuries behind his, but thought better of it, in case I took it as rude. "Please, don't worry, you have only been asleep for a few hours. You regained consciousness before I expected you to. Otherwise I would have trimmed your nails before you woke. Both they and your hair will grow very fast for a couple of hours, it's all part of the growth accelerator I injected you with."

"The what?"

"I'm afraid you tore a ligament in your knee. The regeneration process can be excruciatingly painful so I sedated you."

"Sedated?"

"Yes."

"Right. And when you say, regeneration, d'you mean like stem cell therapy?"

"Exactly like that, the same treatment as your friend, Persalub. You'll be recovered in an hour or two. The meteor has not hit your planet and it will not for some hours."

"How many hours?"

"About thirty I believe."

"So everyone on earth is still alive?"

"Yes."

Blummin' Ada, there was still time, if only I could get off this stupid ship.

"I have to get out of here," I swung my legs round and stood up. For a second it felt fine. Then the pain kicked in, the room began to spin and I felt my legs giving way.

"Easy, little one, not yet," said Apreetik, grabbing me with his flexible antennae to stop me from falling. He lifted me up and sat me back on the bed. "I have the final injection here, then, another hour's rest and you should be as right as rain. Hold out your arm."

I did as he said and he injected me with a syringe full of fluorescent pink liquid.

"Nice, will I glow in the dark?"

"I should hope not. Here." He held out a box of paper tissues before he seemed to realise I could never hold a tissue without shredding it when my nails were this long. "Perhaps you will need these first."

He put the box of tissues down and proffered a pair of nail clippers. However, when I started to try and trim my fingernails the threep clippers were unbelievably stiff.

"Here, let me," he took them from me. "Hold still."

His small kindness nearly started me crying again.

Nails back to normal I took a handkerchief, wiped my eyes and blew my nose with a loud parp.

"Can I ask you something, Doctor?"

"Call me Apreetik."

"OK, can I ask you something, Apreetik?"

"Yes, go ahead."

"What's going to happen to Eric – I mean Persalub?" I asked.

"He's recovering well, another half an hour and he'll be through the worst. My team and I are monitoring readings from his pain receptors, as soon as they reach an acceptable level we'll wake him up."

Although, when I'd asked about Eric, his physical condition wasn't what I'd meant. Apreetik seemed to realise.

"Is there anything else?"

"What I was really wondering is, what will happen to him and his marital partners with Doge Sneeb?"

"I cannot tell you."

"Will it be bad?"

"I—" he was unsure of himself, "it is a grave charge, insubordination."

"Yeh, I had a feeling it was. Can I see him?"

"Yes, when he wakes, which won't be long. In the meantime, there's someone else who wishes to speak with you."

I had a horrible feeling I knew who it was.

"Am I allowed to say no?"

He projected something that, were he human, would have been a sigh.

"I'm afraid not."

In an ideal world, I would not see Doge Sneeb ever, ever again; and now I had to talk to him while I felt like warmed-up poo, and probably looked like a banshee. And he would almost certainly gloat.

"Does it have to be now?" My voice sounded frightened and small but not nearly as much as I felt.

"Yes. I must go and check on your friend and you must make your peace with my commander."

"How can I make my peace with him? He hates me."

"Talk to him. Be honest. Believe me, he is not the monster he pretends to be."

"No, he's way, way worse."

Apreetik seemed stung by my words, sad almost.

"Sneeb is ... it's—" again that hesitation and this time I said the word.

"Complicated?"

He nodded and projected a smile. "I will tell your visitors that you are ready."

Chapter 21
Revelation

I really wasn't in the mood to talk to anyone, especially on such an empty stomach. As if to agree, my tummy made a gurgling noise, starting low and rising in pitch as it tailed off into silence. Great. When the door opened, shortly after the doctor's departure, Doge Sneeb walked in with another threep. It was the same one who had been with him in the corridor when I'd shot him. The absence of any kind of emotional feedback from either of them confirmed my suspicions that the Doge had been prepared for any incidents such as my frying Mingold and brought a spare sage advisor. It didn't exactly boost my spirits.

"Good afternoon," he said calmly. His English was as impeccable as ever with the usual BBC accent. "My time is valuable so I will cut to the chase. I am wondering if you could tell me what, exactly, you think you're doing?"

"Trying to save my planet: from you."

There went my mouth, miles ahead of my brain, but whatever Apreetik said, I didn't trust Doge Sneeb. I couldn't.

"From me: or from the inevitable?"

"Oh from you: definitely."

"That is what you think, is it? That I will stop at nothing, not even genocide on a planetary scale, to advance my political career."

"From where I'm standing, that's how it looks. It's not as if you've shown me any evidence to the contrary."

He cocked his head on one side for a moment and buried the beginnings of a questioning expression.

"Perhaps you are right in one respect. It is certainly my ambition that has brought me here, but if your civilisation had the technology to save itself the point would be moot."

"It does," I snapped.

"Then why hasn't anyone acted?"

They probably couldn't agree what to do for the best but I thought it sensible to avoid saying that.

"They'll have to wait until the meteor is within range of our ships."

"Of course," he said, with withering sarcasm.

"Though you're right, the point is moot because as soon as they get there they'll be blown up."

"So it would appear."

"As you must know," I retorted, "Eric and his partners said the fighters which attacked us were short range. They had to come from this ship."

"And why do you think that?"

"It's obvious. There's no other ship out here. Where else could they come from?"

Silence. I got the impression he was pausing to control his annoyance.

"For someone whose time is so important you're certainly drawing this out. What do you want?" I asked him. "You've obviously let your doctor treat me for a reason."

"Apreetik acted before I could intervene. He has too much compassion for his own good. He will treat anything, given the chance."

'Any*thing*,' I noticed.

"He's a better being than you are, then."

"Yes, he is."

Now what? I wished I was better equipped for this. Almost all of Doge Sneeb's emotional reactions were hidden by the sage advisor: but neither of them could conceal the bitter anger burning in his human-like eyes: or his intelligence, which was clearly considerable, and vastly superior to mine. I doubted there were many life forms in the galaxy more ill-equipped to argue the toss with Doge Sneeb than I.

And here I was.

Just brilliant.

I tried to stay calm and think sensibly about this, while he watched me closely. I didn't want to look into those angry eyes. It made me feel like potential roadkill staring into the headlights of an oncoming juggernaut.

"In the name of Plort! Talk, human. There isn't time for this."

"Why would I talk to you? How can I ever trust you? You attacked our ship."

"No, I let you go. You and your wayward friends were about to provide me with a very neat solution to a difficult problem. Doubtless I'd have been forced to punish them with the full weight of the law, upon their return, but it would have been tidy."

"Tidy!" I spat. No, no, no. Don't get riled. That was what he wanted.

"The same," he said.

"Yeh sure. If you thought it would be so 'tidy' and let us go why did you attack our ship?"

"I told you. I did not."

"Then who did?"

"I am hoping you will tell me."

"Well I can't."

"Can't or won't?"

"I'm sure you've already spoken to Neewong and Smeesch, and Eric if he's awake. They'll have told you anything I can."

"On the contrary, your friend Eric is still out cold, and why would I waste time on the other two discovering what I can already guess, when I can talk to you? You saw more than they did; more than ships."

I thought about the mind I'd read and my throat went dry. Had it been Doge Sneeb's? Since I couldn't penetrate the defences raised by his sage advisor it was hard to tell. What if it was him? What if he was trying to find out how much I knew? I took a breath and swallowed.

"You already know anything I could tell you."

He shook his head.

"Unfortunately, I do not and the crux of the matter is, I need to: now."

I couldn't feel the sage advisor in my head, but at the same time, I knew he was there, trying to read my thoughts. I realised I'd probably been correct in my suspicions. He'd probably been reading a lot of my thoughts since I arrived back on the ship but

I didn't know how he got in, or why I couldn't feel it. But how else could my pursuers find me so easily when I ran? Why else had I forgotten my way around, especially when I remembered again now. Someone had been blocking my personal access to bits of my own brain. That was extremely creepy. I felt the hairs rising on the back of my neck.

"If you continue to be so obstreperous I will be forced to reclaim the information you contain another way. Except, this time, I will use the services of someone a little more powerful than Mingold," said Doge Sneeb.

A couple of his eye stalks swivelled towards the sage advisor, next to him.

"More mind fusion? That's a very lazy way to negotiate. Go on then. Give me all you've got. What do I care? I've nothing to lose."

"I take it you are not willing to cooperate with me."

"You know this colonisation is wrong and you can stop it but you won't. Are you surprised?"

"When you put it like that, I suppose not, but it really is a pity. It would be very much easier if we could work together."

"Why would I help you? You're going to kill us; the entire human race."

"Kill you? Hardly: that would be unethical. The meteor will do it."

I glared up at him.

"I can read thoughts. I'm sentient."

"Yes, you are. But you are also illogical and foolish. The behaviour of your species, on your home planet, suggests the human race might even be a pestilence. The Galaxy may be better off without you."

I thought about the wars, the destruction, the human rights abuses that went on, daily, on Earth. We never seemed to learn. Doubtless his sage advisor read those thoughts and passed them on to him. I didn't bother to try and probe his defences to find out, I reckoned I would need all my strength for what was about to come. He waited. Perhaps he was expecting me to argue but I had no answer.

"No I-can-change speech?" he mocked.

I shook my head.

"No," it was probably the truth. I took a deep shuddering breath. "Mister Sneeb, sir, if you want to do something decent please can you put me back with my mum and dad, and find my brother and put him with us too. I'd like to die with my family, if that's OK with you. And please apologise to Mingold for me. I really, really didn't mean to hurt him."

He stood still and silent for a moment, scrutinising my face. Trying to meet all seven of his eyes at once was doing my head in so I picked two and stuck with them. I could still detect little from him, only the impenetrable smoothness of his mental guard and the omnipresent bitterness. The sage advisor was concealing all other thoughts and emotional signals. Except that I began to believe there was more to this. I picked up a momentary flash of bemusement, surprise and something else I couldn't place before the sage advisor shut down everything.

"I will pass your message to Mingold," said Sneeb, "but as to your leaving? I think it's a little early for that."

"Do you? Well listen, Mister. You've just admitted I'm sentient! Your code of ethics demands you save my planet. If you're going to ignore it and refuse that's between you and your conscience, but the least you can do is let me go back there, so I can try."

He said nothing.

"For God's sake! Help us. It's the right thing to do."

"Yes. But this is politics, human. It's a little more complicated than right or wrong."

"It shouldn't be."

"I am aware. Nonetheless, it is. There are seven hundred Gamalians on this vessel and I have to think of them, too."

"There are billions of people on my planet! You could always try thinking about them."

"Do you dare to preach to me? There is, as far as I am aware, only one sentient human and she is here talking to me. I have already adhered to Gamalian ethics by saving you. The rest is simply a question of whether or not I preserve your complicated, planet-sized habitat. If you are as adaptable as the rest of your species I wonder if you would require such an extravagant gesture."

"It's not my 'habitat'."

"On the contrary: that's exactly what it is. And now, since you refuse to cooperate, I'm afraid you leave me no choice," he turned to the sage advisor and switched to Gamalian. "Do it," he ordered.

The other threep began to move towards me. No, please, please no.

"As the governor of a planet I should warn you that when I retain the services of a sage advisor, I require someone with a little more mental sparkle than Mingold. He is assigned to Commodore Pimlip, who is in charge of the Eegby. This, however, is Borridge, and he is assigned to me."

"You want me to fry his brain now do you?" I tried to sound bullish but even to my own ears it came out more like begging. Unperturbed, Borridge stepped forward.

"I don't think you will. Oh you're exceptionally gifted, I'll give you that, and you may be a match for someone like Mingold but you have no training and Borridge ... Borridge has quite a lot. And he is very, very intelligent whereas you ..."

He wasn't wrong, already I could feel Borridge's mind in mine; circling the wall, testing my defences. I put my hands to my head, as if it would stop him, as if it would help.

"You can't do this. It's against your code of ethics. I have to agree," I said.

"In this instance, bearing in mind what's at stake, your agreement is not required."

"No!" I wanted to back away from him, into the corner of the room but I also wanted to hide my fear. Somehow, I stood fast.

There was no pain like there had been with Mingold, no horrible sensation of worms burrowing into my temples. Borridge was way too subtle for that. I felt the usual tightness, as if my skull was contracting and squeezing my brain and the same sensation of being dipped in cold water as I'd felt on the Thesarus when I'd accidentally fused my mind with someone else's. Borridge was good at this; better than me, a lot better than Mingold and better than Eric. If he decided to get hostile I was going to last about as long as an ice cube in an industrial furnace.

Without realising what I was doing I shut my eyes, grinding the heels of my hands into my temples. I prepared my defences as best I could. I felt as if my mind was being pushed sideways to make room in my head for his or as if his consciousness and thoughts were trying to engulf mine. Strangely, instead of panicking, I became calm. I pictured a brick wall this time, towering between his mind and mine, keeping the two apart, keeping me safe while I racked my brains for a way to force him out.

"Interesting technique but it won't get you anywhere," said Borridge, in a voice of unruffled calm that went close to smugness. Perhaps it was that which made me snap. Whatever it was, instinctively, I attacked, before I could stop myself. The fact I didn't know how to fuse my mind with another one failed to enter my subconscious thinking. I lashed out by instinct. I caught Borridge completely by surprise. He recoiled, I could feel the energy in the connection lessen, feel him retreat, trying to break the link as he did so. But I was in control now, and he couldn't let go. I felt him struggling to escape. I'd defeated him, for the moment at least, so now I had to break the connection, but even after Eric had helped me on the Thesarus, I still couldn't remember how. I felt the first hints of his discomfort as I began to overpower him. I felt his fear as he realised I had even less idea what I was doing than he'd thought. I needed information from him, fast before I hurt him. Then, exactly as with Mingold, when it seemed I had held my own, the strength of my opponent quadrupled.

My temples throbbed as Borridge fought back, but this was different, a little faux almost, as if I'd reached him and floored him: as if someone else had stepped in to play the part of pretend Borridge while the real one was out cold. There was another kind of intelligence behind this second attack; incisive, ruthless and very, very angry. I gasped and my breath caught as I realised what it meant.

He overpowered me instantly. My moment of shock was all he needed. Still I tried to fight. The wall flickered and disappeared. I tried to rebuild it but my new wall had no substance. An ethereal, transparent ghost of the original, it gave me no protection. There was nowhere to hide. Still I fought and I couldn't believe how hard it was to stand my ground. I felt myself beginning to weaken, sliding into unconsciousness, into nothing. There was another sage advisor on the ship. Perhaps I could have held my own against just Borridge but with his new ally, I was toast.

I felt the pressure in my head increase.

"I'm going to ask you one more time," said Doge Sneeb, "what did you see?"

Even if I'd wanted to tell them, it was no longer possible. They were going to kill me. I could feel their resignation, a hint of regret, even, but they knew that I must die, that it was the only way. I prepared myself to try and face the end with as much dignity as possible: while going out fighting, of course. I kept picturing the wall, imagining it was real, imagining I was safe; and all the while, the pain carried on building until my screaming temples, and the burning fire coursing through my nervous system, told me I was close to the end. As I threw the last of my strength into my defences, I cried out in anguish at my failure; for myself and for the sixty billion humans who needed me to save them; and then I begged.

Please, Borridge, please, help me. Make him stop.

And then I saw a glimpse of something, just for a second: frustration, impotent anger and a sense of despair and utter anguish that was so deep and so acute that it almost surpassed my own. The connection was broken, swiftly and painfully.

As Borridge stumbled backwards, holding his pincers to his head, I collapsed on the ground at Doge Sneeb's feet. I could forget the soreness in my newly knitting knee but I couldn't ignore the lancing agony in my temples. It was like the worst brain freeze ever – the ice cream effect magnified a hundred million times – and my whole body buzzed and prickled with pins and needles.

But I was still breathing.

I was still alive.

I rolled around on the slimy floor sobbing and panting, as I waited for the pain to subside.

Why had they stopped? I'd seen enough in their minds to know that they believed I had to be killed. I looked up at Borridge but he could not meet my eyes. He seemed exhausted and a little flustered as if he was in shock.

Slowly I got to my feet and stood between the two of them. I turned my snotty-nosed, snivel-stained face to Doge Sneeb, squared my shoulders and stared him down. I met the eyes of my planet's nemesis without fear because I had something on him now. I understood, for certain, who the third sage advisor was and I knew that telepaths were not allowed to enter politics in the Gamalian Federation of Planets. And though it was going to take all my courage, I realised what I had to do. My mouth was dry and my voice was croaky when I spoke but I kept my eyes on my enemy's, my gaze steady.

"OK Mister Doge Sneeb. Here's how it's going to go. You and Borridge are going to take me to the captain of this ship and he's going to blow up the meteor right now."

"Oh really," he laughed in my face, but behind his snarling contempt there was a hint of brittleness, and more importantly, nervousness. "Why would I do that?"

"Because I know what you are and if you don't help me, I'm going to tell everyone."

The gimlet green eyes narrowed.

"You know nothing."

Abruptly he swung round, squished over to the door and wrenched it open. "Borridge," he barked. Wobbly legged and slow, Borridge made his way to his master's side. I was surprised when, as he stumbled, Doge Sneeb steadied him, gently, with one pincer: an uncharacteristic, almost tender gesture. They left without a backward glance and the door closed behind them with a click. Shakily, I fumbled my way to the bed. I was so tired I could hardly move and I must have been asleep the instant I lay down.

Chapter 22
Reunited with friends

Muzzy headed and confused I struggled to the surface of consciousness and looked into seven blue eyes on stalks.

I sat up.

"Eric!" I hugged him. "How are you feeling?"

"Better than you I suspect."

"It's OK. I'm a bit stiff and achy, and weary as if I am a thousand years old. And after hugging you without thinking I'm also covered in your yucky life matter, but otherwise, I'm fine."

"Yeh right." He transmitted a smile.

"What about you, how's your thorax?"

"They've fixed me up pretty well."

There was a high stool beside my bed and Eric sat down.

"The doctor, Apreetik his name is, he told me you were lucky," I said.

"More likely he's a really good doctor."

"Yeh," I thought of Doge Sneeb's sneering words, that Apreetik would treat anything and it occurred to me, for the first time, that in ministering to me he might have gone against orders. "He seems a really good bloke, all round."

My knee was still sore and so was Eric's thorax. We compared and shared the pain, using our minds, in companionable silence.

What happened there?

He waved a pincer at my knee. I described my efforts to escape and my eventual capture and shooting.

Doge Sneeb shot you?

Yeh.

Plort, that's awful.

I shrugged.

To give him his due, Eric, I shot him first.

"When I came round, they wouldn't let me see you. Apreetik said you were with Doge Sneeb," he said, out loud.

"Yeh."

"How did it go?"

Where to start?

"I learned some stuff." It seemed that every time anyone tried to tamper with my brain I absorbed some of their training. Doge Sneeb and Borridge had trained extensively.

"Come on then, dish it."

"I can't put my finger on what it is, but let's just say that, while being telepathic has felt like carrying a large bomb around with no idea how to defuse it or what might set it off, now I feel a bit more ..." hmm, confident was exaggerating, and to say that I was anywhere close to actually being in control was far too optimistic, "better equipped?"

"You feel a bit more better equipped! It hasn't improved your grammar then."

"Plonker! I just mean I feel more comfortable with being able to read thoughts."

A bit more comfortable, but if I ever made it home, knowing what everyone around me was thinking would be quite interesting and probably not in a good way. Not that it looked as if I ever would get home.

"Good."

"Yeh. Eric I—hang on," I used thoughts because I got the impression that they would be more difficult to monitor. *There's another sage advisor on this ship.*

You think?

Yes. Doge Sneeb made Borridge try to fuse his mind with mine. I was winning but then someone helped him, someone stronger. That's what happened with Mingold too. He was beaten and I couldn't disconnect so someone else overpowered both of us and did it. That's why I got stuck on the Thesarus, when I was trapped in that scary mind, I still couldn't disconnect, because I never learned how: same with the second time on here. I was ahead for a bit but not for long enough to realise what to do. It was the third one who disconnected us both times, not me, not Mingold, not Borridge.

And this sage advisor, do you know who he is?

Yes.

Who?

I can't say yet. He's too powerful. He might be in my head now and I wouldn't know.

Trust me Andi, you would.

I'm not so sure, and if he finds out you know about him too, he'll kill you. It's pretty dynamite, his identity, and I may be able to use the information to bargain with, but if I fail, he'll kill me and if I tell you, ditto.

Eric whistled out loud but carried on speaking in thoughts.

Shouldn't you insure yourself by telling me? If they realise you're the only one who knows their dirty secret they might kill you. Then the knowledge dies with you.

I think they already tried that but when it came down to it, they couldn't go through with it. But if they try again or get an assassin or something, I don't want to risk you, too.

Eric stared at me, projecting an expression of glassy incomprehension.

Andi, this is attempted murder. Who tried to kill you?

I shrugged.

Him; the secret sage advisor: when he rescued Borridge. But that's the thing, he didn't really try, neither of them could do it. It's probably because I begged for mercy, gets 'em every time in films.

"Andi, this is not funny."

Eric was trying to read my mind to gain access to the knowledge I was hiding but after my last encounter with Doge Sneeb and Borridge I'd absorbed a lot more training. I could feel my friend's emotional response to being thwarted; a mixture of mild annoyance coupled with admiration and pride at my increased ability. I smiled at him remembering to think 'smile' at the same time.

"I will tell you Eric, I promise, when it's safe."

He couldn't stop himself from transmitting his worry although he put in a fine effort.

Andi, you realise we Gamalians take blackmail a bit more seriously than you humans do.

I kind of got that.

So, this sage advisor, is he the guy whose mind you fused with on the way to the meteor?

No, and I'll tell you something else, I know now, that wasn't Doge Sneeb either.

Then what's he doing?

Doge Sneeb? I don't know. There's something going on. He's wound up so tight you wouldn't believe. He's ... he's in torment. He's trapped and frustrated, and the only way he can cope with it is anger. Doge Sneeb's head is not a happy place.

Eric did the mental equivalent of scratching his head.

Maybe it's a blind to fool you.

I don't think so. He's proud of his pointy brain and I think someone's got the better of him. That's half the anguish, because he thinks he's smarter than everyone and he hates to be outplayed.

Then maybe it'll do him good to learn some humility.

Maybe but I doubt it will help us.

Listen, d'you think Doge Sneeb diverted the meteor?

Now that Eric had asked it, I was sure of the answer to this question.

No. If anyone did, it was the guy on the Thesarus—

And you're sure they're not one and the same?

Yes. OK, look even if Doge Sneeb is spinning me a line, even if I have fallen for some fake mental projection, the other guy was like no-one else. There was something dark and warped and cracked; far-reaching mental damage underlying everything; damage that cannot be fixed. The more I think about it, the more convinced I am that it was the mind of an insane being.

You could read a little insanity into Sneeb's actions, Andi.

Yeh, I know. But that's frustration and anger, and maybe a dash of hubris at being thwarted in the bald pursuit of power.

Hubris?

Not a good word but you know ... What I'm trying to explain is that this is a whole other thing. The mind I accidentally wandered into; he was full of hatred and bile and yes, he was angry, but he was calm. Doge Sneeb on the other hand, he is so unbelievably desperate it isn't true. And hurt. And so angry with himself for falling into this that he can hardly keep a lid on it. He's—he's enraged.

But is it insane rage?

Well that's the thing Eric. No.

Doge Sneeb was very sane indeed. Was he heartless? Yes. Sadistic? Certainly, but however cruel, he was incapable of killing another being. Even when his life, his career, everything depended on destroying me and accessing the information I was hiding from him, he could not do it. Also, he was most definitely in full possession of all his marbles.

I admit it would be easier if it was Sneeb because he's such a massive git – but I can't damn him just for that.

So what's going on?

I don't know. Doge Sneeb knows I fused with someone's mind. When he and Borridge interviewed me they kept asking me about what I saw. Like they think I'm going to actually know.

Whose mind had I been trapped in? Was it one of the other Doges trying to discredit Sneeb? Did he pose a threat to them? Well yes, he must do, but was it a dangerous threat or a simple being-more-successful-and-them-not-liking-it, kind of threat?

I bent down and picked up my shoes.

Listen, however much you want to protect me, Andi, with this third sage advisor, I think I know who we're talking about. And you're right, if it's really the guy you think, it's pretty dangerous knowledge. If it got out, it would blow the Gamalian Federation right open.

"I guessed as much. Eric, I think, maybe, I have to—"

Both of us jumped when Apreetik walked in. He was accompanied by two armed guards and seemed concerned.

"What are you doing young lady?"

"Putting my shoes on," I said.

"Then you may need these again." He flicked one antenna down towards me and I realised the end of it was wrapped round a pair of nail clippers. "It should be the last time. I can do it for you if you like."

"Er that would be great," I told him in Gamalian. He was nonplussed for a moment and then he nodded. I realised that whatever knowledge I'd absorbed from Borridge's brain did not include improved pronunciation of his language. Never mind. "Thank you," I added, attempting to give it the full Gamalian wellington.

He projected an impressively stoic expression but I suspected the involuntary transmission – the equivalent of a wince – which my attempt at Gamalian evinced from one of the guards reflected his feelings more accurately.

He turned to Eric, "Captain, your partners will be brought here shortly. They are both asking after you; and Andi too. However, before they arrive, Andi, I would like to examine your knee one last time. I haven't treated a human before. I want to be sure I've got everything right. Captain, would you mind waiting outside?"

With a wink, Eric left me.

"Can you sit with your legs out straight, please?"

I swung my legs back up onto the bed, noticed the guards again and stopped. "Are you scared I'll bite?" I asked him, "only, to be honest, I'm a bit scared *they* will."

He transmitted a smile.

"No but—"

"Doge Sneeb is?"

Apreetik transmitted a resigned expression and shrugged.

"Yeh, I can imagine he thinks I'm a health risk. It's the way he said you'd treat 'anything'."

"I treat whoever requires it," he said.

I detected a momentary flash of annoyance. Apreetik lacked the telepathic ability to hide his emotional responses and I got the impression he didn't really care if I saw them anyway.

"The guards are just a precaution. Sneeb is only thinking about my safety but he and Borridge will fuss over me, so."

My mouth dropped open: although luckily, since most Gamalians seemed to mistake any facial expressions for an attack of the palsy, or just a plain attack, Apreetik appeared not to notice.

"Borridge and Sneeb fuss over you?"

"Yes."

"You and Sneeb and Borridge, are you ..." I left the question hanging.

"We're engaged."

"To one another?"

"Yes. Not that it's any of your business."

"I'm really sorry. I didn't mean to pry," I said.

"You didn't. Now, I need to manipulate your knee," he curled one of his flexible antennae round my ankle, "relax," he said as he pushed my leg up, bending my knee back against my chest. "It doesn't bother me who knows about it – does that hurt?"

"No."

"Good – but their other partner died so it's different for them," I got the impression that despite understanding the need for secrecy, Apreetik found it difficult to be patient. He straightened my leg and holding it just above the ankle, he lifted my heel off the bed and pushed his other antenna against the side of my knee.

"Does this hurt?"

"A little."

"There is their previous partner's family to think about. It would be the height of cruelty if they heard about our engagement from the press before they heard it from us—" he explained as he manipulated my knee a little more.

"Ouch!"

"Sorry. Hmm, manicure time and then I think some more pain relief is in order," he gave my nails a final trim, put the clippers in a pouch on his belt and removed a syringe. "I can't give you too much, it's a local, into your knee," he held the syringe up. "Sneeb wants you with your wits about you."

"Sneeb what?" I asked nervously.

"He wants to see you and your friends in his pod," said Apreetik as he took his space-age, no-needle syringe and injected another dose of fluorescent liquid, into my leg this time.

"What? Again? What if I don't want to see him?"

Apreetik stood back.

"You shouldn't be afraid of him, Andi. He's irascible and he can't abide fools, but as I told you before, he isn't a monster." He took hold of my leg again and bent it backwards and forwards.

"At the moment he seems to be."

"Hmm ..." Apreetik did the sideways test on my knee again. "Does this still hurt?"

"No."

"Good. Did Sneeb give you a hard time?"

"Yes. I thought, well, the thing is. I just, do you think that he and Borridge—could they have killed their other husband?"

Apreetik stopped for a moment, clearly taken aback. He seemed unsure as to what he should say.

"Why? Why in Plort's name would you say that? Neither of them can kill anything. I'm the only one of us who can swat a bug, except I can't: because if I do, the doppy pair insist that it died screaming."

Like I'd thought I was going to, the last time I'd met them. I stared up at Apreetik in amazement.

"Really?"

"Yes. How can you even think such a thing? It's—it's horrible."

"I'm sorry, I'm just a bit of a cynical git. I didn't mean to upset you."

"I'm not upset." He lowered my leg gently to the bed, "I'm ... amazed," he transmitted a frown. "What did they say to you? What did they do?"

"Things," my voice wobbled. Oh please not tears. I cleared my throat and started again, "Things that scared me. To be honest, I thought they were going to kill me. At one point, I think they thought they were."

Apreetik's frowning transmission strengthened but now there was an added dash of puzzlement. He reached one pincer up and smoothed the life matter over his forehead.

"I have no idea how someone as intelligent as Sneeb can be so retarded at reading others. I could have told him scaring you wouldn't work and Borridge should have. I suggested he level with you." Apreetik sounded irritated, momentarily, and not with me.

"I think he did: kind of."

"And I advised *you* to tell him the truth. Didn't you even try?"

"Well, I meant to but it's difficult. I was so afraid and he's so ... wound up. It's as if he's in his own personal hell."

"Yes," Apreetik transmitted a sad smile. "He is."

"Why?"

"I think he'll tell you himself soon enough. Trust him Andi."

"He's a politician!"

"I know but he *will* do the right thing. It may not look as if he will. He may not believe it himself but," Apreetik stood up, "he always does. And now you must go and see him and tell him to stop this nonsense. Your friends will be here in a moment. Oh and I meant to ask, are you hungry?"

Was I hungry?

"Just a tad but—"

"I have some Earth food." How? Where from, I wondered. Apreetik carried on oblivious, "Would a ham sandwich suffice?"

Only if it was one of a pile of about twelve ham sandwiches, but never mind, it was a start.

"Could I have two?" I asked, probably bending the limits of interplanetary protocol.

"If that is what you wish; I'll have them sent to Sneeb's pod."

Suddenly my throat was so tight that the thought of eating lost its appeal.

Apreetik might not have been telepathic but he was certainly empathetic. He picked up, at once, on my discomfort.

"If you can't trust Sneeb and Borridge, will you trust me?"

I nodded.

"Good. Then don't be afraid of them. Answer their questions. Tell them what they need to know. They're not going to hurt you. Sneeb, especially, holds you in high regard."

"And you know that because?"

"Because he calls you 'her' when every other Gamalian on this ship calls you 'it' that is, until he corrects them and insists they do the same."

"You called me 'her'."

"Yes because Sneeb ordered me to. What does that say to you?"

"I have no idea. That he's a grammar pedant?"

"You know exactly what I'm saying, Andi. That he sees you as a sentient being, with rights, because if he didn't he wouldn't show you that respect. He has a great admiration for you and your friends. Now wait here, I'll go get your escort."

Chapter 23
Ham sandwiches

Within moments of Apreetik leaving, the door of my room hissed open and six threeps marched in. Two were equipped with guns the size of small cannon and four with long staffs that looked as if they had some kind of electronic stun gizmo at one end.

This did not bode well in my view.

"Earthling, come with me," said the first guard. He sounded almost polite until he grabbed me round the neck with one of his pincers.

"Nooo!" shouted a voice as Eric, Neewong and Smeesch tumbled into the room. Smeesch rattled his pincers angrily and the guard dropped me.

After a bit of coughing I explained about my windpipe and requirement to breathe. Once they'd taken a moment to reel at the onslaught from my hideous Gamalian, the guard allowed me to walk in front of my friends. I really, really didn't want to go and see Doge Sneeb again and I slipped and skidded in the slime as I tried to persuade my shaking legs – or was that knocking knees – to function. After about three paces, the guards stopped and their leader turned and said something which I was too distracted by my nerves to catch.

"I'm sorry, what did you say?"

"You must be carried," said the guard.

"But I—"

"Please do not resist. His Loftiness, Doge Sneeb, has a tightly packed schedule. I am under strict orders to bring you quickly—"

"I'll carry her," said Eric and he picked me up and put me on

151

his shoulders. He flicked his antennae round and I held the ends like reins.

"Gee up!"

"Eh?"

"Never mind."

"No talking."

I tried to look into the minds of our escorts. They were closed to me: by Borridge, from somewhere else on the ship, I suspected. I thought for a moment. They'd told us not to talk but telepathy hadn't been mentioned so I carried on the conversation with Eric using telepathy.

Are you scared? I asked.

A bit: a lot. But dwelling on it won't help.

Apreetik, the doctor, told me Doge Sneeb admires you.

Yeh. How can a mere doctor know?

He's engaged to Doge Sneeb and Borridge.

Eric stumbled.

"He what?!" he said, aloud and I noticed Neewong and Smeesch throwing us enquiring looks.

"No talking!" snapped the guard to our left.

Are you serious?

Yep, straight up. The trouble is I do trust Apreetik but Doge Sneeb? I know I said he couldn't kill me but …

Eric said nothing. Not even a thought.

D'you think he'd be able to have second thoughts? What if these guards are going to chuck us out of the airlock?

They can't do that Andi, it's murder, well, except with you, officially, but even then it's—

Yeh thanks Eric, I'm very reassured.

Seriously, Andi, shoving beings into space is an Earth fiction thing: nobody does it in real life. It leaves too much evidence for a start. If we were going to be killed they'd have vaporised us in the medical bay.

Vaporised as in—

Yes, Andi. With a blaster set to kill there'd be nothing left.

I hiccuped and our escort halted. One of the guards, a different one, turned sharply towards me.

"Shhhh."

"Sorry. Why can't we talk?" I asked.

The guards didn't answer.

"I suppose they think we might be plotting our escape," said Smeesch.

Our escort stopped again.

"Shhh! If you are not silent I will be forced to stun you," said their leader.

We were taken along a passage, through a door and out onto a platform where I was so amazed by what I saw that I nearly fell off my friend's shoulders and Neewong, just behind, had to put up a pincer to steady me.

"Wow!" I whispered before noticing the stern expressions coming from the guards and forbearing to say anything else, I turned this way and that, craning my head to take in every detail of my surroundings.

Can you sit still, Andi? It's like carrying a jumping bean.

Sorry, I just … what is this?

The centre of the Eegby comprised a massive hollow space, which glowed with ambient light. Dark struts curled their way upwards like the ribs of a vast fossilised monster and between them, in places, you could see out through the hull to the stars. One of the guards pushed Eric towards a walkway that ran along the whole of one side.

Remember the central area I told you about?

It's amazing.

Yeh, every Gamalian gets to see this ship and then dreams of serving here.

I can see why.

In the void, level with, above and below us hung a variety of objects. Some were flat with lines marked out on them and Eric informed me, telepathically, that they were courts for a popular ball game played by threeps. There were saucer-shaped living pods for the upper echelons of the crew. Along the sides were four floors of walkways with lifts and docking gates every few yards. Small craft floated backwards and forwards: space hoppers Eric told me they were called. They were shaped like rubber

153

dinghies but they were bigger. On the wall side of the walkways a myriad of labyrinthine passages led off towards the Eegby's outer hull and all the hundreds of nameless offices and departments an intergalactic star ship needs to function. The bridge was at the front, at the top along with the aquarium, which served as the principal hard drive for the computer mainframe, as well as containing spare plankton for the lighting system.

The whole area was about the size of an exhibition centre, and there must be lord knew how much more superstructure surrounding it. The Eegby was a lot bigger than I'd realised when I'd been looking at it from the Thesarus in space: possibly the size of a small town, or at least, close.

What do you think? asked Eric as I gazed around in open-mouthed wonder.

Not bad.

We came to a platform where a hopper was docked and waiting. The guards shoved us aboard, us round the edges and themselves in the middle. We rose higher and higher until I felt I could almost reach out and touch the vaulted ceiling. Hand rails were not a priority, it seemed.We docked at one of the highest pods suspended in the space. My feelings as I climbed out of the hopper must have been very close to those of a French aristo dismounting from the tumbril during the reign of terror. There was a threep waiting for us on the landing platform and it was Borridge.

"You're late," he told the guards, "the Doge has already begun his call."

"Please accept my apologies, sir," said the head guard.

"No matter, they can join him."

He dismissed our escort with a nod of thanks and turned to the four of us.

"Welcome," he said. He looked each of us in the eye in turn, although it was clear he found it difficult making any direct eye contact with me. "Please follow me."

Borridge led us across a balcony to the doorway. Two guards

standing each side of it saluted and motioned us through into the pod itself. Eric, Neewong and Smeesch all stopped. I got a brief, and slightly garbled, stream of thought from Eric that we probably shouldn't go in. So I stopped too.

"Please," said Borridge, gesturing to the open door, "you are invited guests."

Hesitantly, Eric, Neewong, Smeesch and myself followed him inside, on tiptoe. I felt overawed, as if I was making a huge social gaffe by even being there: you know, like wearing nothing but a bikini to visit a cathedral in a devout Catholic country or going into the man bit of a mosque with my shoes on.

We stepped into a small hall. It was very 1960s, all red with a seat running round the outside and a recliner set to one side. A large sphere of plankton hanging from the ceiling shed the only light. There was also a table containing some bottles of water and a huge pile of sandwiches. At the other side of it was a door flanked by another pair of guards who held large and complicated looking blasters across their thoraxes.

"Please enjoy the—these," said Borridge gesturing to the sandwiches awkwardly.

"Sandwiches," I told him, my Gamalian all the more appalling because of my nerves, "thank you and please thank Apreetik for me."

Borridge bowed his head slightly in assent and managed not to squirm in horror at my pronunciation, although I got the impression from the rigour with which he was maintaining his impassive, transmission-free, sage advisor's facade, that he was tempted.

"Sneeb requests that you join him."

"What? Now?" I asked fearfully.

He sensed our nervousness at once. Well, one, he was a sage advisor and two, with his master's help he'd almost killed me.

"He appreciates that you may be," he was covering his thoughts but I didn't really need to be telepathic to know that he was looking for a way to say 'frightened' without implying cowardice. He eventually settled for, "confused," he looked me full in the eye this time, "and he – we – are sorry for it."

"It's OK Borridge," I said, with a magnanimousness I didn't wholly feel, even if I wanted to.

Borridge's thoughts were insanely hard to track, but I'd picked up hints while he and his husband were trying to unpick my mind. I wasn't confident but I felt I might have gained a glimmer of understanding as to the why of Doge Sneeb's anger.

"Please wait here. I will confirm that the Doge is ready to receive you."

"Thank you," said Eric.

Borridge gestured to the platter of sandwiches, "Eat something."

All four of us managed to say 'thank you' at the same time, although what Smeesch actually said was, 'cheers,' or at least, its Gamalian equivalent. With a glance at the sentries either side of the door, Borridge went into the room beyond. The guards snapped to attention as he passed with a perfectly synchronised squelch.

"I don't think I can eat. I'm ravenous but I'm also so nervous that I think I'm going to hurl."

"Ah that's hungry tum," said Neewong. "You know, when you haven't eaten for a while and you feel a bit sick."

"Thanks Neewong but actually, I think, in this case it's just a side effect of rank fear."

Even so, for the sake of Apreetik, I took a sandwich.

The four of us began to relax a tiny bit. Smeesch walked around the table, taking in his surroundings.

"Nice," he said, "proper ritzy."

"Yes, amazing decor," said Neewong.

"Mpfff," I said, as I tried to swallow my first mouthful, "it's quite cool in a nineteen sixties kind of way but the red's a bit much. It's like being in someone's mouth. I prefer the rest of the ship."

"You would," said Eric.

Borridge reappeared.

"The Doge's call has finished unexpectedly. You are to join him now," he told us.

I saw him glance at the sandwiches. He seemed slightly worried.

"The Earth food is to your liking? You have not eaten much ..."

"I'm a bit nervous." Understatement or what?

"Please, take the Earth food with you. After you have spoken with him you may be more relaxed and regain your appetite. Also, he will be grateful. I think he is curious to try some."

He would be grateful? Was that politeness or ironic mockery?

"I regret I must leave you. While Mingold is indisposed," I could feel the gargantuan effort he made not to look at me when he said 'indisposed', "I have been seconded to Commodore Pimlip."

"We thank you for your hospitality," said Eric. Oh so formal.

"Is Mingold going to be alright?" I asked him.

For the first time, he cracked something approaching a smile.

"Yes," he said, "he will be fit for light duties tomorrow."

"I'm glad," I said, "if you see him before I do—"

"I have already told him. He is a sage advisor. He did what he must and he understands that—that so did you."

"Thanks."

"My pleasure." Borridge bowed and left us.

There was a moment of silence after he had gone.

"Here goes nothing," I said, picking up the platter of sandwiches. Neewong took a couple of bottles of water.

As we approached the guards, they saluted Eric and motioned us through. I took a deep breath and followed him.

Chapter 24
The enemy

I crept into Doge Sneeb's personal quarters as slowly and quietly as a woman wading through slime while carrying a platter of sandwiches can. It wasn't exactly a situation guaranteed to enhance my dignity but I tried. From the outside, these quarters were made of a combination of matt black and silver metals. It felt like walking into a photographic negative.

The pod was circular and I saw no chairs, only chaise longue type things – like the ancient Romans used at meal times – grouped around a table.

In the middle of it all stood Doge Sneeb, one pincer resting on the back of the chaise longue nearest to him. Perhaps I was imagining it, but he seemed a tiny bit less ominous and intimidating. Or maybe it was the aura of intense weariness he gave off. His shoulders seemed to be sagging – even though, with a rigid exoskeleton, they couldn't physiologically do so – as if he was tired and fed up with everything.

"Good day to you."

"Sir," said Eric as he, Neewong and Smeesch all saluted. I tried to say 'hi' but I was so nervous that when I opened my mouth, all that came out was some sandwich crumbs.

Doge Sneeb removed two pads from the sides of his head. They were a bit like headphones and had wires coming from them. We waited, mutely, while he reached one of his long flexible antennae down to the table to place them beside a sleek metal box – a personal organiser like Eric's by the looks of things, only a more up-to-date version.

"You are wondering at your presence here."

"Yeh, just a tad," I said.

He transmitted a brief smile.

"Naturally. I will explain. As the being responsible for this colonisation, the hopes of the Gamalian Federation of Planets, not to mention the Arch Doge, rest on me. If I am to cancel it, I must put a watertight case to my comrades in government and I must back up my decision with facts."

"Whoa, whoa, whoa! What did you just say?"

He tapped his foot impatiently.

"I said, 'if I am going to cancel this colonisation—'"

"You're really going to stop it?" I asked.

"Yes. What did you think I would do?"

"Well …" I stammered, "not that."

"As I told you, I believe you to be sentient, human. Cancellation would be expedient, don't you think?"

"Is this because of—"

"Your clumsy attempt at blackmail?"

He concentrated the full force of his gimlet glare on me and I looked down at my feet, blushing.

"No. Through my own blind ambition I have walked willingly into a trap. So, since I am ruined, regardless, I can do what I like. You would be surprised at how liberating that is."

"And you want to save my planet?"

"Yes, if I can. However, as I believe I also told you, human, this is politics, and the situation is complicated. For the benefit of your friends I will explain—"

A jaunty electronic melody interrupted him: his communicator. He transmitted an expression of resigned irritation as he waited a moment to see who was calling. A holographic picture appeared in the air above the organiser showing the head and shoulders of another threep. Below it was the word in Gamalian letters, 'Zebulon'.

"I have to take this. We will continue when I am done."

He snapped one set of pincers together and a small hologram of Arch Doge Zebulon appeared. He turned his back on us and his full attention on the hologram of Arch Doge Zebulon, which he maximised to life sized.

I pulled Eric's pincer, pointed at the exit and transmitted a questioning expression.

Neewong and Smeesch nodded but Eric shook his head. I was certain the Doge had meant us to go outside but if Eric had to go and play with the rattlesnake by staying put then we couldn't leave him on his own. Well, OK we could, but we had to make a token effort at persuading him to leave before we scarpered. As the rest of us drew back, for all his bravado Eric did the same.

Can he see us? The hologram I mean, I asked Eric as we retreated further into the shadow towards the doorway.

Not from there.

The hologram was so realistic that it was hard to tell it was a teletransmission. It was only when the call suffered interference that you could: the 3D image blurring and skipping for a moment before reverting to its original clear definition. The Arch Doge was unlike any other threep I'd seen. So far they had been shades of brown or dark grey, from beige through to dark. Doge Sneeb, with his jet black exoskeleton, was the darkest coloured I'd seen but there were others who were close.

This threep was white. He shared Doge Sneeb's assured air of command only to the power of about twenty. Seeing them together I realised that the other wore his authority habitually, and comfortably, in a way Doge Sneeb did not. The pale threep's manner was cold and indifferent but where Sneeb was projecting all that wound-up tension, this threep was projecting very little. He probably had a sage advisor covering up the rest. Certainly, there wasn't much coming through. There was something though, some undercurrent I couldn't put my finger on that made me distrust the white threep.

"We should leave," I whispered to Eric.

"Yeh, come on," Neewong beckoned from the doorway.

"Go time," Smeesch whispered, pointing to the door but Eric shook his head.

Relations between the Arch Doge and Doge Sneeb seemed strained: definitely not what I'd expect from an adopted father and son. Unconsciously, Eric, his partners and I drew closer together, as if for safety.

"Zebulon—"

"I have a title, Sneeb and I demand you use it," said the Arch Doge.

"Your Munificence," Doge Sneeb corrected himself.

"What, precisely, is wrong with you that you cannot obey a simple instruction?"

"I do not take orders from Doge Vippit—"

"No, you cut the transmission before he could even start."

"Is that what he told you?" Doge Sneeb laughed mirthlessly.

"And you called him a liar."

"I thought he was."

"No. Those were genuine orders from me."

"To colonise?"

"Of course."

"But I explained. We cannot."

"Cannot or will not?"

"Cannot, it is illegal. You have read my report—"

"Supposition! Happenstance."

"No. Gamalian law is clear. Any doubt – which there is – and we must save the humans and leave. This planet is not worth the moral cost."

"*You* speak of moral cost, Sneeb?"

"I do."

"That's ironic, from someone who bends the law to breaking point at every opportunity."

"Bend, yes, break? No. Oh I am culpable for this but it doesn't have to end in disaster. Short of foolhardiness there is nothing illegal in what I have done. Not yet. Not ever if we act now. The findings of the survey team are—"

"You set their word against mine?"

"No, they—"

"Those mutineers will pay for their crimes."

"They are not mutineers."

"They tried to destroy the meteor, directly against your orders, directly against mine."

"Perhaps they have more moral courage than the rest of us."

"Or perhaps this is an open and shut case of mutiny for which they will answer. Rebels, and rebellion, are not tolerated in the Gamalian Federation of Planets. I hope you understand that, Sneeb, and I expect you to make your survey team understand, with the full weight of the law."

"I will not punish them, Your Munificence, neither will I colonise this planet—"

"Then you will face trial with them for *one* human out of sixty billion. Is it worth that?"

"There is more to this than one human. You read the report. You know what I'm talking about and now, we find there is a force field round the meteor. Why?"

"It is there because we have invested time and money in this colonisation, Sneeb; too much time and money for you to ruin my plans," said the Arch Doge. "If you lacked the stamina for this task, you should have asked me to assign it to someone stronger. Vippit would not have given me this trouble."

"Vippit wouldn't have the wit to see what's wrong. It will take longer but we have invested nothing that we could not recover were we to biocreate a vacant world. What are another seventeen years on nearly three hundred? I have even identified a suitable subject," said Doge Sneeb in that special calm manner of the truly enraged.

"Ever thorough. Or did you do this on purpose to make a fool of me so you would win the election?"

"I've made a fool of myself, not you."

"Then you will reap what you have sowed. You will colonise."

"I can't. Zebulon, the human is here as a guest on this ship. She has resisted mind fusion to the point where she now speaks fluent Gamalian and in doing so she reduced Commodore Pimlip's sage advisor to a semi-coherent wreck. It was only Apreetik's swift action which saved him."

"She?"

"She."

"Yet, I repeat. One being out of thousands does not qualify the entire race as sentient."

"I believe it does," said Doge Sneeb. "If you doubt, I have offered to ask Plort."

"And I have already told you that we will not disturb Plort over this. We have requested his guidance already this year."

"I will happily make the journey myself and speak with him."

"No. I will not see him angered and risk his smiting the entire Gamalian Federation of Planets because you have lost your bottle."

"If I travel to him alone, it is only I whom he will smite."

"I have said, 'no,' Sneeb."

"Then let me introduce you to the specimen we have with us. I know she will change your view, as she has changed mine. She is entirely worthy of classification and she has been thoroughly tested."

"How thoroughly?"

Doge Sneeb paused.

"More thoroughly than I appreciated," he said. "She is a brave and honourable creature. She is altruistic and puts the concerns of others before herself. Furthermore, her mind is more powerful than many Gamalian sage advisors. We could learn from her."

"That's as maybe, Sneeb," replied the Arch Doge and the way he said 'Sneeb' was more of a snarl. "But you have your orders, I wish you to colonise, and the planet I wish you to colonise is this one. It is my will that you do so."

"Zebulon, Your Munificence, Arch Doge of the Gamalian Federation of Planets, I ask, no," Doge Sneeb fell to all four of his knees, "I beg your permission to divert the meteor from its present path."

"No. You will do as you are ordered. You will colonise this planet. The only doubts cast on the status of the pestilential creatures living there are your own. The Lofty Syndic is agreed that the colonisation will proceed."

"Only because its members are currently unaware of the facts—"

"Do you accuse me of misleading them?"

"No. Why would you think that? We were all unaware of the

facts but now that we know them—"

"But nothing, Sneeb. This matter is closed."

"Then I would have written orders, if you please."

"There will be no written orders. You will obey my command or you will face the consequences with your survey team."

I wasn't one hundred per cent sure what the consequences were but if Eric's mental images were anything to go by it was pretty grim, involving a hooked implement and a circular saw. I am not intimately au fait with threep anatomy but I could tell that the punishment involved the removal of a varied selection of internal organs and limbs, without anaesthetic, starting with some of the things on the inside.

We should not be listening to this, I thought. *He thinks we aren't here and we should make that real very fast.*

"Please, Zebulon," Doge Sneeb's voice faltered, "Father, I am begging you, listen to me—"

I caught Neewong's eye and pointed at the door, he nudged Smeesch and they began to tiptoe quietly towards it. Eric stayed put. I tugged at his pincer, gesturing to him that we should beat a hasty retreat. I didn't dare transmit any more thoughts to him. Doge Sneeb might also detect them.

"You will do as you are told Sneeb, or you know what will happen," said the Arch Doge and he cut the connection. The holographic image faded and flickered into nothing. All was silent. Doge Sneeb was still on all four of his knees in the middle of the room. He put his antennae wearily down to his face for a moment, rose slowly to his feet. Above the personal organiser on the table a holographic image showed a picture of Arch Doge Zebulon and the legend 'call terminated'. Doge Sneeb turned round slowly and saw us.

"Captain, I believe I intimated you and your friends were to wait outside," he said quietly, ominously quietly.

Well, he had just been humiliated in front of us. He was hardly going to be pleased. In this instance, if he decided to turn nasty, I could almost understand.

"Sir," said Eric as, instinctively, we each took a step backwards.

"I—I apologise. I misinterpreted—" he stammered. He trod on my toe and I nearly overbalanced and fell over. I was still holding the stupid tray of sandwiches.

"It was my fault," I blurted. "I stayed."

Doge Sneeb transmitted a weary sigh, turned abruptly away from us, squelched over to one of the chaise longues and threw himself onto it with a splat. He picked the personal organiser off the table and the display message disappeared. Eric and I hadn't moved. Sneeb looked up. "Captain Persalub, Officer Neewong, Officer Smeesch please sit. Human, this seat is free of life matter." He gestured to the recliner nearest his. "Put the sandwiches on the table here … if you please."

I wished he wouldn't keep calling me 'human' but on the face of it, I supposed it was better than 'earthling'.

"Right, er, thanks." I waded through the slime, put the tray of sandwiches down and sat where he had indicated. I didn't like being this close to Doge Sneeb. Even after seeing him stand up for us, his presence made me nervous. Needless to say he compounded this by directing his first question at me.

"What is your name, human?"

"My name?" I repeated, like a moron.

"Yes, presumably other humans call you something, what?"

"Andi, Andi Turbot."

"Excellent. I hope the nourishment is to your liking, Andi Turbot," he waved a pincer at the platter on the table. "Apreetik was most insistent."

"It's great thanks."

"You haven't eaten much."

I swallowed.

"Fear is a bit of an appetite killer."

"You are afraid?"

Yes, I was; very, "A bit," I lied.

"I see."

"It's hardly surprising."

"No," he said resignedly.

I thought of Apreetik nagging Doge Sneeb to feed me. He must

165

have balls of steel, or ovipositors or whatever threeps had instead. Doge Sneeb cocked his head on one side and fixed me with a searching look. Please God don't let him have picked up my thoughts about ovipositors. It was probably porn, and he could read my mind. He was probably reading it this very moment. No, no, no, la la la laaa. I cleared my throat nervously and tried to make my mind a blank white space. There was something in the green eyes now, over and above the gimlet glare, the merest hint of a twinkle. Instead of relaxing me it made me even more nervous.

"I confess I owe you an apology," he went on, "Apreetik was right, as usual. I should have trusted you from the start but I could not. Now that you understand my situation, perhaps you will forgive me. I hope so, all of you, for I would seek your advice."

"So you said earlier, but why us?" asked Eric.

"The four of you represent the greatest pool of knowledge about Earth that I have at my disposal. Where else would I turn?"

"To someone whose career you weren't sabotaging," I said, before I could stop myself.

"Andi, it's—" began Eric.

"Andi is right to question, Captain," Doge Sneeb cut in. "Although, I never intended sabotage, more, influence."

"You still behaved like a complete—"

"Yes, I did," he spoke smoothly across me. "But in my defence, I was under great stress. My personal circumstances were bleak and I was not thinking with my usual clarity. After—" he stalled, took a moment to compose himself and started again. "After our partner died, it was torment for Borridge and I. To make it worse my father, the Arch Doge, was becoming ill, his great age had led to calcification of his joints and he took pain meds. Over the years, his system had become used to them. He took more: greater quantities than were safe, until he became addicted. Eventually the drugs began to affect his mind. He began to suffer from bouts of paranoia during which he would treat me with suspicion. He would not listen to me when I begged he sought help, and his aides dismissed my concerns as a political ruse to discredit him.

"As a newly elected Doge, I had much to prove and a crushing work schedule. There was no time to join Borridge grieving for our partner, no time for anything or anyone," he paused, "Borridge and I ... our relationship deteriorated. I knew that in time, I wanted to be whole again, together, as a marital unit, with Borridge and another we were yet to meet. I knew he wanted the same. But working and living together was difficult. We had been three for so long. We were unused to the dynamic of two. I hoped that with enough time, and space, we could repair our relationship. So after discussing it, Borridge and I agreed that he would cease to be my sage advisor.

"Advisors and those they help are matched very carefully. I am not always easy to work with. I knew it would take time to replace him. Sure enough, that first year only one of the officer cadets who applied for training was suitable: Captain Persalub here. However, his personality profile was an excellent match. The Academy of Sage Advice, in its wisdom, sensed doubt in him and refused his entry. I was angry. I was emotional and stupid. I had convinced myself that any chance of future happiness together for Borridge and I hung on Persalub agreeing to serve me. I brought every influence I had to bear on the Academy and the Guild of Sage Advice but they would not relent. They believed a setback was essential to test his intent and nothing would persuade them otherwise. When he did not reapply I set out to make him change his mind."

"And he didn't of course."

"No. He merely treated every obstacle I threw in his way as a challenge. The more I blocked him, the harder he fought. Even when I extended my methods of persuasion to his partners' careers as well. Then Borridge found out what I had done. He was incandescent: rightly, it nearly *was* the end of us. If Apreetik had not already been my personal physician by that time I have no doubt I would be alone now. When the two of them nearly left me it forced me to confront the being I had become. By that time Zebulon, my adopted father, was turning against me. I had no living blood relatives and I was about to lose everything of worth in my life." Doge Sneeb shrugged. "Had I continued as I was, I doubt we would be here now. I am still unscrupulous and ambitious, and I do not doubt that I am still a bad husband, but I hope I am no longer so arrogant, so petty, as to believe my own hype.

"You have every reason to doubt me and what you heard the Arch Doge say is true. I do want this colonisation. Plort! I want it so badly; more than you can ever know. But perhaps, now, I am wise enough to realise that, in the rare instances when fate serves up one's dreams on a platter, there will always be a catch. When the Science Corps required a small pre-colonisation survey team, I wanted one with a suitably independent outlook and I jumped at the chance to make some reparation for my earlier behaviour. I manipulated Vippit into appointing *my* choice of reconnaissance team for the colonisation: you, Captain – and your partners. It seems that my attempts to make amends have merely sealed your doom."

There was another long pause. None of us knew what to say. Doge Sneeb clearly meant what he said, but faced with this new and changed being, it was very difficult to forget past recollections of the old one.

"Thank you for your honesty sir, and your understanding, even if it took you a little time," said Eric. He transmitted the equivalent of a shy smile while Neewong and Smeesch nodded in agreement.

"Captain, Officers – and you, Andi Turbot – I have unleashed an abomination. I ask your forgiveness for this and my behaviour towards you, and I ask your help to stop it."

There was a long silence.

"Apreetik told me you do the right thing: always, even if it takes you a little time," I said.

"Apreetik holds a somewhat idealistic view."

"Yeh, well," said Eric. "What matters is that the five of us agree; we have to save Earth. As for the rest, it's done and as far as I'm concerned it's history. Guys?" he cast an enquiring glance to Neewong and Smeesch, who nodded.

"Thank you. I am in your debt," Doge Sneeb inclined his head in acknowledgement. There was another awkward pause, "Enough wallowing in the past. We have a mission: to business."

I jumped as, in one swift movement he stood up, turned towards the guards at the door and snapped his pincers. One guard ducked outside and returned with a metal box which he brought in and placed on the table by the sandwiches.

"Your arms and your datapods," said Doge Sneeb as the guard removed said items from the box and handed them back to my friends. Eric, Neewong and Smeesch fastened them to their belts and Doge Sneeb returned to his chaise longue again.

"I've been thinking ..." I said when we were all settled, "if you're the mission commander and you believe I'm sentient, can't we just torpedo the meteor and all go home?"

"Wouldn't that be neat?" said Doge Sneeb. "Unfortunately, such a simple solution is unavailable to us."

"Why? There must be some serious weaponry on this thing: enough to dispense with a force field surely."

"There is. However, weaponry is not the issue. Let me show you. Neewong, access the Eegby's secure mainframe." Doge Sneeb picked up his own data pod and threw it to my friend who almost dropped it in his startled surprise. "With this one, if you please."

"Sir, I—yes sir," said Neewong and he began to type nervously. It was clearly a multi-layered security system, as once the data pod connected to the opening screen, it asked for Neewong's choice of security level.

This is the highest any of us can go ... officially, Neewong's hacked into level four but only low priority accounts, Eric thought to me as his friend typed the number five.

"Wait!" commanded Doge Sneeb. Neewong stopped, one of his antennae hovering over the return key. "Access level one."

"None of us is authorised to view data at that level," said Eric.

"But I am, and as supreme ruler of Gamma Five, I'm authorising you," said Doge Sneeb.

Neewong transmitted a shrug, changed the number to one and hit return. The next screen loaded, asking him for his user name.

"Doge Vippit."

"Are you sure, sir?"

"You are not?"

"Er … well, impersonating a Doge, is treason."

"Not in this case. The other Doges, Arch Doge Zebulon and I all share the same level of security clearance so I am fully authorised to view the files you are about to see. The Arch Doge's office would never withhold information from any of the Doges who serve him. It would be unheard of. The fact they have forgotten to add permissions for my account on the files you are about to see is clearly a simple oversight. I can access the information easily enough. Why cause trouble?"

Yeh right. There was silence. Neewong sat back and ran one antenna over the back of his head.

"I will take full responsibility if we are discovered, Officer Neewong. Now, please enter Vippet's password. It is, 'Arch Doge Vippit'," Doge Sneeb added, projecting an aura of obvious distaste.

Neewong typed it in. A file menu appeared.

"Choose that one," Doge Sneeb pointed.

Neewong did as he was told.

"Loading …" it read in holographic letters above the box. It might have been ritzy and state of the art but the makers could have given it a faster CPU. We watched the holographic letters rotating slowly.

"It is connecting to the computer mainframe of the Supreme Gamalian Government, which is based on Gamma One," Doge Sneeb explained.

"Then the government needs to get a bigger pipe," said Neewong before noticing how bemused we all were and explaining, "too much traffic, not enough bandwidth."

"Yes. Something I will rectify when I become Arch Doge."

"Always assuming you do," I said.

"Always assuming," Doge Sneeb surprised us all by transmitting a dry smile. "I admit the odds are long but I like to stay positive."

The holographic lettering floating in front of us changed.

"Welcome Doge Vippit," said the letters.

"Excellent. Search for the file entitled Project X."

"Sir."

Neewong tapped away at the keyboard for a moment and we spent a few more minutes watching the word 'loading' spinning round and round.

"I could really get to loathe that graphic," I said.

"Along with every civil servant in the government – not to mention myself," said Doge Sneeb.

The holographic image of a ship appeared and began to rotate slowly. We stared at it. I could tell it was a Gamalian ship but it was not like the Eegby, or any of the ships I had seen in the docking bay with Eric and his partners. Whereas the Eegby looked like some kind of smooth aerodynamic species of plant, with pointy bits, this ship resembled an ocean-going mine – I'd seen one once, left over from the Second World War. It was spherical and covered in spikes except, in the case of this ship, each spike was barbed and sat on a bulbous lump. There was no obvious front or back, top or bottom. It looked like a football with restricted hair growth and really bad acne.

"What on earth is that?" I said.

"This is a top secret prototype called Project X."

"It's plug ugly," said Smeesch.

"It was constructed by Doge Vippit's engineers on Gamma Two," said Doge Sneeb dismissively, as if that explained everything. "I received intelligence that he might be moving against me but I fear it is Zebulon, himself, who ordered this. I dislike being surprised by my contemporaries so I have acquired a portion of the plans through unofficial channels. However, until now I had no confirmation as to the status of the project. This being Vippit's account, the plans, here, will be the most up-to-date version.

"This," he gestured at the holographic image, "is the most advanced piece of Gamalian weaponry in operation to date. It is coated with a specially treated material, which camouflages it with its environment and contains a sophisticated masking system, which makes it undetectable to the most advanced scanning equipment. As it has already demonstrated it is essentially invisible – even if the fighters it despatches are not – and it is capable of destroying the Eegby."

"Are you telling us THAT is out there?" I asked.

"Yes, and if we try to interfere with the meteor, it will blow us out of the sky."

"That's where the fighters that attacked us were from," said Smeesch quietly.

"Yes, they came from Project X, not the Eegby," he turned to me, "I am truly sorry that I treated you so harshly, Andi, but I hope you understand, now, why I had to be absolutely certain of your status."

"Yeh, I'm beginning to get there."

I sat and stared glumly at the hologram while Neewong, Eric and Smeesch started spooling through columns of figures; the weapons system specifications, in search of a weakness.

"Can't we attack it?" I asked.

"No. It contains numerous threeps, sentient beings no less—"

"They weren't too worried about trying to kill us."

"That does not make it right for me to try and kill them. If my sources are to be believed, Arch Doge Zebulon is also aboard that ship and, of course, as it is invisible, where, precisely, would we shoot?"

"I didn't say anything about killing them and I think I might know how you could find it," I said. "How big is this Project X thing?"

"Small. It is a prototype."

Maybe but it had room for three short-range fighters, possibly more.

"So is it as large as this pod?"

The Doge flicked a couple of eyes this way and that at the living quarters around him. From outside his pod looked about the size of a suburban semi.

"No. Bigger."

"It's about three times the size according to these plans," said Eric, answering my question for him.

"According to my own private sources it is an iota larger than that," said Sneeb.

"Let's say it's four times the size of your pod to be safe then, right?" I asked.

He nodded.

That was small fry compared to the Eegby.

"OK. So why don't you provoke it into a fight?" I asked.

All seven of Doge Sneeb's green-grey eyes swivelled round and locked with mine.

"Because it would win," he said as if spelling it out to a toddler.

"Yeh, I know. Listen, what I meant was this, if you could get it to fire one shot you could tell where it was, if only for a second."

"And?"

"And if we know where it is we can fire on it."

"I have told you—"

"Hang on, hang on," I put both hands out in front of me, slow-down-style, "hear me out. OK, so Project X is here to make sure the meteor hits Earth right?"

"Yes."

"So if you fly the Eegby at the meteor in a way that makes it look as if you're planning to divert it, what will Project X do?"

"If it follows protocol it will warn us off and—if we continue on our way—fire a warning shot."

"Right. So you do that and then you back off but you make sure you've traced the source of the shot. Then even if the ship has moved presumably you will have narrowed down the area it's in."

Neewong and Smeesch looked nonplussed but I had a feeling Eric was beginning to get the gist of my idea.

"Interesting, but pointless," said Doge Sneeb. "The ship moves too fast. Our knowledge would be valid for a few seconds at the outside. I fail to see what that would achieve."

I rolled my eyes.

"Nothing on its own but I have an idea: OK, look, one on one, if neither ship was invisible, who'd win, Project X or the Eegby?"

"The Eegby, without question; Project X is a prototype; it has a formidable array of weapons but its invisibility is the key to its invincibility. Ship to ship, it will be outgunned by the sheer quantity of ordnance available to the Eegby. Furthermore, I believe much of it is unfinished or non-functional—it has been designed and constructed on Gamma Two," he transmitted a flicker of a smile. "If Zebulon wished it to be of any practicable use, he should have had it built on Gamma Five. All the best engineers work for me, now."

"Exactly, so he could hardly use them. Not if he was trying to keep you in the dark," I doubted a gnat could fart on Gamma Five without Doge Sneeb knowing about it. "Anyway, we don't want it to be an engineering masterpiece. The less well it works the better for us. What happens if you fire a torpedo at it?"

"Well, Officer Smeesch?"

"Sir, the missile protection system would vaporise it — although I'd like to double-check these plans before I confirm that," said Smeesch.

"What if you fired a torpedo containing something else instead of explosives or warheads or whatever it is you put in your missiles?"

"If the system was scanning for components that occur in a torpedo rather than the actual explosives, then it would still be destroyed by the ship's defences: if the scanners are searching for warheads only, nothing," said Eric. "It wouldn't need to destroy everything that flies at it. The hull of Project X will be meteor-proof as standard, like the Eegby."

"That's right," Neewong cut in. "If it's up and running, Project X's system will examine the approaching object for evidence of weaponry and speed. If it contains explosives, it will be vaporised. If it's going so fast it would damage the hull on impact, ditto. In any other scenario the ship will leave it."

"So anything without a warhead on it would smash harmlessly against the ship?" I asked, just to check.

"Yes, as long as it is travelling slowly enough," said Smeesch.

"How fast is 'slow'? What I mean is: could a threep in a spacesuit get close to the ship without them knowing?"

Neewong and Smeesch exchanged glances.

"Possibly," said Smeesch.

Eric knew my plan now, I was sure, the huge smile he was

projecting, gave him away. Doge Sneeb watched us, his head cocked on one side, his expression one of intense concentration.

"If he was carrying a limpet mine no," said Eric as his eyes scanned the holographic plans, "right Smeesch?"

"Yep," said Smeesch. "Even if he wasn't, his presence might be flagged up by the ship's life support system. Most of our ships are configured to note and monitor threep life signs near the hull. It means nobody gets left outside if there are any repairs going on."

"So even if we find an alternative to the limpet mine, they'll see a threep in a spacesuit."

"I'd say so."

"What about a human? Are we different enough? Could I get through?"

Neewong ran one antenna across his forehead.

"It would certainly take longer to compute you as a life form — the radiation shielding on the suit will dampen your vital signature and you're a much smaller mass than a threep. If we made you a suit with the right kind of mineral and organic coating we might be able to convince it you're space debris. They still may see through it and transport you into the ship."

Damn! Now I only had half a plan. I shared it with them anyway.

"I have an idea. It's not as good as it was, but maybe it's the beginning of a plan. We have this game at home called paintball. You get into teams and you're all given guns full of different coloured paint — say red for one team, blue for the other. Then you all run around and shoot each other with the guns and the team that wins is the one that has managed to put the most paint on the other team." I was sketchy on the exact rules of paintball but I knew they were along those lines.

"So we get Project X to break cover and fire at us. Then we track the source of the shot and fire our first paintball. I dunno, maybe we should fire several so it'll run into one whichever way it goes. When the paintball hits the hull and smashes open, it sprays paint all over the top of the special coating. If we're really lucky, I suppose the rest of the special coating might change to match the paint. It's not perfect. I guess we'll only have visual contact unless your scanners can get a trace from the paint but even if Project X itself is still invisible, at least we'll be able to see the bits we've coloured in."

The four of them stared at me.

"And then?" asked Doge Sneeb.

"Well, I'm not sure now. I was going to suggest we damaged it. If it was possible to make me a spacesuit, and I chugged out there and stuck a limpet mine on the side, I might disable it so we could blow the meteor but if the protection system would blow up the limpet mine …" I shrugged.

Doge Sneeb transmitted a smile, a real one, with actual warmth in it. Perhaps it was a relief to share his troubles after all this time.

"The spacesuit would be easy enough, we are simply required to think of something equally devastating with which to replace the limpet mine," he said. There was a glint in his eye and a confidence to his posture when he rose to his feet. He seemed taller, larger, more alive. He fixed his attention on Eric. "Persalub," no 'captain' I noticed. "How are you recovering from your recent matter loss?"

"Very well, sir," said Eric.

"Good. Your friend has had a remarkably inspired idea. You will organise the paint missiles so we can see our enemy. I will leave the logistics in your hands but work swiftly, if you please. We do not have much time. At its present speed, the meteor will strike Earth in twenty-two hours. However, circumstances may change."

"You mean someone might give it another nudge," I said.

All seven dark green eyes swivelled round to give me a bit of a look. Clearly the Doge disliked being interrupted.

"Yes. And if they do I want room to manoeuvre. I want the missiles ready to fire in three hours: maximum. As many as you can."

"Yessir," said Eric. It sounded like a lot to achieve but he seemed remarkably unfazed.

"I will escort the four of you to the lower deck. If you proceed to the missile bays I will brief Commodore Pimlip and ask him to ensure a work unit from engineering is there to assist you."

"Thank you, sir," said Eric.

Doge Sneeb acknowledged him with a nod.

"Excellent. Come with me," he said, and I made to head for the door. "No this way." He led us through another private room as luxuriously appointed as the one from which we had come and out onto a small balcony. There were plants there and a pond with a fountain. We passed a table with three things like sun loungers round it, presumably the threep equivalent of patio furniture. It was easy to see how the Doge could enjoy sitting out on the platform well – I gave the pond a sideways glance – if he didn't look at the 'fish' too closely. Then again, maybe all Gamalian fish had teeth like that. Despite the piranha-like ornamental pond life the air felt fresh and clean and the view was impressive. It must be a thoroughly relaxing way to keep an eye on the crew and the plants made it pleasantly secluded. Beyond the balcony was a docking platform, and parked beside it, a hopper. It was almost indistinguishable from other hoppers on the ship except that, like the pod, it had that subtle nuance of quality which marked it out as high-class merchandise.

Doge Sneeb didn't hang about. It seemed that no sooner had we got onto the hopper than we were arriving at a docking bay at the bottom of the ship. Unfortunately, as well as driving fast, Doge Sneeb also braked late, skidding the hopper sideways and stopping alongside the landing platform in a manner more reminiscent of a handbrake turn than parallel parking. I lost my balance, falling against Eric who transmitted a disparaging remark about the driving skills of threeps who had chosen a career in politics. Doge Sneeb might be an elder statesman but he drove his hopper like a boy racer, I thought, as we watched him speed away.

Chapter 25
Plan laying and bomb making

Eric, Neewong, Smeesch and I made our way towards the missile tubes on one side of the ship. As Eric and I walked the corridors in companionable silence I tried to think of a way to complete my plan and render Project X disabled as well as visible. When we reached our destination I thought I might have an idea, sort of. Smeesch gave me the perfect chance to bring up the subject.

"Painting Project X is fine but what then?" he asked morosely. "Even if we can see it, we won't be able to defend ourselves and it doesn't look like Doge Sneeb will ever let us attack."

"He will let us disable their ship," said Eric.

"I've been thinking, I reckon we may not need to attack," I said.

"How so?"

"Project X is a prototype. Doge Sneeb reckoned it was about the size of his pod. That's small fry compared to the Eegby, right?"

"Yep, *if* it's the same size as the numbers on the plan," said Smeesch.

"So what about Neewong's transporter algorithm? If I went out there with a spacesuit on and a universal transporter would I be able to move it?"

"Why would you want to?" asked Smeesch.

"I have an idea that's all but if we can't move the ship it won't work."

"Well Neewong?" said Eric. "Could you do it?"

"I've never tried to move anything that big before. In theory if the weight and size specifications on file are accurate enough it's easy to apply the formula. There's no time for testing, though, and the real thing may be different. If I exceed a small margin for error, it will be the end. It's also risky. It causes extreme turbulence and you'd have to be very careful not to get sucked in with it or you'd die."

"I guess there's no point then, I can't go killing the crew," I said.

"Oh no, the crew inside it would be perfectly safe," said Neewong. "The transporter will see Project X as one huge animal, albeit with very complicated innards. The Arch Doge and his crew will be transported along with their ship, without harm. However, if you are accidentally drawn into the transporter, too, it would reassemble you both as one object. You would be scattered throughout the ship's hull and the bodies of the crew. You, yourself, would cease to exist."

"That's quite grim."

"Yes. I should be able to programme in a delay to give you time to get out of range. Nothing that has happened in our experiments with other objects suggests there will be any problems."

"He's right," said Eric. "We've used it all the time on heavy cargo and equipment—"

"Exactly, some of which come close to having the same actual weight."

"But not a ship."

"No, but theoretically, if you can move a few tonnes you can move several hundred, you just have to reprogramme the internal software of the transporter and override the right safety codes. The ones here are a more modern design but that shouldn't present a problem. I'll look into it if you like."

I thanked him and said I would like, even though the very idea of overriding safety codes alarmed me deeply.

"If your plan works and we move Project X where would you put it Andi?" asked Eric.

"In here, inside the Eegby."

"What? Are you mad?" said Neewong.

"No. The Arch Doge is mad. *I'm* perfectly sane."

"Are you sure about that?" asked Smeesch.

"Listen, Project X can't be all that big. It's a top secret prototype so it has to be as cheap as possible and easy to conceal. Think about it."

"I am, and I think it'll blow us apart," said Smeesch.

"Will it though?"

"Of course it will!"

"I don't think so."

"How can you tell?"

"Because I know the mind I read when we were on the Thesarus is Zebulon's mind and there's something I am pretty sure of. Whatever we do, Arch Doge Zebulon is going to kill Doge Sneeb. When I was stuck in Zebulon's head, he was watching the Thesarus disintegrate around us. He was anticipating it, savouring the thrill; he got off on watching them torch us, because he was looking forward to seeing the same thing happen to Sneeb."

"But Doge Sneeb's his adopted son, not his enemy," said Eric.

"Yeh, stuff like that means a lot to us Gamalians," said Smeesch.

"Yes, but Zebulon thinks Sneeb is out to get him. He is really, really ill, mentally ill. Trust me. I've been in his head. I know. Behavioural norms do not apply here."

"So …"

"So, he thinks he's invincible, he believes he'll live forever and he wants to, as Arch Doge. Adopted son or not, Sneeb is in the way. He's ambitious, he asks too many questions and he's smart. Too smart, he's the only one Zebulon can't control. This whole meteor thing is just a scheme to get rid of him. There's no-one out here but us, so if Arch Doge Zebulon blows up the Eegby and tells everyone at home he had to, there's nobody else to believe. If he wants his colonisation, he says that the Eegby attacked and he had to blow it up, but that the battle took so much time he was unable to get to the meteor before impact. Whichever way, Doge Sneeb's name is mud, plus he's dead so it's not like he can put his side across. Zebulon gets to be the one who started the whole journey from your ... the Huurg Quadrant to your alien folks the other side of space you want to see. The whole Captain Cook thing is suddenly his, not Sneeb's. Bringing the Arch Doge into the Eegby is the only way we can keep it safe. Zebulon can't blow it up from inside because, if he does, he'll blow himself up at the same time."

"He can."

"Yeh, but I promise you, he won't."

"That's ... an interesting theory Andi."

"Yeh, yeh, I know the three of you think I'm mad but I'm the one who got stuck in his head, remember, and I can tell you, for nothing, that the mind he's in now is not his right one. At the best, he's criminally insane."

"Doge Sneeb won't countenance it."

"Yeh. I know. That's why I wanted to talk to you guys."

"Our laws don't look kindly on mutiny," said Smeesch.

"It didn't stop you before."

"That was moral versus legal this is ... we can't send you to your death."

"You might not be."

By this time we had reached a wide corridor with double doors at the end.

"Here we are," said Eric.

We stopped.

"Oh c'mon guys?" I pleaded. "My whole planet is at stake. If I can't save the human race then, at the least, help me to die trying."

"Andi, it isn't that simple—"

"Just think about it."

Eric rolled all seven eyes.

"Well?" he asked the other two.

"I think she's madder than the Arch Doge," said Smeesch, "but I'd say it's our only chance."

"Neewong?"

"Yes. I'm in."

"Alright then," said Eric, "but we can't tell Doge Sneeb. He could never officially sanction this."

"What if he reads our minds and—"

"We'll have to pray he doesn't. I'd say the chances are that both he and Borridge will have enough to do. They're trying to get out of this their own way and they'll have to protect themselves from the Arch Doge's sage advisors."

Neewong pressed a button on the wall beside us and the doors slid open to reveal a sizeable room. One side had a huge rack-like arrangement. It looked like a gun magazine only magnified to fire missiles about the width of a pedal bin. It was lit by a glowing red light, except for a rather more utilitarian version of the light globe in Doge Sneeb's pod, which hung over a workbench set in the middle. There were hoists and pulleys – presumably for lifting the missiles, and alongside the bench, a bunch of cylindrical canisters lined up on hoverpallets. They were large, about eighteen inches in diameter, and my height. Beside them was parked a small hovertanker, like the one I'd seen a threep using to feed the lighting system in the docking bay. This one was about the size of a van. Three threeps were waiting, two near the canisters and one beside the hovertanker, nozzle at the ready in one pincer.

Although he was technically off duty, Eric was the senior officer present and they saluted as we walked in. The one next to the tanker forgot he was holding the nozzle and biffed himself in the side of the head with it.

"At ease guys, I'm Persalub," said Eric, "these are my colleagues Neewong, Smeesch and the alien here is a human from Gamma Six – her name's Andi. Who are you?"

They introduced themselves as Engineers Smelk and Ergot while the one with the paint tanker was Gernoidal.

"Brilliant, I see you've brought a fair few warheads. Are they ready for priming?"

"These ones are sir," said Smelk waving one of his antennae at a pallet full of them. "None have warheads but my orders were to remove some of the telemetry and guidance systems as well. They will fly straight but little more."

"Nice. That's exactly what we want. They don't need guidance, not if Smeesch is going to be aiming them. Is that the paint?" Eric gestured to the hovertanker with his pincer.

"Yeh," said Gernoidal, giving the nozzle an experimental squirt. A jet of fluorescent pink paint hit one of the canisters with a loud bong and I started to giggle. The others gave me a bit of a look.

"Sorry, don't mind me," I said.

"Are those universal transporters?" asked Eric, pointing to the pallets of canisters. I realised there was an upright in the corner of each pallet with a matt black control box attached to it.

"Yes sir."

"Excellent, d'you have the docking station?" Smelk hurried forward and pointed to the box on the first pallet, which was plugged into some kind of control console. "Yeh, right, my bad for not seeing it. Can we borrow them?"

Ergot scratched his head.

"The UTs and the docking station?"

"Yes."

"No reason why not sir, but we have a brand new set of spares back in engineering, I can nip back and get them."

"Thanks," said Eric.

We started loading up the missiles. I say 'we' but to be honest, I watched, and after Ergot came back, Neewong went off with the UTs.

With the aid of various pieces of heavy machinery, none of which I had the strength to manipulate, Ergot and Smelk decanted the paint into heavy-duty plastic bags, sealed them up and locked them into the cylinders while I stood around offering encouraging remarks and pretending I was helping. Gernoidal lowered the cylinders into the missiles using a hoist and Eric guided them into position and then put the missiles onto a loader. Smeesch checked and double-checked each warhead, tested the seals with a handheld scanner and then activated the loader which put them into a giant magazine ready for firing.

In just over an hour we were done with the first batch of missiles.

A few moments after Ergot, Smelk and Gernoidal went to collect some more warheads, Neewong returned with the UTs. He squished over to me and held them out.

"Here Andi," he said handing me the first one. "This is for the ship, and this," he put the second into my other hand, "is for you."

"Uh."

"In the case of the ship I've delayed the timer so you'll have to attach it somewhere and let it transport itself. They're a new design, these, and I think it best to use the auto setting on yours. I don't want to risk any mishaps."

"Right." Neither did I.

"All you have to do to transport is point this side at the object you're moving and press the red button," he showed me with his antenna. "DON'T muddle them up."

"No." I cleared my throat. "Run that by me again?"

"This one's for the ship," said Eric coming up behind me, leaning over my shoulder and daubing it with pink paint. "We'll Velcro it to the arm of your suit, and the one without the paint on it is for you." He was a clumsy painter, my hand and half my arm was pink as well. Smeesch squelched over to us.

"Nice. Pink's your colour," he said, projecting a smirk. "Neewong, are you done?"

"Yep."

Smeesch and Neewong exchanged a look.

"You want us to finish off here?" they asked Eric.

"Thanks, yeh," Eric turned to me. "Andi, you and I have just under an hour to get you into a spacesuit and flying a jetpack like a pro."

Chapter 26
Space tailoring

If you are ever offered the opportunity to be fitted for a Gamalian spacesuit, refuse. Trust me, I've never felt so queasy. Eric took me to another room a short distance away. It was empty, save for a huge tube in the middle and a bed. It didn't take a genius to see that it worked a bit like an MRI scanner, in that I was going to be put on the bed and then the bed put into the tube. Definitely a grim option for someone who is uneasy in tight spaces. Which I am. I wouldn't call myself full-on claustrophobic, or at least, I wouldn't have done, but after getting into that thing I'm not so sure.

"It's nanobot technology," Eric told me helpfully. "I insert you into the tube, the machine takes measurements and then it designs a suit which the nanobots build."

"How long does it take?" I asked.

"Not long."

"How not long, exactly?"

"Only a few minutes."

"Yeh, but how many minutes is 'a few'?"

"Thirty."

"Thirty minutes! Half an hour in that coffin!"

"Yes."

"In there, in the dark, with the ends sealed."

"Yes, well, no. Not in the dark, there are strobe lights so you need to wear a special headset with eye protection." He held up a thing that looked like a set of comedy udders. Three of his eyes swivelled to look more closely at me and back at the thing. "It's made for threeps, one eye in each—"

"Yeh, I get it. So I have to lie in the dark, with occasional strobe lighting and a set of space udders over my head."

Eric said nothing. He was concentrating on trying to hide a smile.

"It's not funny Eric!" I wailed and he out and out laughed.

I did it of course. And when I got out, I had to sit with my head between my knees for a minute or two. It didn't help that the process of building a spacesuit seemed to produce the vilest odour I have ever smelled.

"What is that stench? Eugh, it's like fried socks with a side order of rotting flesh, pickled dog muck and a BO jus."

Eric handed me a bottle of water.

"Ah. That's the suit."

"Ugh, does it smell the same inside?"

"No there are filters and you'll be breathing bottled air."

"Ooo it's so evil." Even thinking about breathing through my nose made me feel ill but breathing through my mouth wasn't much better. The smell was so strong I could taste it.

"Thanks for this," I held up the water bottle and took a sip. It helped a little.

"Neewong brought it."

"Was he here?"

"Yeh, he's the one who worked out how to disguise you. That's what the smell is." He stood up with a flourish, "Tonight, Andi Turbot, you are going to be disguised as ... space garbage."

"Does it come with a clothes peg?"

"I told you, you'll be inside it. You won't smell anything."

"Where did you get all the ... um ..." I hiccuped, "special effects?"

"Don't worry, it's not real rubbish, it's all ersatz, made by nanobots."

"Will it work though? I mean, won't they smell me coming? And what about my vital signs? Won't they still pick them up?"

"We put in a dampening layer so your vital signs will be severely muffled and they are already far less powerful than those of a Gamalian. Only the most sensitive equipment would pick them up, even at close range, and if the system works along the standard lines it will scan you once, possibly twice, class you as a rubbish pod and discount you from further sweeps."

"What if it isn't standard?"

"You'll be beamed inside the ship and get to meet the Arch Doge," two of his blue eyes winked. "Come on," he pressed a button by the door and the back wall of the room slid back to reveal a large high chamber, about the size of two tennis courts. "Let's get you flying."

Chapter 27
Learning to fly

I hit the wall going backwards at top speed and even with the protection of the suit I still winded myself. Worse, my limbs seemed to have tied themselves in a knot and I appeared to be stuck there. Eric waved at me from the safety of the control room observation window and waited in sympathetic silence until I had stopped making my usual sea lion noise before he spoke to me down the two-way radio.

"Are you OK Andi?"

"NO. I'm stuck again."

"OK hang on," his voice came back, calm and relaxed, "switching to normal gravity." He waved one antenna downwards for extra effect. I saw him flick the switch and then I slid slowly down the wall and landed in a crumpled heap. I wouldn't have minded quite so much if it hadn't been the fifth time in as many minutes.

A Gamalian spacesuit has a propulsion pack on it which is guided by a system of compressed air jets. It is incredibly responsive and therefore almost impossible to manoeuvre. The fact I was still feeling mind-bendingly queasy after being exposed to the smell of the suit before putting it on didn't help. Eric's voice came over the two-way radio again.

"Great work, Andi, you're really improving."

Bless him, it was such a load of cobblers.

"No I'm not. Why can't I do this?" I gasped.

"You can and you will, you just need to practise. Hold on, I'll be with you in a second," he said.

A few minutes later the doors of the chamber squished open and Eric joined me. If it was hard to move in zero-g it was impossible with gravity restored and I had to lie there like a trussed-up chicken until Eric had plonked me the right way round and untangled my arms and legs.

"I am really struggling here, Eric."

"It's easy, I told you, like riding a bike."

"Eric, I'm quite good at riding a bicycle now but it took me months to learn when I was a kid."

He transmitted a smile and wiped the visor of my helmet. "You'll cope."

"We don't have enough time for me to learn," I told him.

"There is another way."

The smile he was transmitting began to feel less genuine and more fixed. After two unsuccessful attempts to fold my arms with the suit on I gave up on body language and said, "Go on then, what is it?"

"Andi, I can handle a spacesuit but I can't fly this mission. You can leave the ship but you can't handle the spacesuit."

"Thank you for summarising the situation so well: null points for tact as always. What's the plan?" I said.

"You use telepathy and mine my brain for knowledge."

"Like Mingold?"

"More like Borridge, but without the pain I mean."

"No. Mental fusion is right out. Never, ever, ever," I warned him. "I am all power and no control."

"I consent. Fuse with me."

"NO!" I said.

"OK. Let's fire up the anti-grav again and have another go."

I made no move to ready myself for zero-g and neither did he. We both knew I was going to agree, but I went through the charade of having to be convinced anyway.

"You might be needed on the crew – I can't fry your head."

"I trust you. You won't."

"What if I hurt you?"

"It's only painful if you resist – or if the guy doing the probing is a little rough. When you read Arch Doge Zebulon's mind by mistake, that didn't hurt did it?"

"That wasn't mind fusion Eric."

"Trust me, it was: you on him and me on you. You didn't hurt him."

"How do you know? I might have done."

"No, believe me Andi, if you'd hurt him, you'd know. And I didn't hurt you getting you out of it did I?"

"It still felt gross," I said, my resolution beginning to waver, "and even when it doesn't feel gross it feels scary. What if it makes you nervous, what if you fight it?"

"We both know there's no other way," he said.

"Flippin' 'eck."

Planet Earth was asking a lot from me. All Captain Kirk ever had to do was snog stunning, multicoloured alien women who were only non-humans by dint of being green or blue. And where was my sky-blue lovely lady when I wanted her? Nowhere! Instead I got to have my mind probed by something which, best friend or not, looked like a lobster and was covered in Marmite-scented goo. Sometimes reality sucks.

"OK, I'm just—I worry that—I'll try and be gentle, I promise," I said.

"That's what they all say."

"Stop that! And stop laughing! OK, OK, let's get this over with quickly."

He sat in front of me and I closed my eyes and concentrated.

"If you need to, you can put your hands either side of my head to help you focus."

"Na-uh, I'm OK."

"Shut your eyes and think about something nice," he told me. I thought about the stars. "You may feel dizzy but otherwise we should be OK."

I stopped concentrating for a moment to say, "Tell me if it's painful."

Although I was the one doing the fusing, he showed me each step and then he reversed it and I did it to him. When our minds were 'in communion' which is exactly as gross as it sounds, I felt colder as if I was immersing myself in water, the way I had on the Thesarus. Which reminded me—

How come the Arch Doge's sage advisor didn't stop me?

He, or they, were too busy protecting the pilots.

So that's why I couldn't get to them.

Yes. You were searching for a way in and your mind latched onto the easiest target. We were unaware of the Arch Doge's presence and his sage advisors knew this so—

He has more than one.

He's the Arch Doge. Of course he does. They would be concentrating on protecting the things you were most likely to attack, which was the fighter crews, rather than him.

But then any sage advisor could have found him surely?

Only if they were looking and, to be honest, Andi, only if they were you. Humans seem to do telepathy in a slightly different way to us.

Then why didn't I just get someone on the ship?

This is the human mind thing. Your mind was seeking some very specific information. So, it found the mind with the most to tell you: Arch Doge Zebulon's.

Yeh that figured.

"Come on, now, concentrate," he said aloud.

I realised the feeling of coolness had gone away so I shut my eyes and concentrated again. I felt as if I was being sucked towards Eric. I began to back off.

No, that's right, you're doing fine.

Then a rush of cool air seemed to be blowing in through one ear and out the other and I was laughing as Eric asked me if I had noticed any change from usual and whether I was surprised to find I had nothing but fresh air inside my head. I began to giggle. It wasn't a pleasant sensation but it was better than the last time and it wasn't the agonising horror I'd had to endure from Mingold or Borridge.

This is the moment to think about the spacesuit, Andi. Here, I'll help with a memory.

I was in space, looking through his eyes. He flew forwards, backwards, sideways and looped the loop. It was as much second nature to him as walking. In the real world through the goldfish bowl glass helmet of the suit I could see Eric fidgeting restlessly. I wasn't feeling any pain but I didn't wish to inflict any either. We disengaged and I opened my eyes. He was kneeling down.

"Are you OK?" I asked in alarm. "I haven't hurt you have I?"

"No ... I'm dizzy but I'll be fine," he climbed slowly to his feet and shook his head. "I hate doing that!" he said cheerfully.

I didn't like it either.

"Have we finished? Can I fly now?" I asked him.

"I hope you can," said Eric. "I don't think we can try again for a while." He clearly felt queasy and I got the impression that it wasn't the effect of the revolting, stinky spacesuit. Yes, he was definitely a little wobbly on his feet as he checked it over and headed back to the control room. Once inside he sat behind the control desk, which was in front of the observation window, and waved at me through the glass. He switched off the gravity and I tried again.

It was awesome! In five minutes I had changed from Captain Inept to Andi the human hoverfly. I could move with the grace and speed of a hummingbird. The sensitivity of the suit controls, which had been the root of my problems was now a source of pure delight. I was revelling in their responsiveness, able to undertake any acrobatic stunt I wanted at any speed. Eric was good at this and now he had passed his skill on to me!

Practice over, he unscrewed the top of my suit, replaced the compressed air canisters with new ones and transmitted an indulgent smile, while I gleefully expounded the joys of spacesuit travel. Then he tucked the helmet under one arm and me under the other, because there was no way could I walk in the wretched thing, and lugged me to the airlock.

Once there, we checked that the UTs were positioned correctly – or at least Eric did while I tried not to gag at the smell. I was only using my UT to come back. I couldn't risk transporting out from the Eegby to Project X in case their sensors were set to pick up that kind of activity and I was vaporised. One side of each unit had an emitter which would make a field around the thing I wanted to move. Eric had attached a magnetic foot to the pink one and Velcroed it to my right arm. I was to slam it hard onto the hull of Project X and when I'd pressed the button I had one minute to clear the area using the other one. This was Velcroed to my left arm with the beam side facing inwards, so that by bending my arms towards me I could point it at myself and transport to the Eegby. I was so nervous my palms, no all of me, was sweating. Then Eric helped me out of the suit because Doge Sneeb wanted us to report back to the bridge.

Something beeped. He consulted the personal communicator Doge Sneeb had returned to him.

"The guys have finished the missiles," he pulled the retractable pads out of the side and held them to the sides of his head for a few seconds, "I've told them to head for the bridge," he said as he pressed a hidden button and the pads snaked their way back into the side. "We'd better get a move on."

The communicator beeped again, this time when Eric activated answer mode, a tiny holograph of Doge Sneeb appeared in the air in front of him.

"Captain Persalub, where are you?" it asked sternly.

"Er ... by the missile bays, we've just finished," said Eric, manoeuvring himself in front of the most neutral and unidentifiable piece of wall he could find.

"We are ready to locate Project X. I require your presence, and Andi Turbot's, on the bridge immediately."

"On our way, sir."

Chapter 28
A vote of confidence

A few yards up the corridor was a door in the wall, Eric pressed a button and it opened to reveal a lift. We climbed in.

"State your destination," said an electronic threep voice.

"Bridge please," said Eric. It was so Starship Enterprise. The lift lurched into action and stopped almost instantly. The voice waited a few seconds for our stomachs to arrive before it said, "You are now at the bridge," and the doors opened.

Doge Sneeb stood waiting for us in the centre of the bridge. Beside him stood a yellowy-brown threep and around the room, the crew stood or sat expectantly at their stations, including Smeesch at the weapons console with Neewong.

"Is our secret weapon ready?" asked Doge Sneeb with a glance at the pink stains on my arm.

"Yes, sir," said Eric as Neewong came and joined us.

"Good. I have already briefed Commodore Pimlip and the crew. Commodore, when you are ready."

The yellowy-brown threep standing to one side of him bowed and walked over to his station, a large armchair set to one side.

"Go to red alert. All shields up," he said.

It was like every science fiction film you have ever seen. The lights dimmed and that same stupid klaxon, like the one on the Thesarus, started sounding somewhere, although it was less intrusive.

"Head for the meteor. Captain Spoon."

"Sir," said a voice from right beside us, at the pilot's station.

"Scan for ships."

"Scanning ..." said a small beige threep over on the opposite side of the room. "Complete. There are no ships out there, sir, but there is a force field round the meteor. It's a very faint signature, I've had to amplify it to pin it down, but it's there."

"Hmm ..." Commodore Pimlip sounded thoughtful and turned to his superior with an enquiring expression. Doge Sneeb made a curt nod, "Put the meteor on screen."

One wall of the bridge dissolved into blackness and revealed the stars beyond. Eric, Neewong and I moved back against the wall by the door, out of the way. I kept my mind as neutral as possible but I could tell, at once, that Doge Sneeb was onto us. Every time I looked up, one or more of his ocular pieces was pointing in our direction, watching us intently. Eric, on the other hand, was watching Captain Spoon pilot the ship.

The Eegby was only travelling towards the meteor for thirty seconds or so when there was a loud rumble, like a thunderclap and everything shook. The crew and anything else that wasn't nailed down were thrown in all directions. Captain Spoon was thrown from the controls and I remembered ducking to avoid being hit by him as he flew over my head.

"What was that?" I asked in alarm, as I extricated myself from the slime.

"A torpedo," said Eric who was stuck to the ceiling. "But it must have been a huge one."

Captain Spoon lay moaning in the slime next to me.

"I think he's hurt," I said.

Eric finally detached from the ceiling and fell down with a loud splat.

"Sir, Captain Spoon is injured, matter loss," said Neewong as he scooped gloop from the floor over the prone pilot.

"Noon and Kloik, take him to the medical bay. Where are Captains Nomgin and Flange?"

"Already in the medical bay sir, in quarantine, they're suffering from Betelgeusian measles."

"Both of them?"

"Yes sir."

Noon and Kloik took the prone Captain Spoon away and

Neewong left my side and joined one of the crew members at a bank of instruments a few feet away.

"What's going on, Commodore?" snapped Doge Sneeb.

"Our shields took a pounding, and it appears we have no pilot," said Commodore Pimlip, turning away from him and jabbing at a nearby console irritably.

"Engineering: damage report?" he barked.

I glanced over at Neewong but he and the threep at the console were deep in whispered conversation.

"Shields are holding, sir, but they are considerably weakened," replied a tinny voice.

"How 'considerably weakened' exactly?" asked Doge Sneeb.

"Well?" demanded Commodore Pimlip.

"In layman's terms, please," added Doge Sneeb.

There was an awkward silence while the threep at the other end was clearly gathering the courage to deliver bad news.

"We can take two more of those, sir," he eventually said.

"What's wrong with the Missile Protection System?" asked Commodore Pimlip.

"Nothing, sir, but that was a planet-strength warhead," said Neewong from his position at the instrument panel.

"For one measly starship?" asked Doge Sneeb incredulously.

"Yessir. The system isn't geared for a missile so large. It's the equivalent of a simultaneous strike from two-thirds of the Gamalian battle fleet."

"What in the name of Plort ...?" Commodore Pimlip flicked one antenna down to the front of his head and stroked a couple of his eye stalks. "Set the missile protection intercept as far away from the hull as possible, I'll get us back out of harm's way."

"Incoming," shouted Smeesch.

"Plort! It's got through the shields."

Commodore Pimlip turned and dived for the pilot's seat. Even I could see he wasn't going to get there in time to take evasive action. Clearly Eric was thinking the same thing.

"Brace!" he shouted as he leapt forward, wrapped his

196

antennae round the controls and wrenched them sideways. There was a massive jolt and the entire ship jinked left with a suddenness that threw me and several others to the ground.

"The missile's missed us, sir. It's turning for a second pass."

There was muffled rumble and a bump.

"Got it with the lasers!" said Smeesch.

"Why didn't you give us proper warning?" growled Commodore Pimlip.

"My apologies sir, the system didn't detect it until it was a few seconds out. It's as if it was shielded from our sensors until it was right up close."

"Can Project X do that?" he asked Doge Sneeb.

"There's nothing on the plans but it would not surprise me, my scientists on Gamma Five have recently perfected a similar system," said Doge Sneeb.

"Captain Persalub, you can clearly fly. Move the ship back to a safe distance," said Commodore Pimlip.

"Message from the Medical Pod; Captain Spoon will be recovered and ready for duty in three hours."

"That's too long. Can one of the other two not fill in?"

"No sir, they're at the eyeball pimple stage, neither of them can see."

"Then we'll have to make do. Captain Persalub, you have the stick."

"Sir," said Eric. He was bursting with pride and a little nervous.

"Where is our mystery attacker?" asked Doge Sneeb.

Another awkward silence followed. In the heat of the moment, we'd all forgotten about tracking the ship. The Doge fixed Commodore Pimlip with a glassy stare and Commodore Pimlip turned and passed it on to the threep Neewong was sitting with.

"Well, Scanning Officer Boldrort?" asked Commodore Pimlip.

"We don't know—"

"We don't know," Commodore Pimlip held his pincers out

either side of him in a helpless gesture, "what has got into you lot today? Doge Sneeb ordered us – and that means you, officer – to trace the source of the shot!"

"Yes, sir, but we don't know *yet*, sir," blurted Officer Boldrort.

"Readings coming through now, sir," said the cheerful voice of Neewong, next to him.

"Excellent," Commodore Pimlip turned to Doge Sneeb, transmitting an enquiring expression.

"Fire at will," ordered Doge Sneeb.

"Sir," said Smeesch.

I didn't want to disturb any of my friends while they were helping the crew but Neewong winked at me as Smeesch fired.

Everyone on the bridge watched in silence as a ring of missiles headed away from us into space. They grew smaller and smaller until they were nothing more than tiny specks of reflected starlight winking as they spun through the blackness. At last, when they had all but disappeared two of them exploded pinkly.

"We have impact, sir," said Smeesch. "Tracking … I believe the ship is moving left."

"Excellent!" said Doge Sneeb, "Commodore Pimlip, please order Officer Smeesch to fire the rest at his discretion."

While Smeesch was lining up a second barrage of shots at the rapidly moving pink blob on screen, a large dark red threep in the corner cleared his throat hesitantly and said,

"Commodore Pimlip, sir, we have an incoming teletransmission for Doge Sneeb. It's—it's—"

"Arch Doge Zebulon, I assume," said Doge Sneeb coolly.

"Sir."

"Patch it through to the Doge's pod, he will be there directly."

"No thank you, Commodore. Communications Officer Mondock: here, if you please," said Doge Sneeb firmly.

With a static crackle the holographic image of Arch Doge Zebulon materialised on the bridge. The crew carried on with their duties but the hush which descended showed they were paying plenty of attention to Doge Sneeb's call.

"Arch Doge Zebulon," said Doge Sneeb calmly.

"Sneeb," snarled the Arch Doge, "I ordered you to stop interfering with this colonisation."

"Yes, Arch Doge Zebulon, you did."

"Then why are you here?"

"I intend to vaporise the meteor."

The tension on the bridge increased.

"Against my express orders?"

"Yes," Doge Sneeb paused. "I have already told you why; because the humans are sentient and evidence has come to light that the meteor is not on a natural collision course with Earth. Someone moved it."

The tension ramped up another notch as the crew on the bridge took this in. In the silence, the holographic figure of Zebulon jumped and flickered as the signal was disrupted by static.

"There is no reason why anyone, other than you, would move the meteor, Sneeb. Did you? Are you suffering remorse at the last moment?"

"No. I have been duped by someone who wishes to discredit me. Someone who believed I wouldn't examine the evidence too closely and that, even if I did, I would turn a blind eye."

"Well, you were always single minded in your pursuit of power, Sneeb."

"Luckily for the human race, not as single minded as someone anticipated."

The holographic Arch Doge and Doge Sneeb stood glaring at each other in malignant silence.

"Zebulon, father," said Doge Sneeb and the whole bridge projected the telepathic equivalent of a gasp as they realised he had used the Arch Doge's actual name as opposed to his title, "I'm sure you agree that, now this evidence has come to light, the colonisation simply cannot go ahead."

I think he had assumed this would be enough. That once he had divulged this information in front of outside witnesses the

Arch Doge would have no choice but to call off the colonisation and save Earth.

"You call it evidence. I call it speculation. My view has not altered, Sneeb. The colonisation will proceed."

"If there is any doubt, and there is, the colonisation cannot proceed."

"But it will, Sneeb. Now move your ship away from the meteor, or I will be forced to take action."

"No. Zebulon, listen to me, you can't do this."

"Who will stop me?" asked the Arch Doge, "you and your rebel crew?"

Nobody on the bridge was doing anything now except for Smeesch who was still doggedly firing pink paint at Project X. The others were still and silent, listening.

Doge Sneeb stared at the holographic projection in front of him in horrified amazement.

"If it comes down to it: yes."

"I think not. I am sentient and so are the Gamalians here with me. Even if you were able to find my ship you would have to destroy it to stop us. You lack the strength of character to take that step. Do not prolong the agony. Give yourself up now and I may decide to spare your crew."

"I cannot."

"You really are selfish, Sneeb. That beautiful ship and all those Gamalians, the cream of the fleet, wiped out through your intransigence."

"What about the humans?" said Doge Sneeb. "Surely you would not be remembered for genocide? Allowing a sentient race to perish is—"

"Monstrous?" the Arch Doge interrupted him. "Indeed it is, but history is written by the survivors, Sneeb. It is not I who will be remembered for this evil deed but you. Shortly, the humans on Gamma Six will die and when you have witnessed the spectacle, the Eegby will be vaporised and you will join them in the afterlife. You're welcome to try and defend yourselves of course, if you think you can. Upon my return to the Huurg Quadrant, when I have taken care of you, once and for all, I will let it be known that I tried to save the sentient inhabitants of Gamma Six – oh yes, they are sentient, Sneeb, there is no question of that – but that you attacked my ship. I fought you, desperate to get to the meteor and stop it, but I failed. The meteor struck and the humans died: such a shame. And while trying to save them, I was forced to destroy you and your vessel to preserve my own life and that of my crew."

"I thought you said you would spare my crew."

"I shall, if you give yourself up."

"And you think they will allow this atrocity to be suppressed?"

"They will if they want to live. Once you are handed over to me each crew member must sign a document binding them to secrecy on pain of death. Otherwise, I will destroy them and the Eegby."

"There will be an investigation and the Lofty Syndic will want to know why you did not merely disable us."

"A tragic accident – an iota too much power to the weapons system; a small miscalculation, an oversight by a young and inexperienced crew member while using a laser array of far greater power than he is used to; an error which occurs in the heat of the battle for our very survival."

"They won't believe you," said Doge Sneeb.

"Oh they will, Sneeb, they will," said the Arch Doge. "I am the longest-serving Arch Doge in the history of the Gamalian Federation. I am the father of all the planets and you are a precocious upstart. I am loved yes, even on your precious Gamma Five, while you are feared. They trust and adore me. You, they distrust. They will believe exactly what I tell them."

"My followers are loyal, they will ask questions."

"Then I will have to teach them the price of that loyalty," retorted the Arch Doge, "and when I have finished, with every passing minute they will curse you." He laughed: the type of long-drawn-out evil laugh that said, more eloquently than any

201

psychoanalysis could, that he was criminally insane.

It didn't take a telepath to know what Doge Sneeb was thinking; that the Arch Doge was right; that even if both of them survived it was Zebulon's story, and not the truth, which would be believed.

"You are not so infernally smug now, are you, Sneeb?" gloated Zebulon. "You're not as clever as you thought. Neither are your scientists. I am in control here. Tell me, how does it feel to fall victim to your own blind ambition?"

"Zebulon," said Doge Sneeb, though his voice was little more than a whisper. "This is not you. You are very sick. Please, do not do this. I am your son. Let me help you. I will withdraw from the elections. I will withdraw from politics if that is what you want. I will vaporise the meteor and we will say nothing of this conversation. It is not too late, not if we return to the Gamalian Federation, together, and explain."

"I don't think so. And you are not my son. I will give you fifteen minutes to surrender, otherwise, prepare to die."

The holographic image disappeared. The Arch Doge had hung up.

By the end of the call, Doge Sneeb's colour had lightened from black to a dark grey. He shook his head, apparently at a loss for words and regarded the officers and crew around him.

"I would like to apologise for bringing you into this. As you all can see, our situation is bleak. The Arch Doge is out of sorts mentally and I cannot surrender. This colonisation is wrong on every level. I must destroy this meteor or die trying," he cast a sweeping look around the bridge, "but if you wish to exchange me for your lives, I will not hold it against you." He half raised his pincers and let them drop to his sides in a helpless gesture.

A couple of crew members shuffled from one foot to another but nobody actually moved.

"I would rather die well than sign away my honour to live," said Commodore Pimlip. "I believe my crew will be in agreement."

"I thank you, Commodore. But we will put it to the vote and we will do what the majority wishes," said Doge Sneeb, adding, as an afterthought, "if you please."

Commodore Pimlip nodded and turned to his communication officer, "Mondock, relay the transmission to the rest of the ship."

Doge Sneeb swung round suddenly to face him.

"Did you record our conversation, Commodore?"

"Y-Yes sir, I thought it prudent."

There was a long silence as the Doge gave him one of his scary glares.

"It may have been."

Mondock began burbling into a microphone. The crew could vote yes or no with their communicators. I could hear Mondock's voice booming out through the tannoy system on the rest of the ship. The ballot didn't take long and then the ship's computer counted the votes. While all these events had been unfolding around him, Smeesch sat doggedly behind the weapons console paintballing Project X. With each round he fired, the shape beneath the blobs of pink on the viewing screen became more distinct.

After a few minutes Mondock was able to announce the results of the vote. The crew had opted to stay on the ship, almost unanimously. Those who didn't, asked to be taken to the brig.

"I hope our vote answers any questions about our allegiance, sir," said Commodore Pimlip.

Doge Sneeb seemed slightly at a loss.

"I did not expect this," he said. "Thank you, all of you. I am touched by your loyalty. I am only sorry you will die for it."

"Not necessarily, sir," muttered Smeesch from behind the weapons console.

"Yeh," said Eric, "he'll have to catch us first."

With the vote of confidence he had received from the crew, Doge Sneeb seemed to have regained his shredded composure.

By the time he spoke again, he was almost back to his normal colour.

"Is there enough paint to give a reliable signature?" he asked Commodore Pimlip.

"Well?" The Commodore turned to a flustered Scanning Officer Boldrort, who was unwilling to commit himself.

"I think so, sir."

"Is that a yes, giving a safe margin for error or is it a euphemism for 'no'?" Doge Sneeb asked, and before Boldrort could answer added, "a second coat, please, Commodore."

"Officer Smeesch."

"Sir."

Smeesch prepared to fire and Sneeb turned abruptly to Neewong, making him jump.

"Officer Neewong, I require someone to check on the situation in the missile bays. We may need a third coat to convince Scanning Officer Boldrort."

"Yes, sir," said Neewong.

"If you require assistance, I suggest you take our guest."

"That would be most helpful, sir," said Neewong.

"Good. We have," Doge Sneeb glanced down at the communicator on his belt, "twelve minutes. I would like you back in ten."

He was definitely on to us, so we went, but not to the missile bays.

Chapter 29
Space walk

Neewong and I made a dash for the lift.

"Are we going to have enough time?" I asked. In films I'd seen people throwing on spacesuits like a bathrobe, in reality it had taken us a lot longer.

"If we're quick."

It helped, of course, that the suit was enormous and he could pretty much drop me into it.

"Will you be alright?" his voice came over the intercom, as he screwed down the helmet. I breathed a thankful sigh as the air scrubbers on the inside began to remove the rancid smell of its outside. Then, slowly, with the speed of a sedated slug because it was unbelievably hard to move in the suit, I reached one finger round and pressed the button.

"Yes."

"That's good, the radio works," he picked up a small receiver and held it up for me to see. "I'll keep this with me and the frequency open but try not to use it unless you have to."

He put me into the airlock and took hold of the inner door, ready to close it on me.

"Are you sure you will be alright?"

Well yes of course, I was just fine and dandy; tickety boo. He was going to cast me into space and I was going to do a space walk, for the first time in my life, in a suit which was supposed to disguise me as space garbage. A suit which might not work and if it didn't I was going to get vaporised, or transported inside Project X and then vaporised, by the Arch Doge. So this could be the last few minutes of my life and I was going to spend them in space, alone. In short, I was on a death mission. And if that wasn't bad enough, I couldn't afford to fail because the entire human race was counting on me. Of course I wasn't bloody alright. And if he didn't leave very quickly I was going to do something really stupid, like telling him.

"YES." I smiled the special 'I'm in control' smile I'd formatted for job or college interviews. It had taken me ages practising until I achieved that confident, yet friendly, masterful, yet open-minded image. Although, without a mirror I could never be absolutely certain whether I was correctly replicating the expression I had devised or looking as if I was trying to jemmy a fishbone from between my teeth with my tongue. I knew I'd got it wrong this time when Neewong asked me if I'd bitten my cheek at about the same time that I realised I would have had a better response if I'd saved myself the potential embarrassment and transmitted it telepathically anyway.

"Go! Vamoose!" I said.

"Good luck Andi Turbot," said Neewong and did as he was told. I sat for the slowest five minutes of my life while the airlock depressurised. Then the door at the other end opened and I was floating out into the serenity of space. For a moment, Neewong was waving through the glass of the inner door then the solid door at the hull end closed, hiding him from sight. I headed towards Project X.

The silence of space is so complete you could almost class it as anti-noise. I could hear nothing but the sounds that were conducted through the air in my suit: the quiet hiss of the air jets, my own breathing and a deafeningly loud whooshy, thudding sound which I finally identified as my heart. It was beating quickly, and the larger Project X became in my field of vision the faster it went. My worries grew in size as Project X did. Would my transporter work? How long could my heart beat that fast without popping? It was making a sod of a lot of noise, was that because the damping system was keeping it in or was it going to give me away? Would the transporter Neewong had programmed for Project X work? What if there was nothing on Project X to attach it to? What if it fell off and didn't transport the ship? What if Project X was too big to fit inside the Eegby? No, surely it wouldn't be. OK, so I had thought the Eegby was the size of a town, but now I realised I was so, so wrong: it was the size of a small country – Wales for example – you could fit just about anything in there.

I continued my journey and as I watched, a small point of light appeared in one of the invisible spaces between the blobs of pink. As

206

it approached it resolved itself into a narrow metal object heading straight for me! I swore and jinked sharply to the left as it sped past. It was shaped like a rocket with a red-nosed cone and fins. I juddered to a halt and spun my suit round. It was a missile. It looked like every bomb ever launched on Earth – obviously the casing designs for weapons of mass destruction are universally similar. I watched, powerless, as it headed towards the jewel of the Gamalian intergalactic battle fleet, the Eegby: a beautiful vessel which contained some very dear friends, not to mention the only hope of survival for my species. I fumbled the two-way radio button to transmit and said,

"Incoming," quietly, hoping Neewong would hear me. Then I waited, in trepidation, for the missile to make contact. I knew the Eegby had shields and a missile protection system but I also knew that it wasn't strong enough to withstand many of Project X's warheads. I turned my attention back to my destination; Project X. There was another missile coming. I cast another look back at the Eegby and was beginning to panic about what a human in a spacesuit does with no ship to go home to when, despite its huge size, the ship did a neat victory roll. A beam of red light hit the missile and it vaporised.

"Uh-oh." There would be a shock wave wouldn't there? and ... hang on it would hit me if— "Ohmygodohmygod!" I screamed as I spun over and over. "No, no, no, no, noooooo!"

Eric and I had agreed to a telepathic blackout – I didn't want to be spotted by the Arch Doge's sage advisors so he could order my vaporisation with Project X's lasers. Even so it was all I could do not to reach out for help. The world spun dizzily as I tumbled over and over. I was beyond disorientation. I had no clue where I was. On the upside it appeared I was still on course. With a massive bang, I collided with the hull of Project X. There was a hissing sound.

Holy soddy sodding sod it's sprung a leak! I'm going to die in space. Ohmygodohmygod! No ... calm ... breathe ... the hissing sound got louder and more urgent, *but not too much! It's OK, it's OK. Just stick the transporter on the ship and get out of here.*

A glance at the head-up display on my visor showed any number of urgent warnings flashing at me in Gamalian, most of which were of little use to my non astronaut's brain, even after my mind meld with Eric. However, there was a green and red line with graduations on it, like a fuel gauge, labelled O2. That was eloquent enough. It had a pair of arrow-shaped pointers and they were firmly in the red section, a few millimetres from the bottom. Great. That pretty much put my predicament in a nutshell, then. On the up side, I realised I was attached to the ship by my arm because the magnetic foot on the transporter had engaged, and the hissing, most of it, at any rate, was the sound of me venting all my propellant, full throttle. I managed to relax and a lot, but not all, of the hissing stopped.

Slowly, like somebody trying to tie shoelaces with their elbows, I checked that the UT had stuck properly and pressed the big red button to activate it.

Brilliant, part one achieved, now to get free of the ship and get out of here. I heaved and strained but no, nothing was happening. I was stuck, fast.

It's difficult to explain what it feels like to try and do, well, anything in a spacesuit. Imagine trying to use the touchpad on a telephone under water, or possibly under treacle, with boxing gloves on. Also I cannot stress enough how incredibly strong Velcro is in a zero-g environment. It was an amazing enough achievement to press the button but now I had to detach. I had landed awkwardly and I couldn't untangle my legs. At the moment the jets on the suit were pushing me towards the hull, I needed to move just a little bit to point them away from the ship. I felt as if I'd run a marathon, I was seeing spots and the arrows on the graduated red and green O2 line on my head-up display had reached the bottom. With the last of my strength I gave up unknotting my legs and planted the one of my space boots I could control against the metal of Project X's hull. In slow motion, with the strength and grace of a marshmallow, I bent my knee, set the jets to full power and kicked off. I came free suddenly and fast, flying straight into another hard, metal, and this time invisible, part of the ship. I cannoned off, bounced onto something else I couldn't see and spun away into space at high speed. The suit wasn't designed to go that fast and neither was I. I flailed about trying to slow myself down and stop before the suit ripped itself apart or I threw up and drowned most horribly. I couldn't regain control – the power in the air jets was too feeble and I careened on into outer space. I didn't have much time before Project X was transported to the Eegby and my anxiety not to be in the area when it did spurred me on in my efforts to stop and transport away. I had a horrible feeling the propellant in the jets was gone and still I was tumbling over and over at a colossal velocity. After an eternity of panic-stricken effort, seemingly to no avail, the spinning suddenly stopped. Now, I was merely going backwards very fast. Never mind, on the other hand, at least I was heading away from Project X, well, I thought I was but I couldn't see it, or the Eegby anymore, I had no idea which way was up or down and I was dizzy to the point of losing consciousness. I must stay awake to transport or I would die. I shut my eyes and with a gargantuan effort moved my arm across my chest so the business end of the transporter was pointing at me. After what felt like an aeon of impotent, ham-fisted fumbling, I managed to press the button. The next thing I knew, Neewong was removing my helmet on the Eegby's bridge.

"Andi!" he sounded choked.

I was soaked with sweat and until I opened my eyes I probably looked as if I was dead. On the up side, I hadn't thrown up or 'prepared for flight', as my biology textbooks euphemistically called it, in any other embarrassing ways. Yeh, it could have been worse. Then the smell of the suit hit me and nearly succeeded where other efforts had failed.

"Hi," I took a lungful of clean air, which, unfortunately, also contained the smell of the suit. "Ugh," I said and hiccuped, "mission accomplished."

"Am I glad to see you?" said Neewong.

"Seconded," said Eric from the pilot's controls, "I thought you were a goner."

"My ham sandwiches nearly were but I'm all right," I told him.

Neewong, and Smeesch who had joined us by that time, had to pull me out of the suit. I was weak and too dizzy to stand so they also had to hold me upright.

I realised that many of the Gamalian crew within radius were giving off transmissions of total revulsion at the smell of the suit.

"Captain Persalub. Is there a reason for this olfactory assault?" asked Doge Sneeb.

"Sorry, I had to disguise myself as space garbage," I explained.

"Get rid of the suit," he ordered Commodore Pimlip.

"You heard him."

Two of the crew projecting the Gamalian equivalent of wrinkled noses, picked up the suit and carted it away.

"Perhaps you could explain why you needed to disguise yourself as such an impressively disgusting piece of space junk. I am agog to know the reason," said Doge Sneeb, but before any of us could answer, Mondock interrupted us to say there was another telecommunication from the Arch Doge.

"Your time is up, Sneeb. Surrender and I will—" began the Arch Doge and then there was a pop, the hologram disappeared from the bridge and at exactly the same time Project X disappeared from the viewing screen on the wall. Doge Sneeb threw a loop.

"Where is he? Where in Plort's name is his ship? Find it. NOW!"

"There's no trace, sir," said Scanning Officer Boldrort.

"What did you say?" asked Doge Sneeb. The power of his anger was almost physical, his whole body vibrated with it and his voice was quiet but packed with menace.

I wished I could have avoided having to explain myself. He was going to throw his bricks out of the pram and, knowing my luck, me out of the airlock.

"It's gone," I said in a small voice. Slowly the Doge began to walk towards me.

"I know it's gone, human, and I want to know where."

He stood in front of me and bent his head down to my level in a way that made me extra aware of his superior height and size. "Do you know anything about this?" he said. "Because if you've done anything to that ship, sentient or not, in the mood I am in now, my rage will overcome my self-control and I will kill you. Where is Project X?"

I looked into the glowering green eyes and hoped he hadn't noticed I was cowering.

"Look out of the observation window," I said in as steady a voice as I could. The crew were watching us avidly and turned with him, towards the screen along the wall with its view into outer space. I had time to glance the other way and catch a glimpse of pink in the Eegby's voluminous centre beyond the docking station. "No, the observation window *into* the ship," I told him, relief creeping into my voice. He crossed the bridge, put his pincers against the glass and rested his forehead on it for a few seconds. Then he turned round, shaking his head in disbelief.

"Astounding," he said as he faced the rest of us. There was a blob of slime on the window where he had leant. "Absolutely astounding and who should I thank for this ridiculous idea?"

"Me!" said Eric getting up from the pilot's seat at exactly the same moment as I said,

"It's my fault."

"And your logic?" he asked me, adding, aside to Communications Officer Mondock, "reconnect the teletransmission."

Eric started to speak but Doge Sneeb stopped him.

"Do not protect her, Captain Persalub. This action," he gestured over his shoulder to the blobs of pink hanging in the centre of the Eegby, "does not show the hallmarks of Gamalian logic." He held up one pincer, cutting off Eric's attempt to cover me again, "not even yours.

"Andi Turbot, please explain why I should want to transport an invisible ship, which has fired two planet-strength missiles in as many minutes, into the middle of my own vessel. I'm sure it would be an education for us all," he sounded weary.

"Because *he* doesn't want to die: he wants *you* to," I explained.

Doge Sneeb's reaction was utterly against my expectations. He laughed.

"I realise you are not an average human being but even if there is only one other example like you, colonising your planet would be a criminal waste. Have you re-established contact, Communications Officer Mondock?"

"No answer, sir."

"Open a hailing frequency," said Commodore Pimlip.

"Sir: ready to transmit."

"Thank you. Good day to you again, Arch Doge Zebulon," said Sneeb. "Please surrender."

There was a long silence.

"Zebulon, this is done. Surrender your ship."

The speakers on the communications console crackled into life. "No."

"I wonder if you have noticed where you are."

"I know exactly where I am: in a position to blow apart the Eegby, and all its crew, from the inside, starting with you and the bridge."

"That is an option, but you will die along with us and I suspect that is not what you want. I think you want your name to go down in history don't you? I, on the other hand, am at liberty to vaporise your vessel as and when I choose without any risk of damage to my own."

"You will not dare."

"Really? It would be perfectly legal after what you have put us through."

"I am the Arch Doge and I am taking command of your ship. My authority surpasses yours. You are no match for me, Sneeb."

"Ah but I am, aren't I? That's why we're all here. Commodore Pimlip and his crew have elected to stand by me. If any member of your crew wishes to do the same they will press their communicators, now, and we will transport them off your ship. They have nothing to fear. They have both Commodore Pimlip's and my personal guarantees that they will be treated fairly. You have five minutes to give yourself up; then I and my troops will be taking your ship." He nodded to Mondock who ended the transmission.

"What if he won't surrender?" I asked.

"I believe he will."

"What if he doesn't?"

"Then we will have to think of another way to entice him from his vessel."

"But won't that take too long?"

"The Earth and your species will survive Andi. Trust me."

Now that we were no longer in danger of attack, Eric put the Eegby on autopilot to maintain its position and joined me while we waited.

After four minutes Commodore Pimlip reported that the crew of thirty threeps had been transported from Project X to the Eegby, leaving the Arch Doge and a division of forty crack troops from his personal bodyguard.

"Incoming teletransmission, sir," said Communications Officer Mondock. "The Arch Doge has surrendered."

"Excellent."

The crew on the bridge cheered but I was uneasy. The Arch Doge was out of his tree. People like that don't know the meaning of the word surrender. He wasn't going to give himself up. He would fight to the death, our death. A quick exchange of thoughts and I knew Eric agreed with me. It seemed Commodore Pimlip did too, because he ordered everyone to take cover and train their guns on the docking platform. Two of the crew moved among us distributing handcuffs. If it came to a fight, and Commodore Pimlip believed it might, the enemy crew were to be stunned unconscious and restrained.

"No killing, or you will answer to me," Doge Sneeb told the crew of the Eegby. He turned to Eric.

"Captain Persalub, I believe I am going to need your help."

"Yes, sir."

"And you," he told me.

We waited. Borridge and a very nervous-looking Mingold arrived. They came and stood alongside me.

What's this? The sage advisors' corps?

Something like that.

"Borridge," said Doge Sneeb. Borridge stepped up to his side. "The rest of you, wait here," he said. The two of them moved forwards, then, with a flick of three eyestalks, he summoned us to follow.

Chapter 30
The sage advisors' corps

In the central area of the Eegby, the telltale pink splodges which betrayed the whereabouts of Project X started to move. The ship drifted into position in front of the Eegby's bridge. A gangway slid out from the docking station and the locking mechanism clamped into position with a clang. The chameleon coating was deactivated and the dark bulbous sphere, with its occasional clumps of spikes, was revealed in all its ugliness. Where there appeared to have been smooth metal the outline of a door appeared. Doge Sneeb walked a few more yards forwards and waited, in the middle of the gangway, to greet the Arch Doge and the remaining crew as they disembarked. A couple of paces behind, and a little to his left, stood Borridge. Ranged in a row behind him stood Eric, Mingold and I.

Should we be this close? I thought to Eric, *what if they decide not to surrender after all? I bet that ship's bristling with laser cannon and stuff. I bet it could wipe us all out with one gun.*

It could but there's more to Gamalian warfare than weaponry! It was Borridge who answered.

The sage advisors' corps, remember? Eric's thoughts drifted into my head.

Exactly, Mingold agreed. *Although that's not what it's actually called.*

Listen, Mingold—thinking in Gamalian was difficult, there seemed to be less time to get the words right before I sent them somehow, although at least I could imagine a better accent than my human voice box could produce. *I'm really sorry I*—

Forget it. I know you meant me no harm. I should be apologising to you, Mingold thought back.

Pay attention human, Doge Sneeb broke in, *you will need your wits about you and you would be wise to fear the Arch Doge's sage advisor.*

He is one of the most powerful there has ever been, Borridge again.

Yeh, and some, Eric chipped in. *It'll take all our concentration to break through his guard.*

And he will not be alone, from Doge Sneeb.

How many of them can we expect?

At least three, Borridge thought.

Try to confuse them, thought Mingold.

Yes, Andi, like you tried to do with the pilots when they attacked us, Eric explained, *only with five of us we stand a better chance.*

The door in the side of the ship opened and out of the corner of my eye I saw one of Eric's antennae move downwards. I felt it brush my hand in a gesture of reassurance. A couple of Doge Sneeb's eyes flicked backwards, as if to check we, and Mingold, were there.

"Here we go," said Eric, and his thoughts drifted into my head. *Don't be scared.*

Eric, Borridge and Mingold were clearly concentrating. I reached out, trying to find a malleable mind on the ship but there was nothing, only the smooth, impenetrable guard of the Arch Doge's sage advisors.

"Blimey Eric, we're toast," I muttered.

"No we're not. Can't you feel anything?"

"No," I said, trying to hide my panic as I squelched forwards by his side.

OK, here, we'll team up, he handed me his blaster, *I'll confuse them: you stun them.*

The troops came first, marched out of the door and lined the gangway, blasters in their pincers. There was no sign of the Arch Doge. The silence was absolute. Then, a single threep slowly came into focus as it moved out of the darkness of Project X. In real life, Arch Doge Zebulon was even lighter than his teletransmission, a gleaming bright white. I could feel the awe in the crew around me as he moved further into view. Behind him, in the dim half-light of his ship, I could see more threeps, five, I reckoned.

Are those—

Yep. The Arch Doge's sage advisors, Eric's thoughts came back to me.

"But there are five of them," I said aloud.

"Zebulon was never one for half measures," said Doge Sneeb bitterly.

I started to count to ten but Zebulon's troops opened fire before I reached three. Flecks of green and red blaster rounds shot backwards and forwards, and the air rang with noise. It sounded like a street full of car alarms all going off at the same time.

After a minute of heavy fire the air was too thick with smoke to continue and, as suddenly as it had started, the shooting stopped. Behind the Arch Doge, dimly silhouetted in the doorway of Project X, I could see the sage advisors. I knew, instinctively, that they had the kind of power and training that we only had in two of our number. If we wanted to win this battle we were going to have to think creatively. The five of them were way more powerful than the five of us. Three of them would have been.

Now what?

Doge Sneeb hadn't moved. He still stood in full view, seemingly unprotected, with his pincers folded across his chest. Amazingly, thanks to our efforts, none of the Arch Doge's troops seemed to be able to hit him. Then again, thanks to the efforts of the Arch Doge's sage advisors, none of our troops seemed to be able to hit any of his forces either. The enemy sage advisors changed their tactics. I could feel my mind fogging, my brain slowing down. Two of them were concentrating on me, while the others continued to put out general interference and protect them from my companions. I couldn't hold them off. They knew it, too. My temples burned as I fought. Maybe I should capitulate, as I had done with Mingold. I felt a sense of understanding from my adversaries as they took in that previously I had capitulated to the least powerful of our number. I wasn't sure how I hid the truth: that my encounter with Mingold had made me stronger and more powerful, but I did. I felt them discounting me, both as a risk, and as an asset because they believed I lacked the skill to carry out their plan. Clearly they needed a gifted telepath. They concentrated their energy on mithering the mind of one of the others now, Borridge, if I wasn't mistaken. At once I could think more clearly. Softly, gently so they wouldn't notice, I reached out.

The ones trying to confuse the Eegby's troops were using the same blanket techniques as Eric and my companions, ranged beside me. That is: aiming to confuse as many minds as possible on the opposite crew at the same time. Maybe I could make a difference with an alternative approach. Theirs.

I noticed a sudden flash of movement in the corner of my field of vision. One of the Arch Doge's troops ducked back into the opening of Project X but when I tried to follow his movements he shimmered for a moment, as if in a heat haze, and disappeared.

"Dammit, they're jamming me."

I pretended to concentrate on something else, to lull the advisors blocking me into a false sense of security. When I quickly looked again I managed to catch a glimpse of the rogue trooper crouched behind a bulkhead before they raised their guard and he was gone again. What was he doing there? Nothing good, that was for sure. I began to think I might know what our opponents were trying to do and it gave me an idea.

Eric? I thought, in English.

Yeh.

I could feel the tension in my friend as he strained with the effort of defending himself.

I have a plan.

A laser round pinged off the wall beside me and threw a small tidal wave of plastic matter over my legs as it ricocheted onto the ground at my feet.

Good. Hurry up.

That was too close for comfort but now I definitely had a plan. I pointedly turned my head, concentrating on the opposing sage advisors. Out of the corner of my eye, with a hidden corner of my mind, without their realising, I tried to watch the threep trooper they were hiding. Sure enough, he was there, well … sometimes, but still wavy and heat-haze indistinct. The way Eric's projection of his human self had looked in the student canteen, when he'd stopped trying to hide himself from me and I'd first realised he was an alien. Although I couldn't see the enemy marksman clearly, or at all for some of the time, it was the obvious absence of anything when I looked at his position head-on, and the accompanying headache, that told me that he was still there and one of the sage advisors was covering his presence. It was difficult to follow his movements without fighting the enemy advisors openly, and I didn't want to do that. I didn't want them to realise I was onto them, so it was a case of grinning and bearing the headache while trying to pretend their secret marksman was still hidden from me. The sniper was aiming carefully and deliberately and every shot he fired came closer to hitting one of us. He was being clever about it, too, targeting different individuals in our defence in turn. It was only a matter of time …

I had to tell the others so I concentrated on cutting off what I was seeing around me and, instead, sending pictures of words, in yellow letters, and in English, to the two of my telepathic companions who would understand: Eric and Doge Sneeb.

Behind that bulkhead, where there's obviously nothing. The shots came from there. They're protecting him.

The words came back from Eric, rainbow coloured, which was probably involuntary but, looking back on it, it was a nice touch.

I'll try to cover your intentions, you blast him.

No, project me a cover. Make me into the Arch Doge.

Why?

Don't ask, just do it …

I concentrated on planting a tiny seed of doubt in the sniper's mind, a dash of disorientation, a half-formed misgiving and then, stepping sideways to get a better shot, I raised my blaster and attempted to aim it at him. With all the interference from the sage advisors on the other side, I could do little more than wave it vaguely in his direction but it was enough to get his attention. He stared straight at me and then at the blaster he was aiming in confusion. As he glanced sharply back towards the Arch Doge and his sage advisors, I just had time to project a disguise over the nearest one so the sniper saw him as Doge Sneeb. He didn't hesitate. By the skin of my teeth I managed to make him alter the setting from kill to stun before he took aim and fired. The advisor keeled over backwards into the life matter.

One down.

The Arch Doge started towards the sniper as the next two advisors in line wheeled round to trace the source of the shot. But even to me, they now looked like Borridge and Mingold, as disguised by Eric. Our rogue sniper shot them without a second thought, and while the last two were distracted by what had happened to their colleagues, I shot them.

After that it was over very quickly. The number of unconscious enemy threeps grew steadily while none of our guys had a scratch.

I watched Doge Sneeb. He was concentrating. The smoke billowed about his feet like dry ice and the effect was ... well ... dramatic. I thought I saw him turn an eye stalk towards Borridge and wink. While I was still trying to work out if I'd truly, actually seen Doge Sneeb wink, he turned a couple more of his eye stalks backwards, summoning the rest of us.

As the smoke cleared, it became obvious that, at the end of it the only conscious people were on our side.

Commodore Pimlip stepped up.

"Nice work boys and ... it," he nodded to me.

"Her," growled Doge Sneeb.

"Andi," I said.

"Andi," the Commodore transmitted a smile.

While the Eegby's troops kept the doorway and the Arch Doge covered, we counted the comatose forms of the Arch Doge's crack troops. There were forty-one, including the five sage advisors.

"Put the advisors in high security; one to a cell, and assign robot guards. Take the rest of them to the brig and leave them to wake up," said Commodore Pimlip.

"Gently," said Doge Sneeb as one of the heftier crew members slung a sage advisor roughly over one shoulder, "where is Zebulon? I must escort him personally." But the doorway of Project X was empty.

"There!" Mingold pointed. One of the Eegby's troops lay still on the gangway.

"Medic!" shouted Commodore Pimlip as we all ran to the fallen threep.

Apreetik beat us to him. He rolled the unconscious being over and examined him while I pointed Eric's blaster at the door of the ship. I reached out with my mind, trying to be subtle. I could feel the insane presence of Arch Doge Zebulon close by, like darkness engulfing light.

"He's in the ship, can he do any damage?"

"No." Doge Sneeb turned to Eric, "Captain. Bring him out here." Noting that I had Eric's blaster, he drew his own and handed it to my friend. "Here. Use this," he said. He didn't wait for Eric to answer but walked away; an action which put him well out of order, in my view.

"This won't take long," said Eric grimly and he squished off before I could stop him.

"Wait!" I shouted.

He turned.

"D'you want a hand?" I asked.

"No. There's only one threep left in that ship," said Eric. He went up the gangway, into Project X. I havered for a few seconds and decided Eric could look after himself for a minute or two after all and that I'd yell at Doge Sneeb first. I ran over to where he stood talking to Borridge and yanked on his pincer.

"You can't let him go in there on his own like that!"

He looked down at me in surprise.

"Why not?"

"He'll get killed?"

"He will not."

"You can't tell. You're telepathic, not clairvoyant!"

"Andi Turbot, on this one occasion, can you not trust me?" he transmitted a hurt expression and it seemed genuine.

"I do trust you. I know you think you're doing the right thing. I just don't agree with you that's all. Sending him in on his own like that isn't fair and if he dies I hope you'll feel responsible. I'm going in after him."

I turned and ran up the gangway.

"Wait!"

"No!" I shouted over my shoulder as I ran.

"Come back this instant."

I ignored him.

"COME BACK HERE! NOW! YOU PESTILENTIAL CREATURE!"

There was a lot of authority in that shout but I ran on.

Project X was dark inside. Only the emergency lights were on. I crept forwards in the gloom trying not to make any noise. It was difficult because it was even fuller of plastic matter than the Eegby and every step I took squelched. I heard a sharp cry and then Eric started transmitting images to me. Pictures flashed into my mind one after another, scenes from his life, of his fathers, his school, the first time he met Smeesch, the first time he and Smeesch met Neewong. This was bad news. Everybody knows what it means when your life flashes past you like that. I broke into a run, or at least a scramble through the knee-deep life matter. I was terrified that I would be too late and Eric would already be dead. After another twenty yards the corridor opened out into the main control room. In the half darkness I could see the Arch Doge punching and kicking Eric as he lay on the ground. I tried to stop too suddenly and slid over in the slime but I kept Eric's blaster aimed at Arch Doge Zebulon. My fall gave him time to grab Eric from the floor and retrieve Doge Sneeb's blaster from my unconscious friend's antenna but I had managed to stop him from firing. I scrabbled to my feet and took stock of my situation. A maniac was holding my best friend by the neck and had a gun pressed to his temple. This called for a level head and bags of natural authority neither of which I possessed. I took a deep breath and tried to act calmly and thought before I spoke.

"Good evening, Arch Doge," I said, doing my best impression of Doge Sneeb in sarcastic mode, "I hate to break up the party but I suggest you put my friend down."

"No," said the Arch Doge.

Well, cooperation was too much to hope for but I had to try.

Anger is so much more effective if you start politely and work up.

"OK," I said slowly. "I can see you're not getting my point. Let me try putting it another way. I understand that you're really ill but that doesn't mean I won't kill you if you thump my friend one more time. So you do yourself a favour and let go of him. Now!"

I began to move towards them.

"Earthling, listen to the voice of reason," said the Arch Doge.

"My name is Andi."

"Andi," his voice was hypnotic, soft like velvet, or a gentle breeze on a summer day, yeh I know, speaking Gamalian: screeching fax, shouting dolphin and all, but that's how it felt in my head, "I am no more a criminal than you are," he went on, "Sneeb has manipulated us both into thinking ill of one another."

His voice had taken on an even more hypnotic quality and I almost began to believe what he was saying until I remembered that he had just been beating up my best friend and in all appearance, thoroughly enjoying it.

"What do you think I am? A moron? You're a psychopath! Look what you've done to Eric!" I took another step closer.

"Your friend is not dead but he attacked me savagely and I had to defend myself." The voice was even softer and smoother.

"Yeh, I'm sure you did because he's absolutely that kind of guy." The idea of Eric swatting a fly savagely, let alone the hallowed – if psychotic – Arch Doge, was preposterous. "Luckily for you knocking him out and kicking him repeatedly in the head seems to have done the trick."

"Do not be angry human, we are both victims of Sneeb's duplicity and cunning." His voice still had a dreamy, hypnotic quality but I had realised what he was doing now and I was immune.

"No we're not," I said. "Sneeb and I are victims of your duplicity and cunning. Don't think you can talk your way round me now. Let go of Eric and I might not kill you."

"You would not harm another sentient being, surely?" He was still trying to hypnotise me.

"Give it up Zebulon, I'm a telepath!" I snapped. "I can already do sage advice without any training."

"You do not know what you are saying. I may be misguided but Sneeb is evil."

Two days ago I would have agreed with him but I didn't now, I trusted Doge Sneeb.

"He has given into his pride and ambition," the Arch Doge continued. "He will plunge the Huurg Quadrant into anarchy! Thousands of lives will be lost! It is imperative you help me defeat him."

"No chance. You're the one who'll cause anarchy. I heard what you said you'd do to his crew. Even on my planet we don't do stuff like that anymore," I lied, turning a very myopic eye to the human rights records of half the countries on the globe, including my own. "Drop the gun and put Eric down!"

The Arch Doge, having finally accepted that I viewed him as the enemy and that nothing he said or did could change my mind, dropped all pretension of being the good guy, guffawed with evil laughter and said,

"No."

I was five feet away from him by now – nearly close enough to get a point-blank shot at his head.

"Look Zebulon, my civilisation's moral code isn't half as strict as yours. You're the bad guy and sentient or not that means killing you is no skin off my nose—"

"Your feeble undisciplined mind is not capable of killing. I sense you are emotionally attached to my hostage." I winced as he yanked Eric upwards by his neck. "Oh yes," he chuckled as he saw my reaction. "I think I am safe, I do not think you will risk your friend's life, not even to save your planet."

"I wouldn't bet on that if I were you." I was angry now, there's nothing more annoying than trying to argue the toss with someone who's got you bang to rights.

"If you shoot, I will make certain this ingrate dies with me."

"Good word that, ingrate, but still not the answer I'm looking for."

This was hopeless. There was no way I was going to risk

shooting Zebulon unless he put Eric down – I was bound to end up killing the wrong guy by mistake. My only hope was if I could wake Eric up and get him to duck when I fired. I tried telepathy.

Eric! I thought. No reply. *ERIC!* He was out cold. *ERIC! Wake up you idiot!* He groaned and his head lolled to one side. I thought his exoskeleton must be cracked because he was oozing a milky substance. It was either blood or brains and I fervently hoped it was blood – although, I supposed, if it was brains he'd be as good as dead already and nothing I inadvertently did, accidentally shooting him in the head, for instance, could make it any worse. The only thing I was sure of was that the wound was serious. I had to get Zebulon to drop him. I tried telepathy another way. I barged into the Arch Doge's head and started forcing him to let go of Eric's neck. His eyes popped in surprise and he was straining with the effort but he must have had anti-telepath training because he didn't let go. I put my next words into his mind without saying them just so he realised I meant business.

If you don't let go of my friend your brain is going to be custard, I said. *Stuff neural fusion, you will never forget what I'm about to do to you! I have power Zebulon, awesome power, and if you mess with me I'm going to use it.*

He weakened but still held on to the gun, and Eric, and had enough energy left over to indulge himself in a second lengthy cadence of evil laughter.

"Do you not realise who I am? I am the Arch Doge! I am trained to resist the most skilful sage advisor!"

Was he kidding? That couldn't be possible could it? I kept up my telepathic onslaught anyway and he laughed some more.

"Do you think you can defeat me with your puny mind games?"

Obviously not but I had been hoping. Clearly in the confines of the Huurg Quadrant, telepathy wasn't the all-powerful super-weapon it would be on Earth.

"You think it's over, don't you? You think your friend Sneeb has outwitted me but I have arranged a little surprise for him and if you kill me, I assure you, both he and your pathetic species, will be doomed."

"Yeh right; I don't have to kill you to stop you. There's a stun setting on this you know."

"And if you use it, if the slightest thing happens to me, you will all be arrested as traitors, and you know what happens to traitors, don't you?"

"Yeh, yeh: the hooked implement."

"Oh bravo, you are learning. Let me try and explain. I am the Arch Doge, the father of all Gamalians, they have known nothing from me but peace, prosperity and love. I have never betrayed them. They trust me, and with their trust, I control them. They will follow me blindly and believe me, blindly."

"No they won't, they're smarter than that."

"Oh they're smarter than you, I concede, but not that clever."

Eric was coming round. He put one of his antennae to his head.

"Good," snarled the Arch Doge. "You are awake, Captain. I am so glad, it would have been a pity to kill you while you were unable to appreciate the experience." Eric started on another whistle-stop mental tour of his life, all of which he transmitted to me. Zebulon yanked him upright, holding him against his chest, put the gun to the back of his head and whispered.

"Goodbye, Captain!"

"NO!" I shouted over the sound of the Arch Doge's laughter.

I heard the ping in stereo through Eric's mind and my ears before I could even think of firing my own gun and the laughter stopped abruptly. The force of the explosion threw me to the floor and I was showered with red bits, red bits that were horribly reminiscent of parts of Eric. I stood up, numb with shock at what had happened. I could see a threep kneeling on the floor but he was covered with blood and in the dim light I couldn't tell which of them it was. The gun had dropped to the ground by his feet and it sank beneath the surface of the life matter with a gurgle. The flashbacks from Eric had stopped. I held the gun steady and approached, slowly.

"No, wait!" he gasped as he saw the gun. "Plort! Andi, please don't blow my head off! It's me."

I realised his eyes were blue, that he had a crack in the exoskeleton on the side of his head and that it was oozing white stuff. And although he was covered in blood his exoskeleton, underneath, was reddy-brown, not white.

"Eric?" I knelt down beside him.

"Yeh," he said shakily.

"Oh Eric …" I flung my arms round him, not caring about the life matter, and pulled him close with a squelch. I began to cry … "You're … there's so much blood," I sobbed.

"It's not my blood. Andi, it's OK, I promise."

"You mean you're alright?"

"No, yes, sort of," he laughed as he hugged me back.

"You sure?"

"I've a bit of a headache but otherwise I'm fine. It's only a scratch, it probably looks worse than it is. Is it white or red?"

"White."

"There you are, then. No problem. It's not the primary circulatory system."

"You have TWO blood streams?"

He laughed.

"No! It's two circulatory systems but only the red one has a pump, same as yours."

"I don't have two of those thank you very much!"

"Yes you do."

"I do?"

"Yup, one for blood and one for lymph."

"Lymph? Eugh what's that?"

"An important part of your immune system."

Clearly I'd missed something vital in my human biology classes at school. He caught my nonplussed expression and transmitted a grin.

"If you still need to know, I'll explain later," he said, laughing. I was still blubbing like a good 'un and he suddenly stopped and stared at my face. "Are *you* all right?" he asked.

I nodded. "Don't worry, it's just shock. I'll stop crying in a minute." I sniffed and wiped my nose on my sleeve. "I'm fine. Blimey Eric, I thought he'd killed you."

"So did I! So did he, I think, but the gun, Sneeb's gun, you'll never guess what, the devious old scrote, it fires backwards." His voice trailed off as we realised the Fifth Doge was standing behind us. How long he had been there was anybody's guess.

"Sir," said Eric, saluting abruptly.

"Captain Persalub." Doge Sneeb stuck his pincer deep into the life matter and extracted his blaster from where it had sunk, "I am unlikely to use this, myself. Although there is a high chance others will. Were you not aware that the only three Gamalian politicians ever to be successfully assassinated were murdered with their own blasters?"

"No," said Eric.

"Naturally. Please accept my apologies if I caused either of you undue distress."

Neewong and Smeesch rushed past him to Eric's side and the three of us helped him to his feet. We had a group hug and then I stood back and let them have a hug with just the three of them. When I turned to Doge Sneeb, Borridge was standing by his side along with Apreetik, who was obviously waiting for a tactful moment to bring up the subject of examining Eric's sizeable head wound.

"Oh thank you Andi!" Neewong said, reaching out a spare arm to pull me back into the hug too. "We thought we were widowed."

"You weren't the only ones," said Eric, with feeling.

"Captain," said Sneeb, "please forgive me for sending you here to endure what must have been a ..." he chose the words carefully, "harrowing few minutes."

"You were taking a bit of a risk there weren't you?" I said angrily. "Letting Eric do your dirty work. What if he'd had to shoot Zebulon? He'd have shot himself instead."

"Captain Persalub would never have shot Zebulon," said Sneeb sadly. "Try not to think ill of me, Andi. The Arch Doge had to die, and by his own hand," he held his pincers out sideways. "There was no other solution. Zebulon had lost his mind but not his intellect, and he knew the extent of his power – if we had both been alive at the end of this encounter there is no doubt the Lofty Syndic would have believed his version of events. I would have been banished, at the least, along with those close to me – I don't care what happens to me, but I could not allow Apreetik and Borridge to be punished for loving me."

That was seriously Machiavellian.

"What about all the witnesses, the Eegby's crew?" I asked him.

"They would have been banished, or put to death, as rebels for following me."

"Then why send Eric?"

"Because I had to, if I came here and allowed Zebulon to attack me as he attacked Persalub I would have been compelled to tell him about the idiosyncratic nature of my blaster – the moral code of my civilisation demands it – I would have been unable to fire upon him. He would undoubtedly have killed me and you and all your fellow humans would have perished. Had Persalub acted at all dishonourably he would, indeed, have shot himself. However, I was confident he would not," he shot a glance at Eric. "I see you have not disappointed me, Captain. Your behaviour was exemplary and if I am elected Arch Doge you will not find me ungrateful. It will take some years to seed the new planet and when it is ready for habitation it will need a Sixth Doge. Have you considered going into politics?"

"No, sir," said Eric firmly.

"Naturally, nobody with any moral fibre ever does."

"I was thinking more that sage advisor level telepaths are barred, sir."

"There are ways round that. The Guild of Sage Advisors likes to have an inside track on events in the Lofty Syndic. No telepath has the ability to fake the test but the Guild sometimes has ways to fake the results."

Yeh, well that figured.

"Doge Sneeb," I said, "this isn't over. Zebulon told me he'd planned a surprise for you."

"And I do not doubt he has. However, Andi Turbot, there will be time enough to worry about that. First, you and I have a planet to save."

Chapter 31
The Arch Doge's surprise

Doge Sneeb and I ran on ahead of Eric and the others but we were brought up short when we arrived on the bridge, to find eight unfamiliar threeps and an atmosphere of extreme tension. It was the other Doges complete with sage advisors – it had to be – and a detachment of troops. It was only then that I realised the members of the Eegby's crew had their pincers raised and Commodore Pimlip was wearing an apologetic expression.

Had they got their hands up?

Here is Arch Doge Zebulon's insurance policy, Sneeb's thoughts reached me.

"What is the meaning of this?" he demanded as he took in the besieged state of the crew.

"Impact in nine minutes and counting," said a soft computerised voice.

"Nine minutes!"

Patience, Andi Turbot, all will be well.

"Good afternoon Your Loftiness," said the tallest and darkest of their number.

"Good afternoon Your Loftinesses one and all," said Doge Sneeb coolly. "Welcome to the Eegby. Andwick, if you and your colleagues will indulge me and my crew for three minutes, a matter of pressing urgency demands my attention."

"Where is your sage advisor, Sneeb?" asked the smallest Doge in a manner that clearly suggested he didn't consider the Gamalian potentate in the street to be fully dressed without one.

"On his way, Marveen. This human, Andi Turbot, and I are here because we ran. Borridge is walking with the ship's doctor and the Eegby's new pilot, who is injured. If you wish I will fetch him."

The new pilot? Eric?

Yes, he has earned it.

Cool.

I'm so glad it meets with your approval.

He really was sarcastic I reflected, before I realised the third Doge was speaking.

"No, no, no," he was saying, "let Borridge take his time. We wouldn't want to inconvenience him."

"Of course not," Doge Sneeb transmitted a humourless smile, "he might be able to tell me what you are all thinking."

"But—" I blurted before he caught my eye and I shut up remembering his telepathic abilities were supposed to be a secret. Not that anyone would notice if the Arch Doge's ability to resist telepaths was anything to go by.

"No matter. This," Doge Sneeb gestured to the armed guards, "is not necessary, I assure you. Commodore Pimlip will find an officer to escort you to the guest pods and I will join you in the briefing room as soon as I can but, if you don't mind, as I said, I have an urgent matter to attend to first."

"I'm afraid that is not possible—"

"Impact in eight minutes and counting ..."

"—he is under arrest and so are you."

"That won't be necessary, Andwick."

Eric limped out of Project X, leaning on the doctor for support with Neewong, Smeesch and Borridge.

"Ah ... Captain, there you are," Doge Sneeb continued, "this is Captain Persalub, the pilot of the Eegby, may I introduce you to Doge Andwick, of Gamma Four," the tall Doge inclined his head, "Doge Marveen of Gamma Three," the small Doge did the same, "and Doge Vippit of Gamma Two." The last Doge, who hadn't spoken so far, bowed theatrically. Vippit gave me the creeps. His sage advisor was good but I was able to pick up traces of something about his being forbidden to keep pets. I backed away putting Eric, his husbands and the doctor between me and him. I thought I'd been very subtle about it but Vippit was clearly offended, especially when Neewong hugged me and Eric moved further in front of me. Even Doge Sneeb flicked one of his antennae downwards and gave my head a reassuring pat before turning to the last two threeps. I realised, straight away, that one was a sage advisor.

"And you are?" Doge Sneeb asked the other.

"I am Doge Salurian."

Something told me he might have been recently appointed, nothing that I could pick up telepathically, for the most part all their thoughts were a wall of silence. Salurian struck me as a decent, if limited, type – and Andwick, also. It was Vippit and Marveen I was wary of.

"Doge?" asked Doge Sneeb, giving Salurian the benefit of a full-on caustic glare, "of which planet?" I could tell Salurian was not relishing this part of the conversation and when he eventually spoke I could see why.

"Gamma Five," he said bravely.

"Salurian, I know and admire your work but I'm afraid *I* am the Doge of Gamma Five—"

"Impact in seven minutes and counting."

God in heaven!

"—perhaps you were referring to Gamma Six," Doge Sneeb turned slowly towards Vippit as he added, "or do I detect the beginnings of a small coup d'état?"

None of the Doges spoke but if the atmosphere had been tense before, it was now charged enough to satisfy the demand for electricity on a small planet.

"I see I do," said Sneeb, answering his own question.

"Yeh," muttered Smeesch, "the armed guards kind of give it away."

Two of the armed guards under discussion turned and aimed their blasters at him.

"Easy," said Eric.

"We are here, Sneeb, in accordance with the wishes of the Arch Doge," said Vippit nastily.

"What a coincidence, Vippit, so am I."

"Not if his word is to be believed, this is no trivial errand,

Sneeb, we are here to arrest you."

"Really: on what charge?"

"Treason, the murder of the Arch Doge, oh yes he foresaw your plans for him, genocide and hiding your true nature."

Doge Sneeb nodded.

"Naturally. Zebulon was always thorough." His manner was deliberately relaxed, even equable and he seemed remarkably unworried by his predicament. I, on the other hand, was not. We had seven minutes to save my planet, probably less and Smeesch was nowhere near the weapons console. "Why am I not surprised to hear these accusations, Vippit?" asked Sneeb enunciating the word 'Vippit' with an awesome amount of contempt. Eric was right, there was no love lost between these two.

"Presumably because you are guilty, Sneeb," said Vippit who was revelling in his rival's misfortune far too much for my liking.

"I might be guilty of some small indiscretions – none of which I will admit unless you can prove them to be true – but these charges are patently ridiculous."

"Oh but they're not, are they, Sneeb? Tell me, how much does it cost a telepath to bribe their way through our supposedly infallible screening process these days?"

"Perhaps I am not telepathic."

"Perhaps I am pink, with yellow spots but no matter. Try this. We picked up a distress call from one of the Eegby's shuttles, the Thesarus. It was piloted by three of my Science Corps staff, the survey team, no less and we have picked up no traces of it since. The last we heard it was being attacked by the Eegby's fighters."

"If the distress call is the one we intercepted here, they stated that the fighters were unmarked, is that not so, Commodore?" Doge Sneeb turned to Commodore Pimlip.

"Yes, Your Loftiness, Doge Vippit, sir. I can provide you with a transcript if you—"

"The identification markings – or not – of the ships is irrelevant. There is only one place they can come from."

"Not necessarily."

"Six minutes and counting …"

For heaven's sake, were they deaf? I glanced helplessly over at

Smeesch who nodded and flicked a couple of eye stalks towards the weapons console.

"Lay down your arms."

"Of course," Doge Sneeb unhooked his blaster from his belt and to my surprise, he handed it to me. I put it on a nearby control console.

"Commodore Pimlip, Captain Persalub," said Doge Sneeb. "Please excuse me. I must discuss these points of law with our guests. In the meantime; you know what to do."

"Sir," said Eric.

"Stay where you are, Captain," said Vippit and two of the threep guards behind him aimed their lasers at Eric, priming them with a click. "And you, Commodore. You are both as thoroughly implicated in this as Doge Sneeb."

There wasn't time for this! Life on earth was at stake. I waded in.

"No they're bloody not!" I said in my horrendously bad Gamalian, and I could feel the wave of surprise as they appreciated that, bad pronunciation or not, I was speaking their own language. "I was with Captain Persalub on the Thesarus and we were going to blow up the meteor but there was a force field around it."

"A force field, are you certain?"

"Yes I'm certain. If you don't believe me, one of your sage advisors can perform mind fusion on me."

"You would willingly submit?"

"Impact in five minutes and counting ..."

"Yes. I'll do anything to save my planet, you know, the one which is going to be completely bereft of life in five minutes if you don't stop wittering on and blow up the blummin' meteor."

"Arch Doge Zebulon would never destroy the Earth. He came here to persuade Doge Sneeb to call off the colonisation. He sent a distress signal summoning us here and ordering us to arrest those in command of the Eegby. We have heard nothing since, so we can only assume—"

"Oh get a grip! Are you stupid?" I snapped. "That was part of his plan: to kill us and pretend we'd tried to stop him: that we'd held him up too long to save the Earth."

"The what?" asked Salurian as Vippit said,

"Do you dare to call me stupid?"

"Gamma Six," I answered Salurian, "and yes," I told Vippit. "Think about it! If we've really blown up the Arch Doge we're hardly going to hang around here waiting for you to turn up are we? Why would I be here helping Doge Sneeb if he was trying to destroy my planet? Why would I be happy to see my species wiped out? If things are the way the Arch Doge told you, why aren't I with *him* trying to save the Earth? If the Arch Doge was telling the truth why am I here, willingly?"

"The creature has an excellent point—" began Salurian.

"It's she, 'she has a point'," said Doge Sneeb.

"Look, I'm sorry but the Arch Doge was nuts, it wasn't his fault, it was just the insanity talking but he wanted to have his colonisation and discredit Doge Sneeb. What's more, he was prepared to kill to stop Eric, Neewong, Smeesch and I from blowing up the meteor. Unmarked fighters attacked us without warning. We nearly died and I've enough aptitude at sage advice to know that he wanted us to."

"Prove it," said Vippit.

"I just did, you total tool."

"How dare you—"

"No, wait a minute! I see what you're doing. You're just like Zebulon, you want my planet to die, then you're going to blame Doge Sneeb just like he planned, so you get your precious colonisation and do away with your biggest rival," I shouted. "But if you look, you blind plonkers—"

"Impact in four minutes and counting ..."

"Andi," Eric interrupted me firmly, "I know you're trying to help but please, please, please shut up." I stopped, breathless and angry. "Thank you," said Eric. He turned to the Doges. "Forgive my human friend. The meteor is very close to impact with her planet and her nerves have affected her manners." I glowered at him but all he did was wink at me. "However, if Your Loftinesses will indulge her, she would like to explain that the Arch Doge's ship is docked just behind you—"

"Inside the Eegby? That's impossible."

"I agree it is wondrous but my captain speaks the truth," said Commodore Pimlip.

"I fully appreciate that it is a little irregular, Your Loftiness," Eric continued, "but if you move a few yards to your left and turn round to face the observation window then I assure you, you can see the ship for yourselves."

"I assume you will recognise it," Commodore Pimlip chipped in.

"Of course," said Andwick, "we have all been aboard."

"Oh have you?" said Doge Sneeb.

"If you would just follow me," said Eric. Escorted by wary armed guards, he turned round and headed back out onto the observation deck, to the docking platform. From the bridge I could hear the smooth Gamalian tones of the computerised countdown continue.

"Is that Project X?" Eric asked them gesturing to the ship docked in the Eegby's centre.

"I apologise, I didn't recognise it painted pink."

"The crew surrendered," Doge Sneeb broke in.

Vippit stared incredulously from Doge Sneeb to Eric, to Project X and back.

"All of them?" he asked.

"Yes, all of them; including Arch Doge Zebulon's five sage advisors. The sage advisors are being held in secure quarters by security droids, the rest are being debriefed in the brig by Commodore Pimlip's security forces."

"Would you like to see them?" asked the Commodore helpfully.

"That will not be necessary," snapped Vippit.

"Where is Zebulon?" asked Andwick.

Ah. That was going to be a problem. I glanced over at Eric.
What do we do? I can't tell them he's in there in bits.
Yes you can. Just be diplomatic.

Yeb. Diplomatic Eric: that's my exact point.

Doge Sneeb, who had been uncharacteristically quiet while Eric and I argued with his colleagues, spoke.

"I sent Captain Persalub into the ship to arrest Zebulon. It is unfortunate," he hesitated, "but my father was gravely ill and he chose to commit suicide."

Vippit's sage advisor sent some thoughts to his master which I couldn't quite catch, but I got enough to realise they doubted the truth of that statement. Not really surprising, I supposed. Vippit threw me a contemptuous glance.

"Come now," he sneered. "You're going to have to do better than that. We know you murdered him."

"No Vippit. There will be onboard surveillance on Project X. I appreciate it was built by your scientists but if, by some outside chance, you find it has been functioning correctly, feel free to check the recordings. In addition, Andi Turbot has offered herself to your advisors for mind fusion. What further proof do you need?"

I got the clouded hints of thoughts from Vippit's sage advisor this time, something to do with the excrement of a huge creature which roamed the forests of Gamma Three but basically, as far as I could tell, it meant 'rubbish'.

"Listen," I said. "Your sage advisor is right to question. The Arch Doge actually died because he tried to kill Captain Persalub," I remembered, just in time, to use Eric's Gamalian name, "but he didn't know the blaster he was holding fired backwards."

There was a pause. That had made them think. Not enough though; time for a radical demonstration.

"It's a safety feature. Doge Sneeb says the only successfully assassinated Doges were killed with their own guns," I told them. "I'll explain."

The guards surrounding us looked to Vippit.

"Proceed," he said.

"OK, here's the blaster," I took it from the console where I'd left it. "Doge Sneeb gave it to Captain Persalub and sent him into

Project X to get Arch Doge Zebulon. Zebulon attacked Captain Persalub and took it but neither of them realised it shoots backwards. When Arch Doge Zebulon tried to kill Persalub he killed himself instead. If he hadn't been very, very ill in the head he'd be here now because he'd have set it to stun. Now can we please blow up the meteor before it hits my planet?"

"It would appear this colonisation is cancelled," said Sneeb calmly taking the blaster from me and assuming control of the situation before anybody had a chance to say anything else. "I like to be prepared for any eventuality so I tasked my scientists with identifying a suitable alternative," he continued as he moved swiftly back towards the bridge. "They have the specifications of a planet a few galaxies from here. It is smaller and it will require seeding but we biocreated Gamma Five from nothing, I am confident we can repeat the process. It enjoys a slightly less advantageous position than this: we will need two more relay stations—"

"Adding another seventeen years and extra expense—"

Doge Sneeb put up one pincer, indicating, 'wait'.

"—which are but a drop in the ocean in a project of this magnitude."

"But – if Zebulon is dead, who is going to be Arch Doge?" asked Marveen.

"Whoever is elected by the Lofty Syndic of course," said Doge Sneeb in the kind of bemused tone that suggested that Marveen would have worked that out, for himself, had his intellect been up to the job. "I, for one, will stand."

"Over my dead body," said Vippit.

"If only that were possible," muttered Smeesch.

"Shhh!" said Eric.

"You must retire from politics, Sneeb. If you do so today, we may overlook that you are trained in sage advice."

"I am? What evidence do you have?"

"The evidence is overwhelming."

"But entirely circumstantial, whereas I happen to have documents in my possession which implicate you, Vippit in the torturing, for your own personal enjoyment, of animals and less sentient alien species. Isn't that why you are forbidden to keep pets? Marveen, I have some very interesting files implicating you in vote rigging and extortion on Gamma Two, which you do not even govern. Andwick, you gave a contact of mine some excellent stock tips a while ago, but it was foolish of you to send them by email. I'm unsure how favourably the Lofty Syndic would look upon insider dealing. Salurian, I think you know what I have on you. So the four of you can attempt to destroy me if you like, spread this ridiculous rumour about so-called telepathic abilities, but you have no proof. I was tested and found fit to enter politics. If you do decide to slur my good name, I think it only fair that all the information I hold about you is aired just as thoroughly in the public domain.

"That is blackmail, Sneeb."

Doge Sneeb made a mocking bow.

"I merely follow your lead, Vippit."

"You're bluffing! You'll have no proof about any of this. I can guarantee it."

"Really, what if I actually am telepathic? What if I am powerful enough to fake the entry test and go into politics? If, as you believe, I have no proof, I will find it. I will know exactly what to look for, and where. Can you run that risk?"

"If that's so you are little more than a criminal. You cannot stand! I will be Arch Doge," said Vippit and I could have thumped him. I could see a long and pointless argument brewing. An argument my planet didn't have time for.

"Call it a radical idea," I said, "but perhaps you should both stand. Then the Lofty Cynic—"

"Syndic," Eric corrected me.

"Yeh, whatever, can vote on it. Isn't that what you're supposed to do?" I was getting very twitchy. They could probably see the meteor from Earth by now and if these idiots didn't hurry up and finish their bickering, everyone on my planet was going to die.

"To select an Arch Doge there must be the same number of legally elected Doges as there are planets in the Gamalian

Confederation," said Doge Sneeb. "Perhaps, in your haste, you have overlooked the recent death of one of our number? Any election taking place now would be null and void."

"The Lofty Syndic has already spoken, Sneeb. This colonisation, your colonisation, has failed. So despite the death of Arch Doge Zebulon, there are five planets and five Doges present," said Vippit triumphantly.

"I do not believe all the Doges here are legally appointed," said Sneeb calmly. "I suspect Salurian's election was not conducted according to the usual protocol, was it, Vippit?"

"Salurian's election is perfectly legal. He has been voted Doge by the Lofty Syndic and his position ratified by the rest of us."

"Impact in three minutes and counting ..."

"On the contrary, it strikes me that Salurian's election is far from legal. He appears to be under the misapprehension that he is supplanting me as Doge of Gamma Five." Doge Sneeb was still talking but he was beginning to speak faster.

"He is, Sneeb," Vippit transmitted a gleeful smile. "The Lofty Syndic have elected him Doge but they have trusted us to allot him tenure of a suitable planet. They have also voted me special powers to relieve you, as of this moment, of your duties."

"Then there will only be four Doges – and the validity of office of one of them is questionable – and five planets: the result, alas, that an election can be held to appoint another Doge but not the Arch Doge. You can't have it all ways, Vippit. We either do this by the book, or we don't," said Doge Sneeb. "As I understand it, there is nothing illegal in the Lofty Syndic's decision to elect Salurian as Doge without specifying the planet over which he will preside."

"Impact in two minutes and counting ..."

I was getting really fidgety now. I scanned the threeps around me, searching out Smeesch. He was now waiting by the weapons console.

"However," Doge Sneeb was saying, "if Salurian is to assume another Doge's tenure midterm I believe strict rules do apply. If the Doge in question has died, resigned, been found guilty of a capital offence or is too ill to continue in office another Doge may assume his position. As you see, I am patently alive and enjoying the most robust health. I may stand accused of a capital crime but I have yet to be tried – let alone found guilty – and I do not intend to resign. Salurian must wait upon the process of our legal system before he has any hope of assuming control of Gamma Five.

"He may assume the Dogeship of Gamma Five only if I am legally removed from office. As far as I recall, to legally remove me from my position as Doge, the Lofty Syndic must first convene a special session and hold a vote of no confidence, in my presence. Furthermore, I believe I have the right to put my case to them before they vote and that once the result of their ballot is known the remaining Doges must ratify it with a second vote of their own. Finally, as a fellow member of the Lofty Syndic, albeit another Doge, I believe I too, am entitled to cast a vote on my future. I don't recall being invited to do so. What did you say to persuade them to depart from this procedure?"

"I merely told the truth, Sneeb," said Vippit.

"The truth as you saw it – presumably without bothering to check the facts – that I am so ambitious and unscrupulous that I did not stop at deliberately destroying a sentient species, that I would let nothing stand in my way, not even vaporising the Arch Doge and his entire crew; in other words, a complete fabrication. An assassination of character for which, Vippit, I have half a mind to sue you and good case to do so. You have grievously misled the Lofty Syndic and obtained special powers from them under false pretences. Now, personally I would consider that unscrupulous and ambitious. What do you think they would make of it?" he asked and paused to give the idea time to sink in.

"I am sure I don't have to remind you how easily they can remove all of us from office," Doge Sneeb went on. "Technically, the four of you have taken advantage of Arch Doge Zebulon's unfortunate illness to smear and conspire against me, instead of helping him. Perhaps if you had been a little less single minded in your plans to bring about my downfall, Zebulon would be here now. More to the point, in choosing to mislead its members, you have also conspired against the Lofty Syndic.

Remind me, isn't that technically treason?"

In light of the fact nobody said anything I assumed it was treason and that they were thinking long and hard about the circular saw and the hooked instrument.

"You really should fire your legal team, Vippit – or do your own research. This could become very messy and unpleasant couldn't it?" Doge Sneeb continued breezily. "However, I do not think we need to involve the Lofty Syndic. I am willing to overlook your somewhat vulgar eagerness to bestow tenure of my planet, in my absence, upon Salurian. I have no objection to his appointment as Doge of somewhere, which makes that, at least, legal. Are we agreed on this, Vippit?"

"Yes, Sneeb, we are agreed," said the other sullenly.

"Excellent. We therefore have five Doges – all of whom are legally elected – and five planets. All that remains is to decide which planet Salurian will govern and to do that perhaps we should decide who will stand in the elections for the position of Arch Doge. Once we have decided upon these small matters, I imagine that, if we provide a united front to the Lofty Syndic, we will easily persuade them that you did not intentionally mislead them. Especially in light of the precarious state Zebulon's mental health had reached and the fact you were, no doubt, acting under his orders. Does this compromise meet with all our approval?"

Andwick, Salurian, Marveen and Vippit exchanged glances.

"I have no intention of—" began Vippit but Andwick spoke over him.

"Speaking for all of us, I believe it will suffice."

"Good," said Doge Sneeb flatly. "Then it is settled, the Lofty Syndic will not be informed of anything which might worry them unduly – other than the truth, in time: and now, to restore political equilibrium to the Huurg Quadrant, we merely have to make two small decisions. However, Vippit, it should be noted that having had to solve yet another crisis of your making I feel somewhat put upon, so, in return for all this magnanimity on my part I seek a small favour."

"What?" snarled Vippit.

"Impact in one minute, and counting ..."

"That I stand, unopposed, for election as Arch Doge, Supreme Ruler of the Gamalian Federation of Planets; and Gamma Five," said Sneeb.

"Never!" said Vippit.

"Then perhaps we should present the facts to the Lofty Syndic and seek guidance from them."

"This is an outrage!" blustered Vippit.

"Is it? I would be more inclined to describe it as politics," said Doge Sneeb evenly. "May I suggest our new colleague here governs Gamma One?"

"He can't be Doge of Gamma One. That is the seat of Government and has always been governed by the Arch Doge," shouted Vippit.

"There is no law stating which planet the Arch Doge governs," said Doge Sneeb. "It is merely a tradition, which I intend to break."

"You're not the Arch Doge yet!" retorted Vippit. "This is supposed to be a democratic process. No vote has been taken."

"True, but since I am standing unopposed, surely the vote is a technicality. And now, if your guards will release us ..." except it wasn't really a request and the guards holstered their weapons and snapped to attention before Vippit could so much as squeak.

"Thank you," said Doge Sneeb, "Smeesch, Commodore Pimlip?" he barked and the other Doges moved aside as he made his way swiftly towards the weapons console. Smeesch and the Commodore were already there.

"Your Loftiness," Commodore Pimlip bowed to Doge Sneeb. "Communications Officer Mondock, scan the meteor for life forms and beam aboard any that you find."

Mondock's antennae tapped at the keyboard in front of him for a few seconds and he sat back and waited.

"Nothing found, sir."

"Excellent. On screen." The scene outside was relayed onto the huge viewing screen along the wall of the bridge. In the middle of the picture, slightly larger and brighter than the neighbouring stars, with a tail of debris smeared behind it, was the meteor. Suddenly, it grew in size as Mondock magnified the image.

"Impact in fifteen seconds, initiating verbal countdown: Ten, nine ..."

"Vaporise."

"It's close," said Andwick.

"And make it thorough, Officer Smeesch."

"Sir," said Smeesch, "aiming," he tapped rapidly at the panel in front of him, "firing," he pressed a button with a flourish and sat back. There was an electronic humming sound from within the ship, rising in pitch, and then a beam of green light shot into space. The meteor glowed for a moment and then exploded in a cloud of boiling steam. Everyone on the bridge, even Vippit, broke into spontaneous applause.

"Thank you! Thank you so much," I said.

Commodore Pimlip bowed again, "My pleasure."

"Wow! We saved the Earth!" I said as the chaos subsided. I felt a bit jelly legged, hardly believing it was true.

"In the nick of time! The way all the best superheros do it," said Eric.

"Only better!" said Smeesch.

Doge Sneeb transmitted a smile.

"And Apreetik tells me that the correct etiquette, upon averting Armageddon, is to celebrate," he swung round towards me. "The ways of your planet are most interesting, Andi Turbot. Perhaps you would join us for one of your Earth meals before Captain Persalub takes you home?"

I looked up at him and this time, behind the penetrating green-grey stare, there was definitely a bit of a twinkle.

"Alright," I said.

Chapter 32
Aftermath

Eric left to go to the medical pod for a check-up while Neewong and Smeesch, with Borridge, escorted the Doges to their quarters. We agreed to meet at the medical pod in a short while.

With the promise of a celebratory meal, constructed for flavour, earthling-style, I went to the luxury matter-free pod which had been specially prepared for me. There, I washed off as much of the old Arch Doge as was humanely possible; from myself and my clothes. There were still a lot of unpleasantly red stains on my best Danger Mouse T-shirt but I'd managed to wash it, so, theoretically, they were clean red stains and in the absence of anything else to wear, necessity forced me to dry it out and put it back on. While I was waiting for Eric and his partners in the medical pod, he and they had arranged with Commodore Pimlip that I should have a tour of the ship.

"Ah," he hesitated for a moment while he tried to remember what to call me, "Andi, I regret that I will not be giving you the tour."

"No?"

"No," he nodded to where Doge Sneeb, I supposed it was Arch Doge Elect Sneeb now, was squishing out of Project X. The Doge was pushing a hovercart with a closed metal box on it and carrying what looked like a snow shovel. I said goodbye to the Commodore and went out onto the docking platform.

"Andi Turbot," said the Doge. He sounded strained.

"You OK?"

"I have been preparing Arch Doge Zebulon for the next world." One of his flexible antennae flicked down and rested, gently on the metal box.

"He's in there?"

"Yes. All that remains is to send him his body."

"How do you do that?"

"He will be cremated."

"But isn't your afterlife—"

"Real? Yes but ... it is difficult to explain. It is not his actual body we send across. This ritual cuts the ties that tether his soul to his physical form, allowing it to go on."

"'Go on' is that what you call it?"

"Yes."

"Have you finished or d'you want a hand?" I asked him.

"It is done. I am Zebulon's adopted son. His husbands predeceased him and he has no other family so it is my duty to take care of the collection alone," he said.

I looked down at my blood-spattered T-shirt, self-consciously aware that from the moment I got into the shower liberal amounts of the Arch Doge had been washed away forever.

"What about the bits that ..." I shrugged.

He transmitted something like a sigh.

"This is a custom rather than a necessity. Zebulon will manage with ... what he has," he transmitted a sad smile. "He always did."

"It must be tough; the way it ended."

"It is but life will continue and I will ensure that he is remembered for who he was and who he undoubtedly is now, not what he became at the end."

I nodded and we stood together in silence for a few moments.

"I'm guessing you're going to be a bit economical with the truth then, when you write this one up for the history books."

He chuckled.

"Some things are better left unsaid."

"More like most things and surely there are rather a lot of witnesses."

"I would not be the Arch Doge Elect were I not persuasive."

"Right. That sounds a little sinister, you know." I hoped he wasn't going to torture anyone and then I remembered that he could read my thoughts and tried to cover them up.

"You humans are very cynical. Do you still doubt me after what has happened?"

"Not exactly but you have to admit, you're quite scary."

"I'd hoped that was charisma." He sounded weary again.

"Of a sort, I suppose. But you are a politician."

"Through and through: on that reasoning, perhaps you always should doubt me. I assure you, none of the witnesses will be harmed or coerced. It is simply a question of framing the request correctly. They will agree to endorse my version of events. I guarantee it."

"Guarantee?"

"Better, from a politician, than a promise, don't you think?"

A group of four threep guards squished out onto the platform with a fifth wearing a lurid purple sash and carrying a thurible which was belching out some of the most rancid smelling vapours – short of my pretend garbage spacesuit – that I've ever had the misfortune to smell.

"Ah, here is the Reverend Hanabris, he is the Eegby's resident priest," Doge Sneeb explained to me. "These others are Zebulon's guard of escort. He will be treated with full state honours."

"Your Loftiness," said the Reverend, with a low bow.

"Your Holy Reverence," Doge Sneeb returned it with a sweeping bow of his own.

"Hi," I said with a pathetic attempt at a curtsey.

"Sir." The guards presented arms, with a single, uber-synchronised squelch.

Reverend Hanabris pressed a button on the coffin and a holographic text appeared.

"This is my father," read Doge Sneeb.

"Who is also Plort's son," the reverend intoned, two of his eyes flicked upwards, towards Doge Sneeb and I could hear the nerves in his voice.

"I entrust his spirit to Plort and his body to you," Sneeb read smoothly.

"I accept and honour your trust," said the reverend and he swung the vile-smelling censor over the coffin in a figure of eight, the chains rattling and clanking as his pincers shook with nerves. "I will protect and prepare him in the surety of Plort's mercy, for to him we are all weak and helpless as hatchlings."

"Amen," said everyone.

Zebulon will be taken to the Worship Pod.

Do you want me to come with you?

No, he will make this journey with the priest. That is part of the custom.

Doge Sneeb put his antennae on the coffin and said aloud, "I hope I will see you in the afterlife old friend."

He stood, head bowed, both antennae on the casket, for several minutes until, looking up sharply, catching the priest by surprise, he said,

"Thank you Reverend. I have asked Commodore Pimlip to arrange a guard of honour, to stay with Zebulon in the Worship Pod."

"I thank you, your Loftiness. He will lie in state there until we return to Gamma One?"

"Yes. I wish to allow time for his advisors and crew to pay their respects."

Privately, I hoped the Worship Pod was well refrigerated, or that the journey back wouldn't take a long time.

"I have been in touch with the Elders. They are arranging a state funeral."

"I thank you."

We waited another few moments, in solemn silence. Then the priest pressed a button on the casket and music blared out. It was the same beyond-death-metal as the Rites of Twonkot. Plort's musical preferences seemed a little bizarre to me.

Ah the funeral antiphon, Doge Sneeb thought to me, since the music was way too loud to hear speech. He and the others stood still and straight, listening, while I tried to, but the music was almost physically overwhelming. *Such a profound piece, and with the power to move the soul, even after thousands of years.*

It was so loud it felt more like a physical assault. I suspected the only way it would move my soul would be to vibrate it out of my body by sheer volume. Luckily the guards took the coffin away before my ears began to actually bleed.

Doge Sneeb stayed as he was until they were gone. Silent, unmoving, locked in contemplation. We were disturbed by Eric, squishing through the life matter to join us.

"Ah, Captain, I am glad you are here. You will come with me, please, and you, Andi Turbot," he squished off and after a brief exchange of bemused glances, Eric and I followed.

"You've saved your species from extinction," said Doge Sneeb conversationally as Eric and I squelched through the slime alongside him. "I hope you are proud."

"It was more of a team effort."

"You were the catalyst, and you acted with great bravery."

I shrugged.

"Thanks."

"When you return to Earth no-one will know what you did."

"That'll be three of us, right here, in the same position then, won't it?"

"No, I will make the truth of this colonisation known, in time, when the extent of Arch Doge Zebulon's illness can be understood and appreciated in a more charitable light. It is only right that the truth is told one day. You and the others who fought beside me must be officially honoured for your bravery. The Gamalian Federation of Planets should know its heroes and understand its history."

"I'm not sure I'd call myself a hero but the history bit sounds amazingly sensible," I told him.

"It is merely rational. But my point, Andi Turbot, is that you will carry this alone. No-one will ever realise who you are."

"No-one realises who anyone is anyway, even when we think we do," I shrugged.

"That is an interesting view, coming from a telepath," said Eric.

"Well, I wasn't was I? Or at least, I couldn't read minds, not until I met Mingold and … and …"

"Me," said Doge Sneeb.

"Yeh. I guess it would be good if the human race knew how close it had come to Armageddon. People might treat the planet better, and each other. But I really wouldn't want anyone to know I was involved. I don't think it would be much fun, being a famous heroine. Anyway, I won't carry this alone. Eric will know, you'll know, Apreetik and Borridge will know, Neewong and Smeesch will know. I'll bet the crew of the Eegby won't forget it in a hurry either. There are the other Doges, they'll remember – even if they pretend not to. What I'm saying is, even if I never see you again, I won't be on my own, because all of you are still out there somewhere. However far apart we are physically, you're only a thought away and anyway, most of all *I'll* know who I am and what I did. The way I look at it, that's enough isn't it?"

"Not for me. I owe you a debt. You have taught me much that I needed to learn. I will be a better Arch Doge for having met you. Will you not be lonely?"

I shrugged.

"I can cope with being lonely if I like who I am."

He stopped walking.

"You possess great wisdom," he said and then ruined it by adding, "for a human."

I rolled my eyes at Eric who tried to stifle a transmission of a smile. Doge Sneeb didn't react. He seemed to be on edge all of a sudden. For all the calm of his exterior I could feel his uncertainty and confusion. It was as if he had some bad news to impart and didn't know where to begin.

"I can give you a choice about this, Andi Turbot; to be remembered – by some, at least – or not."

Eric and I exchanged glances.

"Meaning?"

"You asked me to put you with your family."

"Yeh, and you said it wasn't possible."

"That is true but ... it was possible, expedient even, that I put your family, and your friends, with you."

"You don't know who they are," I retorted, more in hope than conviction.

"I am fully trained in sage advice and I have fused my mind with yours, twice. I know things about you that you do not realise, yourself." I swallowed. I didn't want to think about that. I didn't want to remember. "I should not have done it. If I had reasoned with you; trusted you ... but I believed there was not time. Please forgive me for causing you such pain but once you had overcome Borridge and Mingold—when you could not unfuse—I had to act; to spare all of you. Had I not you would have been ..."

He stopped, apparently lost for words.

"Fried?" I asked.

"Indeed. If it helps, the second time, with Borridge, you inflicted as much pain as you received; on both of us."

I said nothing.

"And so," he continued, "since I was not entirely confident of the outcome of today's events I have been collecting specimens for a rebreeding programme. Should my attempts to preserve the human race in situ have failed, I had designated the vacant planet, the one upon which we will now be biocreating Gamma Six, to be their home, and yours. I could not let you perish and I did not know what else to do. So I chose two groups; those with particular gifts or knowledge which would be of use, and those who meant something to you, personally. I ask your forgiveness."

I stood watching him, trying to read his eyes. His mind was still open, no defences. Nothing obvious, anyway, other than a hint of admiration for my good sense in distrusting him.

"You've just saved my planet from Armageddon."

I was surprised to find I forgave him so easily and so was he, I could sense his relief.

"As I explained, you saved your planet," he corrected me. "Now, if you will come with me." He squished off down the corridor and Eric and I followed. Soon we arrived at a large door. In order to open it he had to put one eye to a security scanner on the wall.

Uh-oh! thought Eric.

What? I asked.

I think I know what he's been doing. You're not going to like this.

It can't be that horrendous, surely?

How much worse than abduction does it get?

Abduction? Well … I transmitted a mental shrug. *It's turned out OK for me.*

The doorway led onto a darkened room. One wall was like that of the bridge, all screen, but this one was showing different views from surveillance cameras in an area with no life matter. From what I could tell there were communal bathrooms and showers, a recreational area and a canteen. All were empty. At the side of the screen were images from a series of huge dormitories. Rows and rows of beds, arranged with military precision and someone fast asleep on each one. The people were wired up to headsets with a sensor stuck to each of their temples. Threeps with clipboards were moving slowly among them, taking readings, checking pulses, in one case, straightening the sheets.

"What is this?" I asked.

"This is the Ark. Your Ark."

"My—" I gazed open mouthed at the screen. The picture was fuzzy and indistinct but among the supine bodies I recognised the unmistakable outline of my brother's tousled head. Close by were my parents. As I gradually focussed, I realised all of my extended family and my friends from the International School were there. Doge Sneeb had clearly misinterpreted some of my thoughts because he'd also selected the idiots who shared my corridor in the student residency, along with the policemen who'd tried to arrest me, Mr Slimbridge the principal, and Bob the caretaker. On the other hand, he'd also selected Jen.

"Oh bollocks," I whispered before I could stop myself. "What have you done to them?"

"Nothing, they are in stasis. When they wake up, they won't even know they were here."

"But when will they wake up? How long have they been here? Won't they have missed stuff?"

"They have been here just over four hours. Those from your time zone will awaken tomorrow morning, in their own beds, none the wiser. The others may experience some confusion. If you wish I can have them infected with a mild virus so they believe they have been sleeping off an illness."

"No, I don't wish … Oh my days. I think I need to sit down." There wasn't a chair so I leaned forwards resting my hands on my knees for a few seconds to catch my breath before straightening up and looking Doge Sneeb in the eye, "I don't know whether to thank you or scream at you for being creepy," I told him.

"I was attempting to behave with honour and honesty."

"I appreciate that, and I'm grateful, although, I think your delivery needs work."

"Perhaps, but it was imperative that I saved your species," he said it without the remotest hint of regret; as if that explained everything. "You have a choice now, Andi. We can put them back, or we can wake them and they can know who you truly are, and what you have done."

I gave Eric a helpless look. We didn't need telepathy for this. He knew what I'd be thinking.

"We have to put them back, right now. They can't ever know. Not even Mr Slimbridge and the police, however tempting it is to leave them here—"

"Ah yes, the refrigerator: that will be taken care of. The Eegby carries stocks of metals and smelting equipment as standard. For repairs, you understand. There is an element we use for colour I believe you humans value it highly. It is abundant on Gammas Five and Two."

"He's talking about gold, Andi," said Eric.

"I do not doubt that an apology from you, coupled with a suitable donation to your university and a new fridge from me, will smooth over any problems in your residency. I will arrange it."

"How are you going to do that?"

"The same way Captain Persalub, here, assumed a human lifeform. I thought we could add a godfather to your family group."

"Did you take any Earth animals?" asked Eric.

"Of course: they are in stasis in another section of the ship. They will also be returned to their habitat."

"Thanks," I said.

"My pleasure, and now, Captain, Andi Turbot, we have a small celebration to enjoy and then you must return to your home. Tomorrow, the survey party has orders to head for Gamma Six and I shall be returning to Gamma One for the funeral. Also, I believe you have a date."

He turned away from us and spoke quietly to one of the threeps supervising the surveillance screens.

"It is done," he told us, "come with me," and we followed him into the hall.

Chapter 33
A new beginning

The celebratory meal went quite well, really. Eric showed me how to use the standard Gamalian culinary utensil, a food replicator. This one was freestanding; about the same shape and size as a vending machine and it worked on nanobot technology. Eric explained that in the way a seed was nothing more than a machine to turn earth into grass, and a cow was merely another more advanced machine to turn the grass into beef and dairy products, a food replicator was an awesome space-age machine which was able to turn the basic molecules present in everything into anything edible you cared to mention – plus a variety of the other things you wouldn't want to mention let alone eat. You were supposed to speak to it but this one was wired up for telepaths and so I 'cooked' telepathically.

Once I had finished, Eric had a go and then Doge Sneeb did too. Doge Sneeb made a serious beef rendang but Eric's green Thai curry was a snadge better. Preparing food in a way that made it pleasant to eat was as refreshingly alien to the Doge, and the other Gamalians with us, as it had been to Eric.

When Doge Sneeb got up to cook again, I protested. After all, there's only so much a person should eat.

"I will prepare this in a zero calorie format," he told us as one of the guards put a plate in front of me.

Something happened to me. I couldn't describe it as light breaking, or scales falling from my eyes, but it was definitely a revelatory moment.

"Are you telling me I could describe chocolate to a food replicator, ask it to construct something which tasted exactly the same but with zero calorific value and it could do it?" I whispered to Eric.

"Yup."

Something in the back of my head went,

"Ca-ching!"

"Wow!" I said. "You could make zillions on Earth with something like that!"

I thought of Jane and Laura's extensive array of diet, exercise and fitness videos, mostly made by very strange – but slim, I had to give it to them that they were slim – people with the appearance of several facelifts, dyed hair and bad taste in Lycra gym wear. There were a couple of exceptions but I could see it now, the Andi Turbot Weight Loss Foundation. Zero calorie food, guaranteed. No I couldn't. Jane and Laura could keep that. I wanted to be a stand-up comedienne and if I failed at that I could always find some other Gamalian invention to exploit. A part of me was even wondering about sage advice. I was going to have to do some training in that because I definitely needed to learn more control of my gift.

All too soon, it was time for me to go home, and Doge Sneeb got to his feet.

"Your friends and I have something for you," said the Doge. He turned to Eric who stepped forward and handed me a small, sleek metal box.

"This is from us," said Eric.

"It's the Omega Six, the latest version, just out," Neewong chipped in.

"The think and type version because … you know," added Smeesch.

"It also contains your Gamalian documents," said Doge Sneeb. "I would be honoured if you would accept citizenship of the Gamalian Federation of Planets."

I could tell from the way Eric, Neewong and Smeesch were nearly bursting with pride that the Gamalian Federation of Planets didn't make a habit of this kind of thing. It was totally unexpected and I just about managed to stammer my thanks before Doge Sneeb carried on.

"It also contains your citation for the Gamalian Star of Honour, our highest order of bravery, and I have another small gift, here."

He handed me a bag which I promptly dropped on my foot. I was very glad there was life matter to slow it down because it weighed a ton.

"What on earth—"

"Gold. I thought perhaps you might like some."

"There is enough gold in this bag to make it this heavy?" I asked.

"It's only a little."

No. There was more than a little. There was shedloads. I could hardly lift it. Effortlessly he picked it up for me. "I am ashamed to offer you such a paltry gift for the service you have given to the Gamalian Federation. These things are, essentially, rubbish to us but nothing of any value to a Gamalian is prized on your planet." I was shocked. He meant what he was saying. I hoped he was right in the head. He was going to be Arch Doge, two loons running would be hard luck on the Gamalian Federation of Planets.

"This is too much. You don't owe me anything. I should be giving you the present. You saved my planet."

"I saved myself. Your planet was merely a lucky interloper."

"That's not the way I see it."

He transmitted a smile.

"Then may I suggest some spectacles, perhaps?"

"Nope. You can't wriggle out of it that easily, you've more scruples than you'd have us think."

"You are confusing self-preservation with altruism I believe."

"I don't think so. Will you promise me something?"

"Anything."

"It's about Apreetik. Hang onto him. You and Borridge will never find anyone better."

"We know. Good luck, Andi Turbot, it will be strangely quiet without you."

"You lot are always welcome to visit me. You know where I live."

He gave Eric a bit of a look and bowed slightly.

"Yes. Or perhaps you will visit us ... for a Gamalian wedding."

"I'd be very honoured," I said.

Doge Sneeb transmitted an ironic smile.

"Yes," he said, "you would. Is there nothing else I can do for you?"

"No, but I meant what I said. You can visit whenever you like."

Borridge and Apreetik arrived to say their goodbyes and then Doge Sneeb left with them. Now it was time for Eric, Neewong and Smeesch to say goodbye, too.

"I guess this is it."

"Not forever," said Eric, "and you can call us with your data pod."

"And it contains a remote transporter," said Neewong. "If we are round this way, you can visit us on ship."

"It runs on light power but if you happen to be stuck in the dark it can run on the dynamo," said Smeesch, he showed me where to press the casing and a small handle popped out.

"I'm really going to miss you," I told Eric.

There was a pregnant pause.

"You know you don't have to go," he said. "You're a Gamalian citizen now and you'd be wise to train in sage advice."

"Yeh, it's on my list but ..." I looked out though the viewing screen where my home planet hung in the silence of space. From out here it was beautiful but then, you couldn't see the cities, the pollution, the wars ... or the people. "For now, I belong down there. It may not always look like it but that's just because I'm a natural misfit!"

He laughed.

"You will come and see me won't you?" I said.

"Yes."

I hugged him and Neewong and Smeesch, I didn't care about the slime any more. None of us could think of anything else to say. He gestured to my new Omega Six.

"Press the button Andi," he said and I did as I was told.

****

That wasn't the end of it. I returned to my room in the student residency and a few days later I was called to the principal's office where I was informed that my long-lost godfather, 'Silas Sneeb' had donated a hefty sum of money to the university and a new fridge freezer to replace the one Smeesch had partially vaporised. All charges were dropped and I have a clean record with the university and the police.

Making friends is a lot easier, too. Maybe everyone's relaxed a bit. Maybe I have. Saving the world does wonders for your self-confidence, even if you can't tell anyone. The telepathy helps of course, when you can hear everybody's thoughts, you soon stop worrying about what people think of you. Anyway, I can switch that off now, well, except when I talk to Eric, which I do, often. He, Neewong and Smeesch are overseeing the seeding of the planet the threeps are going to colonise instead of Earth. I've been over there a couple of times and it's going to be amazing. I even chat to Doge Sneeb from time to time. I've also been doing distance learning run by the Guild of Sage Advice, which is why I can blank out all those background thoughts from my fellow humans. Damping, as it's called, is the first thing they taught me. The Guild have offered me a place to train fully and I think I will, after all, as my mum says, never turn down a chance to learn something. It's always good to have options, the more the merrier. But for now, I'm keeping it low key. I'm not saying, if I meet you, that I won't have a tiny peek into your brain but you know what? Each one of us may be unique but we share the same hang-ups. Those thoughts you have that horrify you? Trust me: odds are everyone else has them, too.

Three weeks after I returned from space, I moved out of the Paul Weller Student Residency. I sold all that gold and used the proceeds to buy a house. It had been converted into two flats and for the moment, that's how I've kept it. The whole of the top two floors are mine, and I have a roof garden with peppers, herbs and tomatoes in pots. I rent out the downstairs flat to a friend of Jen's. Yes, Jen and I went on our date. She is every bit as fantastic as I hoped she would be. She helps me with my chemistry and sometimes she even comes to my stand-up gigs. I've never felt so comfortable or at home with anyone in my life, and I know she feels the same. No, I didn't read her mind, she told me. So we hang out a lot. It's fun and we're happy. I'm not sure how I'll break it to her that I want to study sage advice, but I'll cross that bridge when I come to it. I have to finish my degree first, and I might be a famous comedienne by then. 'Kismet, Hardy,' and all that. What will be will be.

—The end—

Other Books by M T McGuire

Few Are Chosen, K'Barthan Series: Part 1

Meet The Pan of Hamgee: coward, unwilling adventurer and, by some miracle, K'Barth's longest surviving outlaw. He just wants a quiet life so working as getaway driver is probably a bad career move. Then he falls in love at first sight with a woman he hasn't even met who comes from an alternative reality. That's when things really begin to get complicated.

Meet Ruth Cochrane: she's the Chosen One, destined to play a pivotal role in saving K'Barth from a cruel dictator. She's never heard of K'Barth, though. She's a public relations executive from London and she's totally unaware of the chaos about to hit her life.

Meet Lord Vernon: power hungry psychopath on the brink of world domination. He wants to cement his hold on K'Barth by kidnapping the Chosen One and forcing her to marry him. Only one person is standing in his way: someone who doesn't even realise it, The Pan of Hamgee. For The Pan, and Ruth, that's a deadly problem.

The Wrong Stuff, K'Barthan Series: Part 2

The Pan of Hamgee is not a natural knight in shining armour. Yet he has escaped from police custody in K'Barth, switched realities and foiled Lord Vernon's attempt to kidnap Ruth, the Chosen One, from the Festival Hall. Pretty good, he thinks.

However, Ruth thinks otherwise. Being pursued by Lord Vernon is bad enough. Now, thanks to The Pan, she's on the run. They are both alive, of course, but with Lord Vernon on their tail neither of them can be sure how long for.

To save K'Barth and Ruth, the woman of his dreams, The Pan must introduce her to the Candidate, who is prophesied to be the man of her dreams. And he must do it fast – before Lord Vernon finds her. But the gentleman in question is in hiding and no-one knows where. Only The Pan can find him, if he can bring himself to unite them.

One Man: No Plan, K'Barthan Series: Part 3

The Pan of Hamgee needs answers, although he's not even sure he knows the questions.

He has a chance to go straight but it's been so long that he's almost forgotten how. Despite a death warrant over his head he is released, given a state-sponsored business, and a year's amnesty for all misdemeanours while he adjusts. On the down side, Ruth has left him for his nemesis, Lord Vernon.

The Pan doesn't have a year, either. In only five days Lord Vernon will gain total power and destroy K'Barth. Unless The Pan can stop him. Because even though the Candidate, the person prophesied to save K'Barth, has finally appeared it's still going to be down to The Pan to make things right. But he has no clue where to start or whether he even can.

The future hangs by a thread and the only person who can fix it is The Pan: a man without a plan.

Looking For Trouble, K'Barthan Series: Part 4

The Pan of Hamgee doesn't believe in miracles but if he's going to save K'Barth it looks as if he might need one.

He's not quite as alone as he thought. The punters from The Parrot and Screwdriver are right behind him and he has rescued three of his friends from the Grongolian Security Forces, who are now of course, three of the nation's most wanted, which doesn't make life easy. He even has something of a plan for once. It involves making peace with the Resistance, trying to resurrect the Underground movement, and toppling Lord Vernon.

Now, The Pan just needs to keep his head down and maintain a low profile. He must be brave and clever and stay in control. That's going to be a first. But the hardest part will be staying alive long enough to put his plan into action.

Keep up to date with M T McGuire by joining her Reader's Group at http://bit.ly/MTMailJNB. You can choose to hear about everything or just new releases. You can also follow her on social media:

Website: http://www.hamgee.co.uk
Blog: http://www.hamgee.co.uk/blog
Facebook: http://www.facebook.com/HamgeeUniversityPress
Twitter: @mtmcguireauthor.

Website	*Blog*	*Facebook*	*Twitter*

Lightning Source UK Ltd.
Milton Keynes UK
UKOW01f2010021116

286757UK00004B/357/P